FORGET IT

THE IT GIRLS
BOOK 2

FRANCESCA SHAW

To those learning to speak up for themselves and to the people who listen when they do.

And for Aimee, my Rosie <3

AUTHOR NOTE

This book is set in the United Kingdom where we have free healthcare under the National Health Service (NHS). The NHS is a service for everyone and free to the point of use. I have many friends and family who work in the NHS and we should do everything we can to protect this system from privatization. The hardworking doctors, nurses and admin staff are overworked and underpaid but it's a service that must be cherished.

Forget It also briefly discusses abortion. Abortion is a legal practice in the United Kingdom under the Abortion Act of 1967 and MPs have recently voted to decriminalise abortion in a landmark bill, though there will always be people that would like to see these rights further restricted.

Rosie has the choice whether to proceed with her pregnancy which is a freedom that many across the world do not have access to.

This book also touches on the UK rental crisis specifically in London where there is limited affordable housing and private landlords squeeze the market, trapping working people in an unfair system.

I also would like to take the time here to mention that no Artificial Intelligence has been used in the drafting, writing or promotion of this book.

Remember, reading is always political.

Fxx

CONTENT WARNINGS

Pregnancy, mentions of abortion, death of a parent, bullying, emotional abuse, mental health issues, serious injury (side character), recreational drug use.

PLAYLIST

'Juno' *Sabrina Carpenter*
'The Love' *Dekker*
'Ride The Storm' *Goldford*
'The Victim Card' *Maya Karli*
'Slice of Heaven' *Dave Dobbyn, Herbs*
'The Rest of Me' *Michael Kiwanuka*
'Mean! (with Noah Kahan)' *Madeline The Person*
'Matilda' *Harry Styles*
'Backstabber' *Kesha*
'The Way I Wanna' *Max McNown*
'Robbery' *Lime Cordiale*
'Love Cocoon' *Muroki, BENEE*
'Lady' *Brett Young*
'Tieduprightnow' *Parcels*

1

ROSIE

THE WINE BOTTLE ON THE TABLE IS ALMOST EMPTY BUT I GIVE it a helpless shake as if there's more to come. I put it back on the white tablecloth with a thud and slump in my seat. I reach up to adjust my glasses but remember I'm wearing my contacts and instead end up poking myself in the eye. The contacts weren't even worth it as I ended up crying so much during the ceremony that they just became irritated and foggy.

I cross my legs and swing my foot, my nude heel resting on the tips of my aching feet. Anya and her brand new husband are still dancing across the room, the dance floor empty as the night winds down. Well, it's less dancing and more drunken swaying whilst sticking their tongues down each other's throats. In a classy, bridal, way of course.

I hide my grin behind a sip of wine at the sight. I've dated men before but I've never laughed the way Anya does when Danny says something funny, or been looked at like I hung the moon.

My Maid of Honor duties are officially done for the night. I reminded her to take the hair tie off her wrist, fluffed her lacy dress at the altar, held her bouquet whilst she shared her vows, and cried until my reusable contacts practically disintegrated. And I even finished off the final bottle of white wine at the head table.

I smother a yawn with my hand and brush the hair that's fallen from my half-up half-down hairdo back into place. My foot keeps swaying to the music, and I almost don't notice when the shoe I've been balancing precariously on my toes falls onto the hardwood floor.

I do, however, notice the man kneeling down to pick it up.

Jackson Harper.

We've met a few times, usually in the presence of our joint best friends. When we first met, I'll admit I was a little starstruck. It's not every day you meet a man who you've only ever seen in IMAX. But, by result of being best friends with Anya Bonnet, who managed to get one of the most famous men in the world to fall in love with her by bossing him around on set, I've inadvertently brushed shoulders with Hollywood's elite enough times now that the excitement has definitely faded.

They're all the same as us, just with more money, more clout and easier access to class A drugs. As evidenced the *second* time I met Jackson Harper, when I accidentally walked in on him in Anya's bathroom snorting a line of coke off the porcelain toilet.

There is something about Jackson though. He's effortlessly charming, his pearly white smirk usually accompanied by a wink from dark brown eyes that just ooze sex appeal. His white dress shirt barely fits around his rippling biceps, though he's not as dehydrated as he must be when he appears on screen as Starseeker–the superhero character that catapulted him to global fame and aroused every man and woman with a pulse.

I haven't spoken to him since bathroom-gate, embarrassment and plain awkwardness causing me to avoid any kind of contact with him whenever we're in the same room. Of course, I had to respond to his messages in the wedding group chat when he asked dumb questions like 'can I wear jandals with the tux?' or 'what pocket should I keep the rings in?', but I've so far managed to avoid a face to face conversation with the man.

Until he kneels at my feet and slips my shoe back on my foot.

His finger traces the arch of my foot, sending a shiver up my body like lightning and I clench my thighs together. Now is not the time to be turned on by this man. It's been too long, nearly a year, since the last time I've been touched by hands that aren't my own and I'd be lying if I thought there wasn't a small part of me that was thrilled at the prospect of a wedding hook up, but even I'm sober enough to accept that there's no way in hell that Jackson Harper would be interested in *me*.

"Thanks," I say, quietly.

He stands to his full height, towering over me. He's got at least seven inches on me and I've always been tall enough that the height information on dating apps has come in very handy. Sometimes a girl likes to look *up*. It's good for your neck muscles.

He pulls out the chair next to me, spinning it around and straddling it. I think I almost swoon. The move was smooth and my ovaries are well aware. I tuck my swinging leg closer to my chair before it autonomously gets any crazy ideas about running along the inseam of his tuxedo leg.

"You're welcome, pretty girl," he says with a wink.

I shift, the lust that was fizzling under my skin dissolving to unease. Right. Echoes of cruel laughter ring in my ears and I glance away, willing myself to breathe through my nose like a normal human.

"You having a nice night?" Jackson asks.

I almost swallow my tongue. Am I dreaming? I've never said more than twenty words to this man face to face. I assumed that after today I would only have to see him once or twice a year at most.

He's probably only talking to me because we're both in the wedding party. I'm reading way too much into this.

My stomach twists, reminding me of when I was a teenager and Jake Jones asked me out after school. I'd spent the whole weekend giddy at the prospect of going out with my crush, until I walked in on Monday morning to see him wrapped around my sister, Cleo. He'd laughed when I confronted him.

"Yeah—uh, yeah it's been beautiful." I dart my eyes around the room, taking in the elegant French chateau and glittering decorations. Danny's sister Pip took over the role of wedding planner, much to Anya and I's relief, so the whole venue is perfectly designed. I use the opportunity to take another sip of wine.

Get it together Rosie, he is not *flirting with you.*

"Would have been just as beautiful in a Californian Winery, I'll tell you that much. Better than making us all slog it out here to France."

I roll my eyes. "It's closer to me than you."

Jackson licks his lip, "London, right?"

I nod. Since Anya moved to LA, I've had a significantly smaller social circle. As in I don't have one. The guys at the post production house where I work are always more interested in talking to each other about the latest anime or RPG game. One time I tried to join the conversation and talk about the new game I downloaded and they blinked at me as if hearing a girl talking about video games was like finding a penguin in a chicken shop trying to order fries.

At least I was able to put my head down and concentrate on work instead of gabbing with the rest of them and I eventually earned enough to rent a small flat in South London, which, while complete with moldy walls and a dodgy landlord, has enough room for my whole desk. Taking work home is a lot more appealing than listening to the guys make jokes at my expense or talk loudly about the latest Starseeker movie.

Anya had a hard time in the US when she first went out there, so we spent most of the time on video calls or planning visits around our work schedules. One weekend that was particularly lonely, I ended up at Anya's mum's house by myself for the whole weekend where we watched French New Wave films and drank red wine. It's been nice having Anya home whilst she's been planning the wedding, and the West London townhouse she and Danny bought has been a nice reprieve from my lumpy mattress, but I'm already dreading the six month honeymoon she's about to embark on.

I startle when one of Jackson's electric fingers taps my knee in a silent question. My silky dress has slipped off my lap, revealing my bare leg, exposing it to the chilled air. His hand rests alongside the inside of my thigh, not touching but close enough that if I so much as twitched, his knuckles would graze my skin.

"Oh." What did he ask me again? "Yeah, London." Shaking off the thought of his big hand clasping around my sensitive thigh, I take a last swig of my wine and make a move to rise. "I'm going to get another."

His palm is feather light on my knee, stopping my movement and getting caught in the burgundy material as both of my heeled feet hit the floor.

It's almost lewd the way the dress pools around his wrist, his large palm wrapped around the delicate skin on the back of my knee. I swear his finger gently strokes before he withdraws his hand, lifting it to gesture to a passing waiter. "Hey bro, any of that good champagne left?"

The waiter nods and scurries off, returning with a chilled bottle and two glasses before I've managed to lever myself out of the chair. I don't think my legs are working anymore.

"I've never been to London," Jackson says as he pours us both a glass of champagne. "Dan's offered me a visit but I haven't taken him up on it yet."

"You've never worked at one of the studios?" I ask, letting the bubbles sparkle on my tongue and attempting to compose myself. At this point, I should probably switch from alcohol to an ice cold shower.

The side of his mouth ticks up. That might be the first time I've even alluded to the fact that I know what his job is. That I know *who* he is, other than my best friend's boyfriend's best friend.

"Maybe one day. Maybe you could be my tour guide. Show me the hot spots."

I scoff. "Not likely." The only hot spot I know is the one on my phone that connects my laptop to the internet.

"C'mon, we'd have a great time." I roll my eyes. "You could show me all the fun tourist traps and introduce me to the Queen."

"I would never go to a tourist trap on purpose, way too many tourists."

"Where they are likely to be."

"And the Queen's dead, where have you been?"

He waves me off as he reaches for his glass. "We'll go look at her coffin or something."

I laugh despite myself. "The only thing you can think to do in London is look at the Queen's headstone?"

He tilts his head with a grin, "What else could we do?"

His tone is almost...flirty? I bite down on the thought. No, Jackson Harper is *not* flirting with me. At least, not seriously anyway.

I blow out a breath and gesture with my now nearly empty glass. "I don't know, we could go to a museum or Richmond Park at sunset or get a drink in the oldest pub in England."

His grin widens, his warm brown eyes crinkling at the corners and my fingers twitch to trace the lines. "Sounds like a date, pretty girl."

I feel my face turn red. "I didn't—I don't mean..." I go to adjust my glasses but awkwardly fiddle with my earring instead.

I hear his low laugh behind my closed eyes. "I didn't say I wouldn't go."

I snap my head up, narrowing my eyes. He's laughing at me and the feeling burns in my chest. Suddenly uncomfortable, I stand, draining the rest of my drink. "I have to go."

"Hey." His tanned hand encircles my wrist pulling me to a halt as those infernal sparks trail across my skin. "What did I do?"

I tug my wrist free. "Nothing. I think Anya needs me." I feel like a teenager again, desperately trying to be cool with the guy I'm into but ending up mortified instead.

Jackson stands and turns his head to the dance floor where Anya and Danny are now trying to race to see who can catch the other's tonsils first.

He turns back with a raised eyebrow. His neck-length hair sways with the movement, the glossy strands shining in the light from the candle sconces above us.

"Are you sure about that, pretty girl?"

"Don't call me that," I say forcefully, trying to sidestep him. His broad chest halts me, his arms wide and open.

"What 'pretty girl'?"

I wince.

"Why not?"

"Because it's mean," I snap and finally walk past him.

I don't know if he says anything in reply as I escape onto the balcony, cruel laughter ringing in my ears.

2

JACKSON

The prettiest girl I've ever seen doesn't think she's pretty.

I've known Rosie Taylor on and off for a few years now. She's always lingering at the edges of group gatherings until Anya or a friendly face approaches. It's like she turns on when her people are with her, her lightness brightening the whole room. She makes them laugh, her voice rises and her pretty smile takes over her whole face.

Ever since she walked in on me in one of my less than fine moments, snorting a line in Dan's brand new bathroom ahead of a launch party, I haven't been able to get her out of my head.

She'd walked into the bathroom as I was hunched over with a rolled up hundred dollar bill in my hands, blinked at me like a deer in headlights, before muttering a quick sorry and slamming the door behind her.

I had tried to find her afterwards to what—apologize? Then I realized I didn't need to, I'm a grown man. If I want to do a party favor I'm within my rights. Even if I haven't touched the stuff since that night.

She's always managed to disappear right when I'm ready to talk to her. But not tonight.

I follow her as she storms out of the wide balcony doors and onto the balustrade balcony overlooking the gardens.

My boy does not do things in half when it comes to his woman. Hiring out a hundred room eighteenth century French Chateau and all its grounds for the weekend. If I've spent an inordinate amount of time wandering the halls hoping to bump into the elusive Maid of Honor, that's my business.

This time, I find her leaning against the balcony looking up into the rapidly darkening sky.

I tug my tie loose as I approach. Resting my back on the thick stone balcony, I face the chateau and the warm lights billowing from the windows. The shadows hide her gorgeous face and all I want to do is tilt her head towards me so I can see her eyes.

"Who told you you're not pretty?" I ask, ducking so I can catch her blues with mine.

She hides her flinch but it's hard to miss when you're looking for it. It's the only thing that makes sense, even if it doesn't make any to me. The woman standing next to me with her long dark hair pulled away from her face and a burgundy bridesmaid dress hugging her tantalizing curves, doesn't see how beautiful she is. She lifts her hand to her face before awkwardly stopping.

"I said it because it's true, but I won't call you that if you don't like it," I say gently, leaning back with my arm until it's slightly crossed in front of her. She's like a magnet. Now that she's finally given me the attention I've been desperate for, I can't let her go.

She turns her head towards me slightly, her hair falling over her shoulder. In the dark with the wedding band's music echoing through the doors, I can't stop myself from reaching forward and brushing it back, my fingers dancing across her pale skin and gently brushing her clavicle. Goosebumps break out in my wake as she inhales a shaky breath.

"I can think of some other things to call you if you like." I sidle closer to her. "Stunning." My hand trails down her bare shoulder.

"Ravishing." I reach her wrist and trace my fingers on the delicate skin of her inner arm.

"Jackson," she says with a weak laugh but she doesn't step away. If anything she takes a tiny step closer, until the hem of her dress brushes against the tips of my dress shoes.

I gently lift her arm to my lips as I press a kiss to her inner wrist, her perfume invading my senses. "Breathtaking," I murmur against her skin.

I'd be lying if I said I didn't want to touch her like this. I've been desperate to taste her plush lips and bury myself in her curves since the first second I saw her. Explore the tempting body hidden beneath a dress that hugs her so perfectly and the pretty blush that travels along her cheeks.

I keep my eyes on that pretty face, watching as her throat bobs at my movement. She doesn't brush me off.

"Sexy." At that, her head whips towards me but I don't stop my motion, the backs of my knuckles brushing the side of her full breast. All the blood in my body drains to my groin as I tilt my head towards her and I feel hers shift ever so slightly towards mine. "Beautiful."

I don't look away from her eyes as I watch them drop to my lips. We're so close our noses could touch. I inch forward, gently nudging her nose with mine.

"What are you doing?" she breathes even as she tilts her

head towards me, her chest rising and falling with heavy breaths.

I could wait in this moment forever, slowly descending to taste the lips I've been looking at from afar for years. "This."

I raise my hand until it tangles in her thick hair and I hear her breath hitch in her throat before we finally meet.

Her soft lips tremble under mine and I'm barely able to repress my groan at the feeling. My tongue reaches out to her lip, slowly parting them until I feel hers flicking against mine. I widen my mouth, allowing her entry and I nearly come in my pants at the delicious whimper that I swallow on my tongue.

I take it slow, allowing her curious little mouth to explore mine, chasing her at every movement.

Her hand rises to my hair, tangling in the strands at the back of my head, gently tugging. My other hand slides across her silky dress, clutching her closer to me as my tongue delves deeper. I can feel her breasts pressing against my chest and I can't stop myself from grinding into her just to hear her make that noise again.

There's no space between our bodies as I twist her towards the stone balcony. My hands travel down to her soft thighs and I lift her effortlessly, placing her on the top. She whimpers and tightens her grip on my hair with one hand and clutches my shoulder with the other. She pulls away and assesses her new elevated position.

"Jackson–"

"I've got you, pretty girl."

We line up perfectly, my arms wrapped securely around her and her legs falling apart wider, welcoming me in as she tugs my lips back to hers.

I reach for her foot, tracing the shoe I hadn't stopped

myself from returning to her. I trail my hand up her smooth legs, tugging her dress up until it's pooled across her thighs and I catch a glimpse of a lacy thong that makes me groan. I trail kisses along her neck, gently biting her smooth skin and licking away the sting.

I feel her head tilt back, her long hair brushing the hand I have braced on her waist. My cock is almost ready to burst out of my zipper and it's all I can do to grind against her.

I dance my fingers up her thigh until I reach the lace hiding what I'm aching for. I can feel her heat through the damp material and I gently trace my fingers through her wetness.

"Fuck," she whimpers, as I tease her through the soaked lace.

"Can I touch you?" I ask, against her mouth. She clasps my jaw between her hands as she nods.

"Please," she whispers against my lips.

I slip my hand inside and feel her, soft, warm, wet. I swallow her gasp on my tongue as I flick my fingers across her clit before swiping inside her, feeling her clench around me. The noises she makes reminds me that we're in public and I'm filled with the urge to shelter her, to forbid anyone else from hearing the noises she's making just for me.

"You gonna come on my fingers, pretty girl?"

She nods her head helplessly.

"You look so beautiful riding my hand, Rosie. You're doing so good. Come for me." I whisper against her lips.

My praise is rewarded as her pussy tightens around my fingers and I swallow her cry.

Her hands finally leave my shoulders, squeezing my biceps before reaching between the buttons on my shirt, popping them open and sliding her wicked hands down to my belt.

She makes quick work of tugging my belt free and her hand plunges into my pants, wrapping her palm around me. My cock is leaking precum as I thrust into the circle of her fingers. I rest my head on her shoulder as I continue playing with her pussy, her clit throbbing underneath my thumb.

"Fuck me," Rosie begs, breathlessly. I almost come from her words but close my eyes with a wince.

"I don't have a condom." Why the *hell* don't I have a condom? Why do I hate myself this much?

Rosie looks at me with desperate eyes. "I'm on the pill." She bites her lip. "I'm clean, I haven't been with anyone for—well for a while."

I kiss her before I have to think about her being with anyone else.

"I got tested last month and haven't been with anyone since," I say against her lips.

She nods and tightens her grip, tugging me towards her. "Fuck me, Jackson. Please."

Ask any man in this position, a pretty girl begging him to fuck her bareback on a balcony in a French castle, and see what they say.

Rosie shifts on her hands, sliding her underwear down her legs. I tug my pants down until my cock springs free and allow her to guide me between her thighs. I nudge my tip at her wet heat and nearly black out. I take a steadying breath to stop myself from rutting into her like a beast. I swipe my tip through her wetness, loving the little gasp she makes at the sensation.

Finally, I end both our torture and slowly plunge into her. Her heat envelops me and my head falls to her shoulder at the sensation. She squeezes around me and I think I enter heaven. "What are you doing to me?"

She tilts her hips, swallowing me deeper. My hand grips her thigh as I press kisses along her neck and rock into her.

We groan together at the feeling. It's never been like this. Never.

I pull out and plunge back in, lifting her skirt higher on her waist and pulling back to watch us move together. I bring my hand back to her clit and tease her alongside every thrust.

"Jackson, I can't–" She breaks off with a gasp as her thighs twitch.

"You can, pretty girl," I purr, snapping my hips faster and hooking her leg higher. "Come on my cock, Rosie. I want to feel you. "

My other arm tightens around her back, pulling our bodies flush, our wedding finery in disarray. I take her swollen lips in mine and it doesn't take long for us to both tumble over the edge. Her head tilts back and I press my lips to her jumping pulse point.

We stay like that for a few seconds, catching our breath, until a loud laugh from inside the party has us jumping apart. Rosie gently pushes me backward but I stay in front of her protectively as she tugs her dress back down and jumps off the balcony whilst I do up my fly and refasten the buttons of my shirt. A quick glance confirms it's still just us out here and the laugh was from inside.

Rosie holds her face in her hands and takes a steadying breath.

"You okay pretty girl?" I ask, pushing my hair back.

She lets out a weak laugh. "I thought you weren't calling me that anymore."

"I said I would stop if you didn't like it," I say with a grin. I want to grab her hand and take her back to my room where I can whisper more compliments she won't accept into her skin until she can't take it anymore.

"I'm going to go back inside now." She doesn't look at me, awkwardly playing with the clip in her hair.

"I'll walk you in," I say, stepping closer to her.

"No, it's uh—I'm just going to sneak back to my room." She finally turns to face me, lifting her chin.

I shoot her a wink and can't help the thrill of seeing another blush rise in her cheeks.

"Alone," she enforces with a groan before rubbing at her temple. "We shouldn't have done this."

"Why not?" I ask, finally catching her arm with my hand. I trace my fingers against her wrist gently but she shifts free.

"This was a bad idea."

"It was one of my best actually."

"I think it would be for the best if we just forget it ever happened."

"I don't know if I can do that."

"Try," she says as she turns back to the party. "Goodnight Jackson." She says as she walks back into the party. She doesn't look back.

3

ROSIE

6 weeks later

With a frustrated moan, I pull the black trousers down my legs and throw them into the corner of the room. My usual work uniform of jeans and a faded knit jumper had to be relegated today for something more professional to impress the company bosses who are coming in for a quarterly meeting.

I've never really minded wearing my corporate wardrobe but it's never escaped my notice that the guys at work wear a variation of jeans and a graphic t-shirt every day regardless, but I know if I wear anything vaguely non-professional I get a horrified side eye.

It's fine, whatever, I can dress nicely on occasion. Normally. Not today when all of my clothes are apparently two sizes too small. I glare at my body in the mirror, frustrated tears pricking at my eyes. *Beautiful.* I bite my lip as Jackson's words echo in my ears. I have done everything in my power to forget that night, forget how he made me feel with his whispered compliments, including drinking an unreasonable amount of wine when I got back to my room and vomiting it all up the next morning. I had allowed his words to settle in my heart, I had allowed the way he filled me with confidence to settle under my skin and spread my legs for him. His raspy groans and hot hands made me feel powerful and beautiful. Like a seductress bringing one of the most handsome men in the world to his knees.

Now, in mismatched fraying underwear and with no trousers that fit I feel nothing like I did that night.

"You shouldn't wear that, Rosalie, it makes you look frumpy."

I press the heel of my hands to my eyes and take a steadying breath. I return to my closet and rummage until I find an old summer dress. It's getting unseasonably cold and I've never worn a dress to work before but time is running out. I tug it over my head and with one last cursory glance in the mirror, I go with it.

I've pissed about so much I don't have time for breakfast as I run out the door, hustling alongside my fellow commuters on our way to the station. The tube is over-crowded and busy and I have to stand and sway with the motion, clinging onto the bar and trying not to let the swooping in my empty stomach make me queasy.

When I finally emerge into the fresh air, I immediately bypass the tens of thousands of people clogging the streets in Soho. It's always so busy around here that it's impossible to walk in a straight line without being bumped off the road by swinging arms pointing at landmarks or taking selfies.

I try not to let my crappy mood show on my face as I bob and weave through the crowd.

I wave at Richard, the receptionist, as I take the stairs to the office three at a time. Our suite is on the third floor of an old nineteenth century building, its marble stairs and thick walls a literal nightmare when trying to get enough signal to edit online.

I swipe my lanyard and push open the heavy door on our floor. The guys are all swinging in their seats as they chat, their work open on the computers behind them. Unsurprisingly, no one acknowledges my arrival, but I mutter a quiet 'good morning' as I scooch past them to my desk.

Kevin, the leader of their little pack and the biggest pain in my ass, follows my trek with his chair.

"Morning Rosie, you look nice today."

I don't look up as I power up my computer offering out a "Thanks" in the hopes he'll leave me alone.

"A dress for easy access?" he leers as his eyes rove down my body. "That will definitely help today's project evaluation."

My shoulders stiffen but I don't turn, sitting heavily in my chair and tugging the material further down my thighs. I hear the boys snicker but I pretend I don't.

I learned pretty quickly to not rise to their misogynistic jokes. On the days I have to be in the office, I come in, put my headphones in and pretend I'm actually at my desk at home to get through the day.

Once my computer boots up, I open my project. I'm still collating the raw footage from the action scene of the medieval feature our team is working on. Kevin is the lead editor so he's doing the fun stuff of cutting it together, often having one on ones with the director. As an assembly, my job is to file and organize every single shot filmed, so that Kevin can swoop in afterwards and cut it all together. Unfortunately for me, this director was a bit trigger happy, so I have hundreds of hours of content to organize. By the end of the day, I usually emerge into daylight still seeing mud flying and silver swords swinging behind my eyelids.

My stomach turns but I ignore it, taking a sip from my water bottle in the hopes it will settle it.

A few hours pass and I manage to block out the sounds of my coworkers clicking away and chatting about the latest game 'Baleron X'. I've already played it through and thought it was underdeveloped and boring, but I would rather play it every day for the rest of my life than pipe up in this room.

Eventually our boss, Gareth, enters the suite and announces a meeting. "I'm running behind so it will be over lunch."

My eyes close and I can already predict the next words out of Kevin's mouth. "Sweet," he says, rubbing his hands together. "Sushi?"

I stifle a groan as the others chorus their agreement. I hate sushi. Just the thought of the stuff makes my stomach roll uneasily. I know it's no use arguing though. Kevin's obsession with eating raw fish everyday is something he needs to speak to his doctor about, but I know as soon as I say I don't like it, I'll be overruled on purpose.

I stay quiet and return to my battle sequence. By the time lunch rolls around, hunger is already gnawing at my stomach. Thankfully, last time I worked in the office I stored a granola bar in my drawer. We're not technically allowed to eat at the computers, so I glance around quickly before scarfing it down in two bites.

Instant regret. The granola disintegrates in my mouth into a giant ball of sand that I have to force myself to swallow. Before I can take a swig of my water, Richard arrives with Kevin's order and the guys all jump up.

Cradling my bottle to my chest, I slowly make my way to the meeting room.

I take a seat at the large table furthest away from the raw fish.

I try to roll my seat away from Kevin when he sits next to me with his food, but there's only so far I can go.

"Right, lads. Let's check in, where are we?"

Kevin leans towards me and grabs a small packet of soy sauce. He slathers it over his sushi and takes a bite before speaking with his mouth wide open.

The smell of fish surrounds me on all sides and I glance frantically at the windows but they're all bolted shut. The scent of the multiple men in this room, more than a few who haven't discovered deodorant, on top of the smell of uncooked fish is enough to bring up my granola bar.

Horrified, I stand, my chair rolling into the wall at the motion. I clap my hand over my mouth as I frantically round the table and stumble into the hallway, desperate to make it to the bathroom before my nonexistent breakfast makes a reappearance.

I rush down the narrow hallway and stumble into the toilet, barely able to fumble with the lock before I fall to my knees over the toilet.

Heaving, my body convulses over the bowl until I have nothing left. With shaking hands, I wipe my eyes and rub my palms over my face.

I must be coming down with something. Maybe I shouldn't have reheated the rice I ate last night. Or maybe it's the flu. It's probably the flu. Whatever it is, I'm not going back to that meeting room.

Swilling my mouth out at the tap, I stare into the mirror. I'm pale but my eyes are bright and there's a little color in my cheeks. I don't feel hot but I've also never had the flu before, so maybe that's normal?

Taking a shaky breath, I leave the bathroom and slowly make my way to the meeting room. The thought of encountering the smell of that room again causes me to knock gently and quietly request to speak to Gareth.

He sighs and comes to the door where I linger on the threshold.

"Yes?"

I gulp. "I—I'm not well, so I'm going to go work from home the rest of the day." He blinks at me so I add, "If that's okay."

He huffs and glances at his watch. "Fine, but make the time back before you log off."

I nod. "Thanks, I will."

He narrows his eyes. "Are you contagious?"

"Uhm, I don't think so?"

"Let me know when you're back online." He turns back to the room, the door closing slowly behind him.

Before it closes completely, I hear a snort from inside the room. "Maybe she's pregnant."

I freeze, staring at the wood of the door as if I can see the words imprinted there.

No. No way. Absolutely not.

I stumble back to my station and gather my belongings, my mind swirling with the word.

Pregnant.

The thought is ridiculous. Me? Pregnant? I've only ever had two boyfriends and I broke up with Adam over a year ago.

It's only when I'm on the tube, squished in the corner, that I allow myself to think of the only other person I've been with. The only person who I've ever had a one night stand with. The only person who I fucked over a balcony in a French Chateau whilst he whispered praise across my skin.

No, it's not possible, I tell myself as I stop in a pharmacy on my way home.

Not possible at all.

4

JACKSON

IN MY HEAD, LONDON IS A MYSTICAL PLACE FILLED WITH RED telephone boxes and men walking around in top hats. In reality, the London I'm in is a large hotel next to a motorway near a place called 'Uxbridge'.

My assistant Eric came recommended by Danny, and he assured me that this is the best place for me to stay. Close enough to the film lot and away from the hubbub of the city.

I did want to tell him that I wouldn't mind the hubbub but I figured that was an argument that wasn't worth the effort.

Instead, I gaze out of the floor to ceiling window and look over the gray landscape of tower blocks and terraced houses.

I wonder, not for the first time, where *she* lives. How big is London anyway? Can I see her house from here? Maybe she's in one of the tower blocks on the horizon, or one of the houses dotted along the motorway.

After the wedding, she made it very difficult to approach her. As soon as Danny and Anya escaped on their honeymoon, I tried nearly every door in the chateau hoping I ended up at hers. No luck, but I did spend at least thirty five minutes listening to Anya's mother relay every aspect of the ceremony, reception and after party as if I wasn't also there.

I should let it go, let *her* go. It was one hook up almost two months ago, but I would be lying if I said that it didn't have some sort of impact when my agent finally got this latest action movie over the line.

Six months of shooting, a combination of stunts, location and studio filming. I told my agent and PR team that I'm mostly excited for the stunts and typically that's true. There's nothing I love more than getting harnessed to a rig and flipped around a few times over a green screen mat. But if I'm being honest with myself, I'm most excited to be in the same city as the girl who walked away from me in France without a second glance and an order to forget it ever happened.

Resting my hands on my hips, I finally admit that I'm probably not going to be able to sense where in London Rosie currently is just from standing at the window.

I have already scoured social media for any hint of her. I pull up Anya's profile and scroll to my favorite photo, one from the wedding of Rosie and Anya before the ceremony, Rosie's dark dress hugging all the curves that felt so delicious under my hands. But it's her face that I linger on, the dazzling smile that she shows her best friend and the shiny blue eyes sparkling with joy.

I've done this multiple times but I tap the picture, desperate to see if maybe Anya has tagged her since. No luck. I can't blame her. Anya has a very small follower list now, with only a few hundred personal contacts and she doesn't tag anyone anymore. I'm just glad that she's allowed me in enough to be able to keep returning to this picture.

Even though she has so few followers, I've already

maxed out every account desperate to find Rosie's. It's getting stalker-ish now and I am almost ready to admit I have a problem. I'm almost positive it's a private account with a tiny picture of a girl who's almost Rosie shaped but it's too vague to tell for sure and the last thing I want is to accidentally follow a random stranger.

Collapsing on my bed, I fall back onto the sheets with a sigh. I need to see her again. I have to. I haven't flown half way across the world to give up now.

I have to see her, even if there's no chemistry (impossible), even if she doesn't want to be with me (possible). I have to know.

Call it closure or call it obsession, I have to know.

A knock on my door disturbs my musings and I cross the room to answer.

Eric is about half my size and always wears the same button down shirt. I've only really met him in person a handful of times. Maybe he has many of the same shirt. Maybe he doesn't wash it between wears. Maybe he washes it every night. My sister Tara would lose it if that's the case, what a waste of water.

"Hello, Mr Harper," Eric says, puffing his chest up.

"Jackson, please." I open the door wider and allow him in.

"The car is downstairs when you're ready to head to set."

I nod. "I'll just grab my shoes and I'm good to go."

As I tug on my sneakers, I glance up at him. Eric is politely staring at the floor by his feet.

"Hey, would you be able to do something for me?"

He looks up. "Of course Mr Har–Jackson. What can I help you with?"

I rub my beard, "I need to get in touch with someone, but I don't have her number."

Eric looks at me suspiciously. "Uh—"

"Not in a weird way," I assure him in what I hope is a convincing tone. "It's the Maid of Honor at Danny's wedding. I uh—I have something for her that she left at the wedding."

Eric looks doubtful. "Wasn't the wedding in June?"

"Yeah, I completely forgot until I was packing my suitcase and then figured I could just deliver it in person."

He purses his lips before nodding to himself. "Yeah... yeah I could probably find some details for her."

I stand and cross the room to him, clapping him on the shoulder as I grin. "Perfect, her name is Rosie Taylor, she's Anya's best friend and she lives in London. Is that enough?"

Eric nods nervously. "Yeah, yeah, I'll see what I can find."

"Excellent, now let's get moving."

Today is a prep day and I spend most of it in costume fittings. Unlike Starseeker, this film is pure action. I'm an ex-spy just trying to get by working construction before my old partner pulls me back into a conspiracy. Basically, I just get to fake punch a lot of people and shoot some fake guns. Excellent.

Sometimes this job feels like what I wanted when I was a kid. I wanted to be a hero, fighting bad guys and saving the day. My dad used to pretend to be a villain, sneaking in the house to press a kiss to my mother's cheek, and I used to hide behind doors and prepare to tackle him. He would go down pleading mercy as I climbed over him, pretending to be bested.

Then one day he didn't come home. In real life, bad things don't happen to bad people and good guys don't save the day. Sometimes, a father of three trips in the street and smacks his head open on the curb.

The play fighting stopped, replaced by rugby and then

an acting class that my mum was convinced would help me process my feelings and the panic attacks that would grip me. I don't know how many feelings were processed in the class but at least I found something I was good at.

It was when I started stunt work that I fell head over heels. The adrenaline that would race through my body when I was suspended by a high wire or when I threw myself onto the crash mat would get my heart pounding in my chest. My body felt like it was jumping off a cliff though my brain knew I would land safely. The contradiction was addictive and I've spent the rest of my life chasing the high.

I'm crossing the lot to the craft services when I hear a familiar accent. "Jackie."

I look up with a grin as Tony Butler saunters towards me with open arms.

"Get out of here," I laugh as I return his hug, slapping his back for good measure. He's got a slimmer build than me, better suited to the type of gymnastic stunts he's known for. "Are you working this one?"

I've known Tony for nearly fifteen years on and off. We started out together back in Wellington but he pivoted to being a professional stunt double whereas I was more than happy to have my face on the big screen.

"Nah, bro. I'm booked on a couple of TV dramas. I'm just here as a favor to Marky, he wanted my eyes on the plans for some of the rigs. This is going to be a big one." He wiggles his eyebrows at me. His face is slimmer than I remember, his dusty blond hair cropped short and a familiar grin pulling at his cheeks.

"Don't I know it," I say, flexing my neck muscles.

He nudges my shoulder. "How've you been bro? I haven't seen you for years, feels like."

I rub my beard. "Yeah I'm good, ready to get this one under my belt so I can retire the Starseeker suit for good."

"But you look so handsome in it." Tony snickers, fluttering his eyelashes.

I grab him in a headlock and we're teenagers again joking around on the rugby pitch. "Yeah, yeah, laugh it up."

"Jackie, I need his head on his body." Marky shouts from across the lot and I let Tony back to his feet.

"I was letting him win!" Tony laughs back at Marky, the silver haired stunt coordinator I've worked with on more than one occasion.

"How's Masen? And Kaia?"

"Yeah, good bro," Tony says as he readjusts his jacket. "Masen's doing well in his exams. Loves maths and science, don't know where he got that from."

I laugh. "You barely know how to count to fifty."

"Hey, I can make it to at least a hundred now."

I see Eric edging closer to me. "Guess that's my cue, bro." I offer him my hand to shake. "I'll see you around, yeah? Don't be a stranger."

"You got it." He claps my hand, and slaps my shoulder. "Good luck with this one yeah? And give me a buzz when you want to let the professionals take over."

I laugh. "Should have stuck with the acting Tony, maybe then you could have had a shot at the big leagues."

"Alright, *Starseeker*," he calls over his shoulder as he heads towards Marky.

I laugh under my breath as I turn to Eric. "I love that guy."

It's only when we slide in the car that Eric clears his throat from beside me and hands me a piece of paper.

I unfurl it and can't stop the grin that spreads across my face.

"My man," I say to Eric and offer him my fist to bump.

5
____

ROSIE

I called in sick to work the rest of the week and migrated from the bed to the sofa, getting up only to visit the bathroom and vomit up whatever I'd managed to keep down that day.

It's been four days since I took that test. Since my whole world upended with the two little pink lines on the screen. *Pregnant.*

It's been a long four days of panicking. Anya has texted me a few times, sending our usual messages of inside jokes and memes, but I've avoided speaking to her on the phone. I don't want to tell her yet. What would she do? I never thought I'd be in this position with my best friend on the other side of the world. I have a feeling she'd be on the first flight over and as much as I love her, I will not be responsible for pulling her away from her six month honeymoon. She was more excited about traveling with Danny than she was for the wedding.

I also don't want to tell her before I tell the father.

The *father.*

Jackson Harper. The thousands of scenarios of what he

might say have been rattling around my brain. The most likely outcome is he'll be horrified, demand I terminate or sue me. Can I get sued for getting pregnant? I mean, I did tell him I was on birth control, even if I didn't know that modern medicine is apparently not enough protection from his super sperm.

It was one fuck against a balcony in the middle of a wedding. And we somehow conceived a child.

God, I hope it doesn't ask any questions about its conception.

How am I even supposed to tell the man? He lives in America and has sixteen million followers on Instagram. Even if I messaged him, it would be a drop in the ocean. He likely wouldn't even see it. Danny's sister Pip did set up a group chat for the wedding party on a fancy high security app, mainly so no details could get leaked to the press, but that was closed after the happy couple left for their honeymoon.

I could ask Anya, but then I'd have to answer questions about why I even want his number. And then I'd have to describe how I defiled her wedding, because if I know my best friend she will demand every single detail. I know Pip and our other friend Cassie would have his number too, but I'm way too shy to message them out of the blue.

I never really considered if I would be a mother. My own wasn't exactly a shining example. I never had dreams about a white wedding or a gaggle of children, but when I took that test in my empty flat, with no one to share the news with, I couldn't help but feel...warm. It wasn't just me anymore. I had a little sidekick.

The doctor handed me a bunch of leaflets when I had my appointment and talked me through all my options. I know I can schedule an abortion. I probably should.

Jackson will likely want that right? He won't want to be saddled with this for the rest of his life.

When I'd idly consider my future, I always thought I'd have an abortion, at least if it happened before I had a husband and a mortgage and a *plan*. I thought for sure that would be what I'd do if this exact circumstance happened.

But I can't make that decision without telling him. I couldn't do that to him. He deserves to know all our options.

I nibble on a plain cracker, one of the only foods I've been able to keep down ever since sushi-granola-gate. My phone buzzes on the arm of the sofa and I glance at the screen with surprise.

"Mum?" I ask, confused as I pull the phone to my ear. I can't remember the last time she called me without a date scheduled in the diary or an important life update. "Everything okay?"

"Rosalie, how are you?"

I stumble. Should I tell her that I'm potentially making her a grandma? "Uh—"

"Lovely, look I'm just calling because Cleo's birthday is coming up."

"Oh," I say, quietly. "Right."

"What are you going to buy her?"

"Uhm." What am I going to buy the sister who has literally everything she's ever asked for? "What does she want?"

"Really Rosalie, you should ask her," Mum scolds.

"Okay." I rub my eyes behind my glasses. "Yeah, I'll text her."

"I have to go now, but make sure it's a good gift this year, yes? Let's not have a repeat of her twenty fifth."

I bite back my sigh. For Cleo's twenty fifth a few years ago, I bought her a signed vinyl of our favorite band growing up. I was so pleased, I was convinced she would love it.

When we gathered for her party in a fancy restaurant and I handed it over, she looked at me disgusted and said, "I haven't listened to this since I was a teenager. Can you return it?" It was awful, and my family has not let me forget it.

I open my mouth ready to keep her on the line, but instead I get her dial tone.

Would I have even told her?

I don't know much about pregnancy yet but I'm ready to blame it for the tear that gets caught behind my glasses. I yank them off and throw them on the coffee table before rubbing my eyes.

Get it together, I think to myself as I attempt a steadying breath.

I keep my hands over my eyes, the darkness allowing my racing thoughts to settle slightly.

The intercom buzzes and I do not have the capacity to direct a stranger to leave their parcel for my neighbor. My building is an old house converted into three flats so I often get asked to open the main door for deliveries, but the speaker is so old it's impossible to ever speak clearly to the other person. It's a game of telephone that I do not have the energy to play right now.

It buzzes again, this time for longer. With a growl, I roll off the sofa and snatch the intercom off the hook. "Yes?"

"Eh, delivery?" The voice is staticy but I heard enough to open the door and reply, "Please leave it in the hall."

I wish I could open a bottle of wine right now, but I am literally forbidden by my little sidekick. Instead, I pour a glass of water and attempt to stop my tears from falling.

The knock at the door makes me jump. I haven't ordered anything, is the delivery for me?

Suspiciously, I cross to the door and tug it open.

A bouquet of flowers are thrust in my face. Mauve calla lilies, dark pink roses, and foliage invade my vision before the bouquet is pulled down to reveal the cheeky grin on Jackson Harper's face.

I blink a few times and wish I hadn't left my glasses on the coffee table. My surprise must show on my face as his smile strains slightly.

"For you," he says like a dream.

I gape at him, my blurry eyes roving across his face. Same dark hair drifting to his shoulders, same tan skin and trimmed beard, same twinkle in his chocolate eyes.

And then I burst into tears.

6

JACKSON

"Well hey now, that's not what I was expecting to happen when you saw me." Rosie looks adorable in her oversized sweatshirt and messy bun, but I'm more focused on her red face as tears stream down her cheeks.

I gently step inside and place the flowers on the console table. "I'm coming in, is that okay?"

She nods behind the hands she's clasped over her eyes.

I gently rest my hands on her elbows. "Hey, hey. What's going on?"

Right, that didn't help. It just makes her cry harder.

"Okay, let's go sit down, hmm?" I try to hide the panic in my voice as we stumble across to a small kitchen and I tug one of the mismatched chairs free from the table, guiding her to sit on it.

"How about some water? Would you like some water? Let's get you some water." What am I doing? I've obviously triggered this and I'm most likely making it worse.

But there's no way in hell I can leave this girl sitting at her kitchen table, sobbing. I rummage through her cupboards until I find drinking glasses, filling one up at the faucet. Do English people drink from the faucet?

I place it gently down next to her and pull another chair free. I sit side on, my thighs bracketing hers.

"Come on, pretty girl, you're scaring me here." I gently move some of her hair away from her face, tucking it behind her ear.

I tug on her wrists until she shows me those big blue eyes. A little bloodshot with some tears sticking to her lashes, but still gorgeous.

"What are you doing here?" she croaks.

I lean back, the chair creaking beneath me. "Okay, well." I run my hand across my beard. "I'm shooting in London."

"You're working here?" she asks, swiping at her cheeks. "For how long?"

"Uh, six months. Give or take."

Her eyes widen. "Six months. In London?"

I nod, biting back a grin. "Yep. Funny how that worked out."

Her big eyes stare up at me for a few seconds before she stands up.

I stay seated, settling further into the wooden chair. I watch as she paces the small room. An impressive feat considering she only can take two steps before she needs to turn around again.

She stops suddenly and puts her hands on her hips, eyes narrow. "How did you know I lived here?"

I tug at my beard again. There's just no way of saying this without it being weird. "I asked my assistant to find your address."

She gapes at me. "What? How is that even possible?"

"He's a good assistant." I shrug, awkwardly resting my hands on my thighs. "It's weird I know, but I didn't have another option. I didn't have your number and I couldn't find you online—"

"You looked me up?"

"Of course I did. I've been dying to talk to you since the wedding. I'm just sorry it took me so long."

"Why?" she asks.

"Huh?"

"Why did you want to talk to me?"

I blow out a breath. "Well hell, I don't know. I didn't really have a speech prepared or anything, but I haven't stopped thinking about you."

She leans back on the kitchen counter, her hands placed on her stomach.

"Wow, uhm," she stumbles. "Okay." Her gaze goes unfocused, like she's thinking really hard.

"Are *you* okay?"

"Hmm?" She looks up distractedly, resting her hands on the counter behind her. "Yeah I'm—I'm good." Her voice rises an octave. She remains by the counter, clutching the marble with her hands and staring into space.

I stand and approach her slowly. "I think this has gone a little bit off the rails here. Shall we try this again?"

She blinks at me confused.

I wink and step around the table, picking up the flowers I left on the side. "Take two!" I throw over my shoulder as I step into the hallway.

I let the door close behind me and then knock a merry tune on the wood.

Rosie's adorably confused face greets me as she pulls the door back open.

I thrust the flowers towards her. "Hi Rosie, I'm so sorry to just barge in like this, I brought these for you."

I can see a smile pull at her lips and I know I've

somehow fixed it. She takes the flowers out of my hands and brings them to her nose. "Hi Jackson, this is a surprise," she drawls, playing along.

I place my hands on either side of the door frame and lean in conspiratorially. "A good surprise?"

She hides that gorgeous smile behind the flowers as she says, "We'll see."

We smile at each other for a few moments and I know I'll do anything to make this girl smile after her tears.

"Come in," she says softly, opening the door further.

I step inside, not once taking my eyes hers.

"I'll just get a vase for these."

I love how she says that. V-ah-ss.

"I love your place," I say as I allow myself to take a look around. The kitchen is small but full of color, glasses hanging from a rack over the fridge and a large orange pot sitting on the stove top.

"Thanks," she throws over her shoulder at the sink. "How *ever* did you find it?"

I grin impishly at her as I come to lean beside her. "I have my ways."

She tries to hide her smile, but I catch it.

"You have any roommates?"

She shakes her head. "No, it's just me." She seems to stumble over that last word but quickly recovers, yanking open a drawer with a clatter.

She lays out my flowers on the table and starts cutting off the ends with a pair of scissors.

Did I even plan what I wanted to say to her when I saw her? Or was I just hoping that she'd jump into my arms as soon as I walked through the door?

"I haven't stopped thinking about the wedding," my mouth says before my brain can catch up.

She jumps with a gasp. "Shit," she hisses, holding her hand. "Ow."

Concerned, I step forward and gently tug her hand free. "Let me see." I rotate her hand, a small bead of blood visible on the tip of her index. Without thinking I raise her finger to my lips and kiss away the pain.

Her finger is warm under my lips, reminding me of the last time I kissed her skin. She blinks up at me until I finally let go, the taste of her blood in my mouth singing to me like I'm a vampire and she's my muse.

She yanks her hand away and rushes to the sink. Turning the faucet on she says quietly, "I'm such a mess."

"You're not a mess, pretty girl. I'm just a very overwhelming person."

She laughs under her breath.

"Bandaid?" I ask.

"Bottom drawer." She gestures with her chin.

I rummage around until I find a little box of bandaids, slipping one out and spinning her towards me. Gently, I wrap it around her finger, and I can't help pressing a final kiss to her wound. When I look up, we're much closer than anticipated. I can almost count her eyelashes.

"Jackson," she whispers.

"I should probably go," I say reluctantly. I've barged into this woman's home, made her cry, wounded her with my flowers and essentially sucked her blood. Overwhelming indeed.

"Oh," she says, taking a step back and not looking at me. "Yeah okay."

"Can I get your number, pretty girl?"

Her head snaps up. "Don't call me that," she says reflexively as if I haven't said it multiple times today.

I bite my lip. "Can I get your number, Rosie? Please?" I add on the end.

She nods. "Yeah, yes. That's a good idea." She says it formally, like this is suddenly a business transaction. "One second."

Rosie darts through the door I presume leads to a living room and returns a moment later with her phone. "Put yours in here too so I have it."

I dutifully take her phone and send myself a text before saving my number in her contacts.

"Can I call you?" I ask as I hand it back.

She tucks it in the pocket of her sweatshirt. "Yeah, we should meet up. To, uh, to talk."

I nod my head. "Talk. I'd like that."

She doesn't say anything else, instead wraps her hand around her bandaged finger. "Okay, well."

"Yeah, I'm leaving, I'm leaving." I lift my hands up.

She follows me to the door. I turn just before she closes it. "Don't keep me waiting too long, pretty girl." I wink as she nods her head and whispers a quiet, "Bye."

I can't help but laugh to myself as I head down her hallway. Not how I expected that to go but I still find myself skipping a few of the creaky stairs on my way out.

7

ROSIE

I THINK I BLACKED OUT SOMEWHERE BETWEEN JACKSON Harper knocking on my door and him closing it behind him. Or maybe I've imagined it. Maybe I've never even met him and I'm actually still seventeen and going to see Starseeker on the big screen for the first time and my imagination has run away with me.

But, when I wake up the next day and throw up in my bedroom bin, I know it's not a dream.

I'm still pregnant and the father unknowingly walked back into my life with a cheeky smile and a devilish ability to make me laugh.

I panicked. As soon as I saw him on the other side of the door, any control I was clinging onto disappeared in a flurry of tears and sobs. He immediately went into protective mode, sitting with me and offering up his strength, even when he had no idea what the hell was going on.

Throughout the whole bizarre twenty or so minutes he was in my kitchen, I felt like my body was floating above the room.

I struggle through my day at work avoiding the annoying questions from Kevin and the guys.

It's early evening by the time I take my headphones off and pack away. I check my phone reflexively and my heart stops at the text on the screen.

JACKSON

Hey, pretty girl. How was your day?

I blink at the screen. How was my day?

I shove my phone in my bag and leave the office without acknowledging anyone. Those seven words tumble around my brain on the long commute home.

How was my day? Does he *know*?

I don't know what I thought he would do with my number but I knew that I would need to use it first. And soon.

I need to tell him. I need to tell him the next time I see him. I should have done it when he first barged into my flat, but the shock didn't wear off until after he'd left.

I swear to myself that the next time I see him, the first words I speak will be "Hello Jackson. I'm pregnant, and you're the father."

I tap my card on the barriers, escaping the crowded tube station to the equally crowded street. I've lived in London long enough that I can dodge and weave pedestrians like a pro, but today I barely notice when I'm stuck behind an elderly couple taking up the entire pavement, adding at least forty-five seconds to my journey.

How was my day?

My day? I threw up this morning and can no longer drink milk because your super sperm has had a pretty inconvenient consequence.

I stumble up the stairs to my flat, finally taking my phone out in the safety of my own four walls.

My phone buzzes again as soon as it's in my hands and I jump out of my skin. It's just a news notification.

This is ridiculous. I need to get a grip. If this were Anya, I would tell her to rip the bandaid off and tell him. It's not something I can—should—keep to myself for much longer.

Jackson Harper literally walked back into my life right when I needed him. I have to tell him.

Taking a deep breath, I type out a reply.

ME

I'm good thanks, you?

He replies immediately.

JACKSON

Better now, pretty girl

When are you going to let me take you out
on a date?

The thought of blurting out my news in a crowded restaurant is enough to make me type out my reply.

ME

You can come over to mine. I'll cook.

JACKSON

I like the sound of that? When?

I tug my glasses off and throw them on the kitchen counter, rubbing my eyes until I see spots. I already sound desperate, what's one more comment? Once I tell him, he'll run a mile the other way anyway.

ME

Tonight at 8?

JACKSON

I'll bring the wine ;)

Please don't, I think miserably.

BY THE TIME eight pm rolls around, I'm as calm as I can be given the fact that my unwitting baby daddy is about to walk through my doors and I'm going to change his life over a vegetable curry.

I check my reflection in the mirror. I still look pale no matter how much blush I apply. Whoever said that pregnant women glow was a cruel liar.

The intercom buzzes and I take a deep breath before letting him up.

The walls in this building are old and thin and I can hear him bounding up the stairs before I hear a polite knock on the door.

I brace myself as I open the door. He's wearing a smart button down and jeans, his hair neat and tucked behind his ears, a few strands curling across his forehead. He grins, his eyes crinkling in the corners and I can't help the smile that returns.

"Hey pretty girl," he says, leaning forward to kiss me on the cheek.

I let him and try to stop my eyelashes fluttering as his lips meet my skin.

"No tears this time, that's what I like to see," he says, lifting his hand for a high five. I laugh and lightly press my palm to his. It's a weak attempt that he rectifies by clasping his fingers around mine and tugging me closer until our hands rest against his hard chest.

I can't help but admire the way our hands look, mine swallowed by his. I've never been small and dainty; my ex-boyfriends' clothes have always just fit instead of looking oversized. But Jackson's hands are twice the size of mine and I can still remember how they felt worshiping my body.

I gently tug my hand free, avoiding his gaze as I step back. "Come in, I've got food ready to go." I return to the table, anxiously straightening the plates so I don't have to watch him follow.

"I brought wine," he says once he reaches my side.

I nod mutely. How long should I keep up the charade? *Can't have wine, sorry. You put a baby in me.*

"Glasses are over there." I gesture to the bar rack installed above the fridge where wine glasses dangle upside down.

He reaches around me and plucks them off the shelf. He's so tall, and my flat so tiny, that he barely has to stretch to reach from one end of the room to the other.

"I hope you like vegetarian," I say, allowing him to hand me a glass that I know I won't touch.

"I didn't know you were veggie," Jackson says as we finally take a seat at the table.

I nod. "Yeah, I picked it up a while ago and got hooked on some of the food I made. I experimented a lot with fake meat and I got a bit obsessed with trying to perfect the perfect dish."

"Is this your perfect dish?" he asks.

"Close enough. I once tried this amazing vegan couscous when I was visiting Anya in LA, but I haven't been able to find all the ingredients over here. Also the measurements are all weird over there. How do you even measure a cup?

It's a nightmare because you have to translate everything into measurements you recognize before you can even begin to cook, and then all the recipes have the writer's most recent marriage problem that you have to scroll through just to get to the good part."

I look up from my food and see Jackson's staring at me with a bemused look on his face. I feel my face flush. "Sorry, I'm rambling."

"It's okay, I like your rambling."

I take a bite to distract myself from the look in his eye.

"Send me the restaurant in LA. I'll have to go when I'm back Stateside."

My heart flutters in my chest. Soon he'll be back on the other side of the world. What are me and the baby going to do then?

Stop it, I tell myself. *He might want nothing to do with either of you. At least then he'll be far away.*

"When do you go back?" I ask, taking another bite so I don't blurt it out too soon.

"Shoot for six months and then I'll probably head over. My family is back in Wellington, so it's not like I'm heading back for them."

"How often do you go to New Zealand?"

He shrugs his broad shoulders. "When I can. It's a long flight, but I miss home. They come over sometimes. My older sister loves coming to LA."

"How many sisters do you have?"

"Two. One older and one younger."

My smile grows. "So you're the middle child"

"Yeah, but the only boy so I still get all the attention." He grins.

"What about your parents?"

"My mum is the best."

"And your dad?"

He shifts in his seat. "He died when I was a kid."

"I'm sorry," I tell him, wanting to reach across the table and grab his hand.

"It's fine," he brushes me off. "What about you? Where are your family?"

"Oh, uh. I'm the youngest of two and my parents live back in Wicklow. It's near Gloucester."

At Jackson's blank look, I laugh and say, "North east of here."

"Are you close?"

I stare at my hand as I grip my fork. "No, not really. I have a grandma that I'm really close with, but she was put into a home just after Christmas. I try to visit her every few weekends though, and we talk on the phone every Sunday."

"I bet that makes her day."

I laugh. "Yeah, the nurses said she waits by the phone for my call and doesn't stop talking about me afterwards. The first time I visited, all the staff already knew me by name."

I don't tell him that I ring her so often because I don't want her to forget me, because I want to have one member of my family who wants to spend time with me.

Jackson lifts the wine bottle and motions to my empty glass. I quickly halt him by covering the rim. He looks at me with concerned eyes. "You don't like white?" he asks, as if he's horrified he got the wrong bottle.

"No, no," I say, swallowing against my dry throat. "I—uh, I'm going to have a Coke instead, do you want one?" I jump out of my seat and head to the fridge without looking at him.

"White wine and coke, I've heard that before."

I wince at the memory of catching him doing drugs in Anya's bathroom. I've never done anything more than the half a spliff Anya split with me when we were nineteen and watching the Da Vinci Code. I spent the first half of the evening loudly rewriting the film, and the second half holding Anya's hair as she threw it all back up.

"Just to get it out there," Jackson holds his hands up. "That time at Dan's party wasn't my...finest moment. It's not something I really do anymore, I think that was the last time I even touched the stuff."

"You don't have to explain," I say awkwardly, though relief washes through me.

"I know, but I wanted to," he says softly.

I hold the fridge door open, letting the cold air cool me down but instead all I can smell is the garlic that has probably passed its use by date. I grab the drinks and breathe through my mouth as I rejoin the table.

"Thanks. Are you okay?" Jackson asks when I sit.

"Yeah, yeah I'm fine," I say, unconvincingly.

He eyes me warily. God, I probably look like a loser who can't even hold a conversation with the man without stumbling or rambling. I need to just get it out. Just get it over with. I can't keep it inside for a second longer.

"This rice is gre—"

"I'm pregnant." I announce, placing both hands on the table. I take a deep breath before I let my eyes rise to his face.

Jackson is frozen, his mouth hanging open like he is ready to continue the sentence I just interrupted. He slowly adjusts in his seat, his large body causing my old wooden chair to creak.

I reach to my face for the glasses that I'm not wearing before bringing my hands back to my lap.

He's not saying anything. Why isn't he saying anything?

His mouth moves like he's trying to form words. He tries a few times before he croaks out, "How?"

"Oh, uhm. Well, you know your sperm met my egg and fertilized—"

"Rosie."

I take a breath. "At the wedding."

"You said you were on the pill." A flicker of something washes across his face.

"I am!" I insist. "Honestly, I never do anything like—I would never have let—I mean I wouldn't have taken the risk if I thought for even a second that I wouldn't be protected, but I spoke to my doctor and they said it's not one hundred percent effective, and because I'd been running around in France and drinking and throwing up, I don't know, it just decided to not work."

He doesn't blink. I don't think he's blinked once since I dropped the bomb.

I wring my hands together. "It was definitely the wedding," I say. "I mean I haven't been with anyone but you for at least ten months. And I really don't think sperm can live in the womb for that long. And even the last few times I saw my ex, I don't think he even came anywhere near my vagina so it's been more like ten and a half months without any sperm in the vicinity of my eggs apart from yours."

"Rosie," Jackson says, running his hand across his face. "Please stop talking about sperm."

I nod my head and mime sealing my mouth shut.

"Pregnant," he repeats. "You're pregnant."

I nod again.

"With my baby."

"Yeah," I say quietly. "I only found out last week and I've been trying to figure out how to reach you. And then you literally showed up at my door."

"Well," he says wryly. "That explains the tears."

"It has been very overwhelming."

He's silent, staring at the table between us. He releases a breath as he runs his hand through his hair, messing up the combed strands. A wave falls near his face and I almost want to brush it away.

"I think I need some more wine for this conversation." He reaches for the bottle and tops up his glass. "You don't have a beer, do you?"

I jump up. "Yeah, of course."

I grab a can of IPA from the fridge. "It's not like I'll be drinking this for the next nine months, so you can have as many as you like."

He takes it from me, his fingers brushing mine. "So, you're keeping it then?"

I sit down in my seat, unable to stop my hand brushing my stomach protectively. It's never been flat to begin with but I know it's way too early to show.

I've been asking myself the question for days, but it's only when he asks me with that earnest look in his eyes that I know my answer.

I nod slowly. "Yeah, I think I want to keep it. I thought about having an abortion but I wasn't going to do that without speaking to you about it first. But I just…" I shrug, "I don't think I want to."

He's staring at me, his usually tan skin slightly pale behind his dark beard.

"I'm sorry to put you in this position, Jackson. I honestly didn't plan for this at all—"

"Don't say sorry," he says, taking a gulp of beer. "This is half on me too."

I bite my lip, unsure what to say. I thought for sure he would be mad at me.

He nods again, his eyes softening as they land on me. "Okay."

"Okay?" I ask.

"Okay, let's do it."

"Do what?"

"Have a baby."

"Oh, I mean I didn't expec—"

He raises his hand, "It's too late to unbutter the bread, pretty girl, all we can do now is eat our sandwich."

An incredulous laugh escapes me. "You're the one who wanted me to stop talking about sperm and you talk about *buttering bread*?"

He sends me a cheeky grin, "My butter, my sperm."

I roll my eyes but can't help the giggle that bubbles in my chest.

8

JACKSON

That was not how I expected my first date with Rosie Taylor to go. I thought I'd go over, bring her some wine, eat some good food and preferably end the evening with her legs wrapped around my head.

Instead, she dropped a veritable bomb.

Pregnant.

I've never considered having children, never considered settling down full stop. I'm happy being the fun uncle to my sisters' kids, meeting beautiful women and enjoying their company, before heading back to my condo and getting into my own bed. I have a pretty perfect life.

But almost as soon as the words came out of Rosie's mouth and echoed around her quaint kitchen, that perfect life I imagined for myself changed instantly.

I've always been safe, always double bagged, even going so far as to pull out when I get paranoid. My sister got pregnant at seventeen and I saw how her life changed instantly. It was enough to make me triple sure there were no eighteen-year consequences for one night of fun.

But Rosie was different. I was too in the moment, too lost in her big blue eyes, her soft curves, and her tight pussy to even consider any consequences.

And they sure caught up with me.

The date I had envisioned changed from lust-filled flirting to practical planning pretty quickly after the news.

I left with a gentle kiss on her cheek and a promise to call her the next day after work.

With nothing to do other than think and plan, as soon as I get back to my hotel I open the notes app on my phone and start a list.

Doctors Appointments
Live where?
Names
Tell Mum??

That last one makes my stomach twist. Gloria Harper had a meltdown when my little sister Ella announced she was pregnant. Well, she was just shy of seventeen. I'm a grown man. It's natural for a man my age to settle down, have a family.

The settling down might come as more of a shock than the baby news.

I'm getting ahead of myself. We're not even in a relationship, despite my best efforts.

I can't tell my mum but I can probably get away with speaking to my sister.

My phone is in my hand before I can talk myself out of it.

"Hi Jackie," Ella's chipper voice echoes down the line, slightly out of breath. "What's up?"

I take a seat on the bed in my room, running my hand through my hair as I ask, "Why does something have to be up to call my favorite sister? Where are you?"

I can hear a loud rustle on the other end of the line followed by a yelp.

"Don't ask. Nina's fostered another dog. But it was following her around and tripping her up so she handed me the leash and told me to go for a run. So that's what I'm doing."

I huff a laugh. "And Cody?" I ask, referring to my nephew. "Is he banished too?"

"No, he's been playing that new game you got him for hours, so he's not even left his room."

My twelve year old nephew is a quiet one. It's hard to get him to say more than twenty words each time I see him. Nothing like the rambunctious toddler I used to carry around on my shoulders. I figured early on that bribery will get me everywhere, hence the copy of *Lanes 7* that I managed to get on pre-release.

Perks of the job.

"Right, I've had enough of this, I hate running. Why did I agree to this?"

"Because you love your wife." I reply.

"Ugh, not right now. So, why are you calling again?"

I clear my throat. "Do you uh, remember when you got pregnant with Cody?"

"Uh, yeah it's kind of hard to forget the birth of my one and only child, Jackie."

"What do you..." I start with no idea what I actually need from her. "What did you do?"

There's silence on the other end and it causes me to wince.

"Jackson," Ella says quietly. "Why do you want to know?"

"Uhm," I muse, in what I hope is a convincing tone.

"Jackson Harper." My sister repeats, more firmly.

"What!" I exclaim, "Am I not allowed to ask?"

"About events from thirteen years ago? You're allowed to ask but I'm allowed to ask why."

"Y'know what? Forget I said anything, forget we had this conversation."

I could hang up, but I don't. Instead I listen to the dead air, and occasional yap from Nina's new puppy.

Finally, Ella sighs. "Fine, I'll drop it for now."

"Thank you," I say, pulling at my beard.

"Yeah, yeah. Listen, I'm nearly home now and I have to get this one inside, so I have to go."

"Okay," I say. "Say hi to everyone for me."

"I will. Jackie?" she asks.

"Hmm?"

"Is she okay?"

I nod my head even if she can't see me. "Yeah." I let out a long breath as a smile tugs at my mouth. "Yeah, she's fucking amazing."

I hear Ella's smile through the phone.

"Okay, next time you call me I want a real update," she announces.

I huff a laugh, "You got it."

Well I don't know what I wanted to get from that conversation, and I can't tell if I got it.

I can't tell them yet, even if Ella now basically knows. I don't know if Rosie wants to tell anyone, if we even *can* tell anyone. Don't they say to wait a few months?

Why? Why do they say that? God, I literally know nothing. I dipped out of Ella's pregnancy, only reappearing when Cody was old enough to be entertaining.

I pull up the search on my phone and start adding books to my cart. I can't remember the last time I read a physical book, but at least it feels like doing something.

I click checkout after I've added enough books to fill a

small pregnancy and early years library and rest my phone face down on the bed.

I stare at the wall for a few seconds before picking up the phone again, pulling up Rosie's text chain. The messages from my wooing attempt stare at me. God, was that just a few hours ago that I was flirting with her? The girl I still can't get out of my head? The mother of my child?

Without thinking too quickly, I type out a message.

ME

Thank you for telling me

I see the bubble pop up before disappearing a few times.

ROSIE

Of course, I wouldn't have ever kept this
from you.

ME

I know, I just meant thank you for

My hands hover over the screen. I don't know what I'm thanking her for. The baby? I erase the message and try again.

ME

I know you wouldn't have pretty girl

How are you feeling?

ROSIE

Good, craving a ham sandwich

ME

Get one

ROSIE

I don't even eat meat! Plus no processed
meat allowed according to the internet.

ME

Damn

I'll eat one for you

ROSIE

My hero

ME

What else are you craving?

(That's acceptable, safe and legal)

ROSIE

Ha nothing yet but I'll let you know

ME

Please do

ROSIE

Yesterday I really wanted salted caramel ice
cream

It takes me less than two minutes to open a food delivery app, and I send her the screenshot of the confirmation.

ROSIE

You didn't just do that!

ME

Anything you want pretty girl, I told you that

My phone doesn't leave my hand for the rest of the evening. I barely manage to brush my teeth and text with one hand. This girl.

It's later, when I'm just climbing into bed, that the picture comes in. It's her curled up in a big sweatshirt, glasses perched on her nose and a smile hiding behind a pint of ice cream.

The grin that splits my face makes my cheeks hurt. I save the photo and make it her contact picture.

9

———

ROSIE

THE TUBE CARRIAGE SWAYS UNDER MY FEET LIKE I'M SURFING and my stomach flips. I take a deep breath through the thin gap in my lips to prevent my breakfast spewing over the other passengers in the carriage.

At what point can I wear one of those cute 'baby on board' badges so I can haggle for a seat? Do I have to be showing? When will that be? Maybe I should start doing some real research instead of just googling 'Can I eat rice whilst pregnant?'. I make a mental note to start buying some baby books.

At the next stop, someone gets out of their seat and I maneuver my way through the crowd towards it. Just before I sit, a guy in his early twenties wearing an expensive tennis kit sits down, spreading his legs and taking up more space on the aisle. Great. Getting that badge has now become the number one priority.

I used to love the tube, used to love the commute that would take forty minutes of my day. I used to swan around in a trench coat and smile at tourists visiting my city and meet friends for brunch in central.

But then, one by one, all my local friends moved away. Anya went to America, my friend Penny from work left to go to a different post-production house in Manchester. Even my old boss Kathleen retired and had a mid career switch, leaving me with a team of guys who would rather talk *around* me than *to* me.

Gareth sent out an email late last night telling me I needed to come in on Saturday to catch up on my missed work. I asked if I could work from home but he ignored the email, his way of telling me an obvious *no*. I had thought the others would be there too but no, just me. Gritting my teeth, I had hooked my phone up to the office speakers and spent eight hours logging transcripts, only emerging into the late afternoon sun when my eyes started to cross.

I need to tell work that I'll be going on maternity leave, but I looked it up and I have until I'm twenty five weeks before I legally have to tell them. Predicting that Gareth is going to sigh heavily at the news, I'm more than happy to wait another few months before confessing. He can complain all he wants but I'm within my legal rights to have fifty two weeks off, though I'm under no illusions that whoever comes in as my maternity cover will undoubtedly be a crucial member of the team by the time I'm ready to come back. My statutory maternity pay will only cover the first few months of my rent, and that doesn't even begin to cover the added expenses of raising a baby.

I can't think about it all too hard without panicking. The train judders to a stop and I cling to the metal railing to avoid toppling into the lap of the wannabe Andy Murray. All I want to do now is unbutton my jeans and eat my weight in the salted caramel ice cream I saved in my freezer. The craving gripped me about an hour ago and if I don't eat it soon I will most likely burst into tears. *Again.*

I've never cried as much as I have in the last week. It's like my face is just a water balloon prone to leaking. If this baby is going to play with my tear ducts this much, I don't know how I'm going to survive the next seven months.

The tube launches to a stop and I shuffle through the crowd onto the platform. When I emerge into the fresh slightly chilled air, my phone buzzes in my pocket.

JACKSON

How was your day?

I bite back a smile. It's nice to have someone ask me that, to have someone care.

ME

I had to work so not great. How was yours?

He types for a few minutes and I tuck my phone back in my pocket.

Finally it buzzes.

JACKSON

How well my day is going kind of depends
on you pretty girl.

Huh? I scrunch my brows in confusion before turning the corner onto my street.

"Hey," Jackson says from outside my front door, his hands in his pockets and his pearly white grin pulling at his cheeks. His hair is tied back behind his neck and he has a baseball hat pulled low over his head. He basically looks like a male model. Which he *is*, I remind myself.

Good lord, what have I gotten myself into?

"Hi," I reply dryly, unable to stop the smile from escaping.

"I swear I haven't been waiting outside for you all day like a creeper." He steps closer, hands raised innocently.

"How do I know that?" I ask, lifting my chin.

"I promise. I showed up a few minutes ago but I didn't want to make it weird and just ask you where you were. So I thought I'd be clever about it."

I laugh as I take my keys out of my bag. "You can come in."

"Yes," he cheers. "Are you going to cry this time?"

I roll my eyes trying to hide my smile. Why is this man sexy, sweet *and* funny? It's like a cruel triple threat. My poor womb had no hope at all. "No, I'm not going to cry."

He chuckles softly behind me as I lead him up the stairs.

"I like your place by the way," he says as I unlock the door.

"You've only seen the kitchen." I reply dryly.

"You don't sleep in here?"

"Well, this is the living room and then the bathroom is down that little corridor and the bedroom is opposite. Don't ask me where a baby is going to fit. I haven't got that far yet." I bite my lip. Maybe I shouldn't have said that. "I'll find a place for it, obviously. I mean the baby, not *it*. I figure they will sleep in my room for the first part anyway, so I think that'll be okay. Or maybe I could, like, move into the living room. I'll just need to get a new sofa, since my one is pretty small at the moment. But maybe I should probably spend my money on the stuff for the baby rather than a new sofa—"

I'm halted by a finger on my lips. "Where does that brain go, pretty girl?"

I clamp my lips together behind his finger, the warm digit making me remember what it felt like when his hands were–*Rosie, concentrate.*

I hold my breath until he removes his hand with a smirk. My blush probably gives away where my traitorous mind took me.

"Cool set-up." Jackson gestures to my desk, wandering closer.

"Yeah, it's for work and play." Jackson tugs the chair out from under the desk, glancing at the two consoles underneath. "I have this one for work and then this one for gaming. I spent an afternoon folding away all my wires so I could switch between without having to get on my hands and knees and unplug. And so my work wouldn't slow down when I want to play games."

"You're such a nerd," Jackson teases with a smile. "It's cute."

I hide my blush by fiddling with my glasses. He spins in the chair and sits, the familiar squeak at the movement filling the room.

"Rosie." He shifts his large body, the chair protesting under his weight. "What the fuck is this chair?"

"What do you mean?" I laugh.

The look he shoots me is a cross between bewildered and concerned.

"This is like some sort of medieval torture device."

"I love my chair!" I say defensively. "I saved up for this for ages."

"Why does it feel like I'm simultaneously sitting on a steel bar and a yoga mat?"

I laugh, my hand resting along the back of the fluffy chair. "It's ergonomic."

"Rosie, there is no way this thing is good for you. You'd be better off sitting on a metal fence. Why is it so wide?"

"It's so I can sit with my legs crossed."

The look Jackson gives me makes me snort with laughter.

"I don't understand this. I'm getting you a new chair."

"No!" I protest, shoving at his shoulder until he takes the hint and rises. "Look, it's perfect." I sit on the chair, the thin padding that has definitely seen better days barely cushioning my butt. I fold my legs up and tuck them underneath me, shooting him a smile. "Ergonomic."

He shakes his head with a laugh. "You're delusional."

I slide the chair under the desk and out with just my hands, ignoring the creaking.

"Look, and it rolls."

He laughs. "Rolling *is* the point of the wheels."

My hand accidentally taps the mouse, lighting up my screen, The Sixth Temple bursting into view.

"Is this your game?"

"Yeah."

"Can I play?"

"Oh." I jump up to let him get the chair. "Oh, yeah of course,"

"Can I play with you?" My vagina takes *that* in a very different way. A very sexual way that has nothing to do with the innocent role playing game.

"Uhm, yeah. Well, we can't on this console but I have the game on my other one." I gesture to the TV.

"Let's do it." He claps his hands together before spinning towards the living room. I didn't think my flat was small until this six five giant stood in the middle of it. I'm tempted to see if he can reach both walls when he opens his arms.

"Huh," Jackson says, picking up my decorative cushion with the crocheted words 'Calm Your Tits' in bright red.

My cheeks heat. "That's my nanny's work. She's always crocheting or knitting. She made me that when I moved in here." I gently take the cushion out of his hand, running my hands over the seams before placing it back on the sofa. "She's a bit slower now but but she hasn't forgotten how to make some scandalous slogans."

Jackson laughs. "I can't wait to meet her."

I glance up at him. "You uh, you don't have to."

"Well"—he glances down at my midriff meaningfully—"We're about to be family right?"

"Oh, yeah of course." Family. Jackson and I are going to be a family.

"Have you told your parents yet?"

I quirk my brow. Tell them? I'd rather lick a brick wall than willingly pick up the phone to tell them the news. I already know how that conversation will go, and I don't have the energy to have it yet.

"I'm thinking they'll find out eventually."

"Nine months from now?" Jackson says wily.

I laugh weakly, "Just about."

"I'm probably going to tell my family soon, if that's okay?" Jackson asks, carefully.

"Oh yeah, of course." I nod so quickly I'm surprised my head doesn't fall off. "You can tell whoever you like."

"I'll just tell them for now," he says with a smile. "But it's kind of an all-or-nothing thing with my family. We're not the best at family secrets."

I smile softly. "They sound amazing."

He grins. "Yeah, they are."

He takes a seat on the sofa, his large body making the cozy two-seater look like a child's play furniture.

"Let's play this game. Where's the controller?"

It only takes him a few minutes to get the hang of the rules and we spend the next forty minutes side by side and playfully nudging each other.

Eventually my alarm blares, the opening chords of the Strictly Come Dancing theme song making me jump.

I fumble with my phone until I turn it off, returning my attention back to the screen.

"You good?"

"Yeah!" I say brightly.

"What's the alarm for?" he asks, gesturing to my phone.

"Oh, it's uh—Strictly Come Dancing, the dancing show? I used to watch it every Saturday with my Nanny and so I still watch it even though she's, well, y'know. When I speak to her on Sundays we talk about it and guess who's getting voted out that night. I have an alarm when it starts so I don't miss it."

Without missing a beat, Jackson saves the game and sets the controller on the coffee table.

"Put it on," he says, leaning back into the sofa and handing me the TV remote.

"Oh no, we don't have to."

I put the remote back on the table. Suddenly it's back in my hands with Jackson's larger ones wrapped around mine.

"I want to watch it with you, Rosie." His hands are so large around mine, and I shiver as his fingertip grazes my wrist. "Unless you don't want to."

I blink up at him a few times before I remember what he just asked me, "Uh, sure."

I switch the TV on and flick through to the right channel. The opening song starts as they start listing all the acts.

"Shall we get a pizza?" He asks, pulling his phone from his pocket. "You do like pizza right?"

Pizza, I think my mouth waters at the thought. "Oh, uhm, it's not really in my budget."

Jackson laughs. "Rosie, if you think I'm going to barge into your home and demand you pay for my dinner, I'm doing something wrong." He places a hand on my thigh and squeezes. "Plus, you're cooking my baby, so feeding you is literally my main job."

"Okay fine," I acquiesce, as my gaze gets caught on his large hand. "Because your baby is craving a veggie pizza right now."

I leave him with my order and head to the kitchen, spinning back to him before I cross the threshold. "I still have the wine you brought, but you'll have to drink it alone." I gesture to my midriff. "Or you can have a Diet Coke."

"I'll go Coke. We can save the wine." He winks at me as he takes the cold can out of my hands. I almost jump at the tingles that erupt at my fingertips. It's from the cold can, that's all, I tell myself.

I settle beside him on the sofa. It is definitely too small for him, his arm stretching across the back showing me the taut line of his side and feeling his hand resting behind my head. I reach forward and turn the volume up.

"Who are all these people?" Jackson asks, taking a sip of his drink.

"You wouldn't know any of these guys," I giggle, as a TV Chef, News Presenter and pop culture icons that no one outside of the British Isles would know about dance onto the screen.

He wiggles in his seat along to the music and I can't help but laugh as I readjust on the sofa with my legs curled underneath me, my knee facing his. "Do you want to know the Taylor rules?" I ask.

"Absolutely," Jackson says seriously.

"Okay, in the first episode you have to pick your favorite, your winner and your dark horse and then throughout the series whoever has the winner wins."

"What's the prize?"

"Well, they play for the glitterball trophy but we'll just play for glory," I shrug.

"Oh, I am all the way in, pretty girl."

"Absolutely not," Jackson insists forty minutes later around a slice of pizza. "You think two left feet Patrick and Kat are going to win over Thatcher and Julianna? You need to up your prescription, pretty girl, because we should be worried."

I laugh as I pick a pepper off my slice, "Trust me he's going to be the best one there. I'm a seasoned pro at this now. One year, a fifty-seven year old retired news anchor won, but he had the best Charleston."

"What's a Charleston again? The slow one?"

"No, this one," I say, shaking my hands in a poor imitation of the moves.

"What was that?" he laughs.

"That's what they do! It's a lot of hand shaking and leg pumping. Watch." I tug the remote off the table and pull up a compilation of the best dances. "Prepare to be educated."

It's gone midnight by the time we've got through nearly every season of Strictly showing all of my favorites and I have to stifle a yawn behind my hand.

His eyes crinkle. "You should go to bed, Rosie."

"No no, I'm sorry, I'm just not used to being up this late. This pregnancy is not for the uncaffeinated."

"I'll leave you to it," Jackson says, fishing his phone out of his pocket and stifling a yawn of his own.

"You can uh—you can stay if you like," I offer lamely. I wring my hands together as I glance around the room awkwardly.

Jackson's fingers freeze on his phone.

Oh my god, did that sound like a proposition? It did. It sounds like I just asked to sleep with him.

"I mean the sofa's not too bad and I have a spare blanket and everything," I stumble out.

Jackson stands up gently taking my hand and halting my fidgeting. "I need to get back, I've got an early morning training session."

"Oh, okay," I say awkwardly. Of course he doesn't want to spend the night on my sofa. It's practically half the size of him.

"Can we have dinner or something this week maybe?"

"Uh, I'm working late all week," I spin awkwardly in place and start sorting through our leftovers, stacking pizza boxes and wrappers.

"Saturday then?" He follows me into the kitchen. "I've got to watch the next episode. Got to support my boy."

I place the plates on the counter, "Uh—" The man wants to come and watch Strictly with me. I should say no, I should reaffirm some boundaries although it's clear I've already lost control of my senses. *I have spare blankets and everything.* Ugh!

But the thought of not spending another Saturday night alone...

"Sure." The word falls from my lips before I can stop them.

Jackson grins. "It's a date." He slides his jacket off the kitchen chair.

"It's not a date." I follow him around the kitchen as he steps into his boots and turns to the door.

"Sure it is, pretty girl."

"It's not a date." I insist one more time.

He pauses with his hand on the doorknob before shooting me a wink, "See you, Saturday."

10

JACKSON

"Jackson Harper," my mother scolds over the phone. "You may be thirty two years old but I still know when you're keeping something from me."

I should have known as soon as I told my sister that my mother would come calling soon enough. In my trailer in between scenes, I can't escape my mothers critical brow she levels at me through the phone.

"What did Ella tell you?"

"Nothing, nothing," Mum says, dramatically. "Just that you had some interesting questions."

"I was just checking in with my sister, you're all blowing this out of proportion."

She says nothing but I can feel her probing stare through the camera. Whenever Ella, Tara and I would get in trouble as kids, she used to just stare at us until we couldn't take it anymore and confessed whatever we'd done. She's still got it thirty years later.

"Okay, but you can't freak out."

"Freak out?" Mum freaks. "What are you talking about? Are you sick? Oh my god, you're sick. You need to quit your job and come fly home right now. We'll get you in with Dr Hansa immediately and he'll be able to help."

"Mum, I don't think my old pediatrician will want to see me."

"He'll know other doctors. My friend Kim's daughter is a doctor, she could help. I'll message her right now."

I bite back an exasperated laugh. "Mum, please don't start messaging people."

"She'll reply, it's not a problem. What are your symptoms?"

She moves the camera away from her face so I can only see the top of her head and her lightly graying hair as she types on the phone.

"Mum, please," I say. "Can you hold the phone up? Let me tell you what I need to tell you."

"Okay, okay," she grumbles, pulling the phone back to her face.

She looks just like my older sister Tara, with the same nose and mouth. We all got Dad's eyes though, and Mum always says she loves seeing him in us.

I take a deep breath. "Well, I met someone." This is probably the easier way to break the news. *Gently.*

Mum squeals. "You did! Oh Jackie this is great, who is she? Where's she from? America? Are you long distance?"

"No she's here, in London."

"An English girl! How did you meet?"

"You remember Danny? The guy whose wedding I went to a few months back?"

"Oh yes, the one with that song about autumn leaves. We listened to that at book club and I told all the girls about it. I told them that you're friends and they all say to let you know to let him know that the song is lovely but he needs to stop using so many metaphors. It's too many Jackie."

"I'm sure he'll love that," I tug at my beard with a chuckle. "Well, this girl, Rosie, she's best friends with his wife. She was the Maid of Honor."

"You've been together since then? Is it serious? When can I meet her?"

"Well," I say, "we're still figuring things out but Mum..." I take a breath. "Rosie's ah—she's pregnant."

Silence.

I think the screen is frozen for a second as my mothers jaw dropped face stares back at me. Then in a flurry of motion the phone is dropped and I hear a tinny screech through the speaker.

It's impossible to tell if it's a happy screech or an 'I'm going to fly twenty-three hours and murder my son' screech.

I rub my eyes as I wait for the noise to stop.

Suddenly the phone is back in her hand and her blurry face is back on screen. "Oh my God, Jackson. A baby! When is she due? When can I come visit? When can you come here? Where will you raise the baby? Are you moving to London? I was okay with LA but London is a new one. What about your house in America?"

I don't want to tell her that I've already set plans in motion to make a move. Eric's hooked me up with a real estate agent and I've got my team in LA sorting out my lease. I was already itching to make moves before this happened, so I'm taking it as a sign.

"Mum, Mum," I say, cutting off her barrage of questions but unable to stop my grin. "Please enough with the questions. I will figure it out. All you need to know now is that there is a baby coming."

She squeals again. "My baby's boy's having a baby!" She yells into her house. "Oh, Tara's here! Let me get her. TARA," she yells off screen.

I can hear my sister yell back, "What!", and can't help the chuckle that escapes me. "What's with all the yelling?"

Tara bursts onto the frame behind mum. "Jackie? What did you do to Mum?" she asks bewildered as our mother grabs her in a hug.

"Jackie's having a baby!"

Tara's eyes bug out as she picks up the phone. "He's what?"

I can't do much more than nod my head.

"With *who*?"

I open my mouth to reply, but Mum cuts me off. "Her name is Rosie, she's friend's with Danny's wife, you know, with the song."

"Oh, the autumn leaves guy?"

"Yes! They met at the wedding and have been together for months."

"Well—" I try to interrupt.

"He kept that to himself!" Tara exclaims, peering at me. "I can't believe this. What's her last name? I'm looking her up."

"No, don't do that for Christ's sake."

There's a knock at the trailer door and I glance at the time on my watch. "Right, I've got to go back to work now, but thank you for being happy for me."

"For you?" Tara says, "This is all Mum being happy for herself."

I laugh. "Okay I'll talk to you guys later."

"Ooh Jackie, I want to talk to Rosie soon. I need to meet her!"

"Okay, I'll see what I can do."

I don't need to remind them to not share this news around. There's been a few moments in the past where my personal business was in the public eye. Rosie hasn't really acknowledged the fame aspect of my life yet, and I don't want her to. She sees me as a guy with a job, not baggage that she'll get dragged into one way or the other, and I need it to stay that way for as long as possible.

"Love you, Jackie,"

"Love you too. Bye." I hang up the phone and hand it over to Eric who is waiting outside the trailer with my daily sides.

"Thanks man," I say as he beams.

The backlot we're shooting on is the size of four rugby pitches stitched together so we get a fun little golf buggy to zoom around in. Eric lets me in the driver's side and I shift it into gear. No matter how old I get, zooming in a fake car on a fake road always gives me a thrill. It's like being behind the bars of my Harley. I love that bike.

I might have to import it over here if I'm staying. And I will be staying. I never liked LA much anyway. I'm much more comfortable with the dramatic seasons you can get in England. It reminds me more of back home. It's unnatural to not have rain.

Though, I don't think I'll be riding the bike much when the baby comes. It would be way too small for a helmet.

Pulling onto set, I park the car and climb out, the frame shaking with the movement. I shake hands with Sam the director, and Shaun the 1st AD and listen carefully as they explain the layout of the scene. It's low on action, heavy on plot so I rub my hands together. It's not that I don't love the action scenes, the high stakes and physical demands that get my heart racing. Get me a harness and a water tank any day, but my agent made the wise choice to get me doing something that can show off what I can do without the explosions and crashes.

I'm ready. I've been prepping this film for months. Rehearsing my lines day and night.

Apart from the last few weeks, where I've spent every spare second in Rosie's cramped apartment eating vegetarian food and watching a reality TV dance competition.

I can't even bring myself to worry though. The words are in my head and they're coming out correctly.

My mind switches off, zeroing in on the lines I've memorized and the blocking Sam took me through in rehearsals.

My scene partner, Ashley, is renowned for her blonde bombshell looks. She's the sassy love interest to my brooding anti-hero. We get on well, having been around the industry for a similar amount of time.

In a break between the scenes, she approaches as I'm taking a sip of the water Eric's fetched for me.

"So, how are you finding London?" She asks almost breathlessly. Her soft Irish accent hidden behind the American monotone she's picked up for the role. It doesn't really suit her, a bit too low for her natural voice.

"Yeah, good," I say with a friendly smile. "You? Where have you been staying?"

"Oh I've got an amazing little flat in West London. It's got amazing views of the river at night. You should come see it some time."

I open my mouth to respond, but before I can Sam is calling her over for some notes.

"See you," she says with a wave.

"Bye," I say, turning back to Eric whose mouth is hanging open.

"Wow," he says, breathlessly. "I can't believe she just asked you out like that."

I laugh, "She didn't ask me out, Eric."

His brow scrunches. "That's what it sounded like."

"She just wants to hang out."

"Alone. In her house. At night."

A frown pulls at my lips as I glance off in her direction. Ashley is already looking at me as Sam talks to her and she sends me another smile.

"Nah," I shake my head. "She wasn't flirting with me," I insist. Was she?

"I don't know. That's what it looked like from here." Eric shrugs.

It doesn't matter if she was or wasn't, there's only one woman who I want to flirt with and she's waiting for me in a one bed flat with my baby inside her.

11
____

ROSIE

THE WAITING ROOM IS QUIET WITH ONLY ONE OR TWO COUPLES sitting in chairs, all engrossed in their phones. Which is great for me as the man currently sat next to me is about as incognito as an elephant.

"I can't believe you think the hat is working," I grumble under my breath. Jackson is decked out in jeans and a black hoodie showing off his broad shoulders and rippling muscles, and I have to remind my ovaries that we're already fertilized.

Jackson sits back, the seat creaking beneath him, widening his jean clad legs until his knee nudges mine. "I thought a full balaclava would scare the poor nurses."

"I don't think scaring them is the worry."

He leans closer to my ear to reply before my name is announced by a woman in a nurses uniform.

I jump, almost knocking Jackson's hat off his head in my eagerness to stand up.

We follow the nurse down the hall. I've had a handful of appointments so far but this is the first time we're going to see anything exciting. It's also the first time Jackson's been able to get away from set and I'm not used to his presence beside me, his hand brushing mine as we walk. I hook my hand on the strap of my handbag and plunge the other into my pocket, desperate to keep them occupied.

"The midwife will be with you shortly," the nurse says as she ushers us inside.

The room is covered in dioramas of fetuses and other paraphernalia, almost every wall covered with pictures of babies. It's enough to be overwhelming. I really don't want to think about how the child of the giant man behind me is getting ready to exit my body through, in my opinion, a very small opening.

"I think that's your spot, pretty girl," Jackson says, gently nudging me towards the bed in the middle of the room.

"Right," I say quietly. I pull my bag off my shoulder and he gently takes it from me, looping it over his own.

"Do I—do I take my clothes off?"

He glances at me with a wry smile. "I'm new here too, baby."

The casual endearment is barely enough to distract me from my nerves. What's more embarrassing? The midwife asking me to take my clothes off or greeting her stark naked?

Clothes on, I think.

I take a deep breath as I fidget with my fingers. My feet barely touch the floor on the bed so I swing them mindlessly.

Jackson peruses the artwork before coming to my side, resting his hand on my knee and stilling it.

I'm quickly getting used to his absentminded contact. Each time he reaches for me, my heart rate speeds up and calms down at the same time, like the most intoxicating drug.

His thumb rubs across the seam of my jeans, his fingers sliding between my thighs

Instead of my own twiddling fingers, I stare at his. Tan skin and prominent veins, the hint of a tattoo peeking out the bottom of his sleeve. I stop myself from tugging the material back so I can assess them all. I haven't been able to take inventory of all of his tattoos yet, but I'm itching to. How many does he have? Twenty? Thirty? Where are they all? How many have I had a glimpse of? I can't stop my finger from gently tracing the ink, lightly fingering the edge of his sleeve.

I hear Jackson suck in a low breath before the door opens and an older woman with a cheerful smile enters, her blonde bob bouncing around her shoulders. She's matronly, exactly as I'd expect a midwife to look.

"Hello there, my name is Christine and I'll be your midwife today. It's lovely to meet you Rosalie." She offers her hand and I remove mine from Jackson's.

"Rosie." I shake her hand. "And this is Jackson. He's the —y'know."

Jackson leans forward for her hand.

"Oh, I already knew you were here. The girls at reception have already talked my ear off about you." She says with a warm smile, "But don't worry, we're very discreet."

"I appreciate that, Christine. Trying to fly as under the radar as possible."

"You got it." Christine assures him before turning to me.

"So Rosie." She pulls out a clipboard, "I'm just going to check your blood pressure and ask you some questions if that's okay."

"Yeah sure," I say, pulling my sleeve up.

Christine slides the blood pressure cuff up my arm. "When was your last period?"

"Uh, May sometime." Christine nods and writes it down in her notebook.

I shift in my seat, "The uh-conception was the 24th June."

Christine doesn't look up from her notebook, "That's great, love, but I don't need to know that. We go from the date of your last period."

I blush as Jackson chuckles softly beside me.

"You'll be around twelve weeks. Perfect, we can go ahead with the scan now. If you lean back on the chair and lift your shirt above your tummy. Dad, you can go around that side for the best view."

Jackson stands frozen for a few seconds before he jumps into motion. "Yep, that's me."

Dad.

Whoa.

Swinging my legs onto the bed, I hike my shirt up. I ignore the awkwardness of Jackson seeing my belly. It looks mostly the same as usual, if with maybe the slightest curve indicating there's something in there other than bread.

I can't help but let my hand cover the exposed skin as I wait for Christine to prepare the ultrasound wand.

I turn my head away from Jackson's, pretending to be engrossed in Christine's fascinating process of sliding gloves on and clicking buttons on the computer.

His hand comes to cover mine, gently curving around my fingers and tugging my hand away. "You okay there, pretty girl?"

"Uhuh," I nod, offering him an awkward smile.

The man has literally held me as I sobbed in his arms, not to mention impregnated me. Why am I always so awkward?

"Okay, here we go. It will be slightly cold." Christine says, approaching my side.

My skin jumps as she applies the jelly, before she firmly presses the wand to my stomach.

"Let's see here. Ah, there they are." Christine smiles as she turns the screen to face us and my heart stops in my chest.

I'm suddenly glad Jackson hasn't let go of my hand as I squeeze his tightly.

I'm also glad Christine uses a gloved finger to gesture to the blob on the screen. "There's your baby."

"Wow," Jackson says under his breath, cradling my hand in both of his and leaning closer to the screen. "There she is."

I let out a watery laugh. "They look like a little smudge, how can you tell it's a girl?"

"I have a feeling."

Christine moves the wand further and presses a few buttons. "There. I'm going to give you two a moment, but all looks healthy. Congratulations."

I think I thank her but the room around me fades away. All I can feel is Jackson's hands on mine and all I can see is the little smudge on the screen that's growing inside me.

"She looks like you," Jackson whispers in my ear.

I huff a wet laugh and wipe my tears.

"Look, can you see that?"

He leans over me and points at the screen.

"See what?" I whisper, leaning closer.

"Tiny little glasses."

I playfully nudge him with a laugh. "Shut up, she's going to have twenty/twenty vision, I'm manifesting it."

We stare at the screen until the midwife comes back in, turning the lights back on and making my eyes flutter.

Jackson listens intently as Christine hands him pamphlet after pamphlet and his arm lingers at my back as we leave the hospital.

He opens the door to the car and waits until I'm inside and buckled before closing it and rounding to the driver's side. I take the ultrasound out of my bag and stare at it as the car pulls out of the car park.

I glance at Jackson as he shifts in his seat, one arm outstretched on the wheel with the sleeve rolled up. My eyes linger on the veins on his forearms and my mouth goes dry. His forearm is probably the size of my calf. I bite my tongue to quench the urge to trace it along each vein.

"Can we go somewhere?" I ask before I can stop myself.

He glances at me with a slow grin. "You taking me on that date, pretty girl? We really do everything backwards."

I blush and readjust my glasses. "No—uh, never mind."

His large palm connects with my leg, squeezing gently. The warmth travels from his hand all the way to between my legs and I have to concentrate not to clench them together and trap his hand there. "Where shall we go?"

I look out the windshield, and bite my lip. I have no idea. We're on the M25 and I glance at a sign. "Take this exit."

Concentrating, Jackson easily pulls across all five lanes and it's not long before the motorway turns to country roads. I offer up vague directions until we're eventually pulling into a long manor house.

Jackson reverses into a space, his hand on the back of my chair as he twists his body.

We step out into the frigid air, breathing in the fresh country air. Jackson waits for me to round the car before we head towards the old manor house.

"I've wanted to come here for ages."

"How come?"

I shrug. "I don't know, I used to drive past it on my way back home and I used to tell myself that I'd come have a look but I never did."

"Who lived here?" he asks.

"No idea."

Jackson laughs and rubs his hands together. "Let's learn. I hope they have an audio guide."

He orders both our tickets and pays despite my protest. He also pays extra for us both to use a personal guide and he fits the orange headphones over my head.

"You're taking this so seriously," I laugh after he lines both our guidebooks up so they start at the same time.

"Shh, you're going to miss it."

"Welcome to Ealbury House. This tour starts to the right of the grand staircase," the automatic voice drawls in my ear.

"This way," Jackson says eagerly, grabbing my hand and tugging me towards the starting point.

I can't help the giggle that escapes as he doesn't let me go, dragging me along the predestined route and stopping at every single picture, artifact or talking point.

"Did you know they used to use this as the prayer room?" Jackson asks when we walk in the room.

"Yeah, I learned that when you did, you dork."

"Fascinating." His earnest expression is adorable. I've never spent this long on any kind of museum tour, instead walking at a regular, if not speedy, pace and taking in everything in the periphery. I can barely even concentrate on the droning voice of the tour guide, eventually pulling the headphones around my neck and waiting for Jackson to burst out with tidbits and fun facts. ("This is where they bathed!")

Eventually, the tour ends and we are thrown outside into the setting sun. The air is significantly chillier now, summer officially on its way out and a light fog settles on the horizon, the sprawling garden bathed in sunlight.

"That was fun," Jackson says with a grin.

"I didn't expect you to enjoy it as much as you did," I laugh, rubbing my cold fingers together before tucking them in my coat pocket.

Jackson gently eases my arm out of my pocket and loops it around his own. "I love an audio guide. My dad used to load us all up in the car and take us somewhere new every weekend. If the weather was bad, he'd drag us out to museums and would get each of us a guide. Then he used to test me and my sisters on everything we learned on the drive home. We used to be so competitive about it but the older I get the more I think he just wanted a few hours of peace without us screaming and running around. Then I just got used to them."

"I love that," I tell him softly. I've heard a lot about his mother and sisters, but he's never brought up his dad willingly. "What's your dad's name?"

"Oliver." He says, gazing out over the quiet gardens. "He didn't really believe in a lazy weekend, so we were always doing something."

"I don't think my parents ever took us anywhere that wasn't a shopping center, and even that would usually end in a screaming match. Well, no, they went to Buckingham Palace one year for Cleo's Duke of Edinburgh award."

"The what?"

"It's like a torture regime they give teenagers in England," I say dryly. "It's a week of camping in the Brecon Beacons with a map and a soggy tent. But at the end of it there's a fancy trip to the palace to get a certificate."

"I can imagine teenage you in waterproofs," Jackson teases.

"I uh—I didn't do it." I say, glancing out into the distance. I came home from school after the teachers announced it was time to sign up, and I was thrilled to tell my mum. To go shopping for supplies and get a hug as soon as I got off the bus when I came home with a tired grin, then later dressing up fancy with my parents and going to London without my sister. Just me and them.

"Why not?"

My mum left the permission slip on the counter where it stayed until the winter.

"I—I just didn't, I guess." I can feel Jackson's gaze warming my face so I plaster on a smile, "I would have hated it anyway. I hate camping."

"Have you been since?"

"Once, just after university. I wanted to go traveling but it didn't happen either. Kind of like coming here. I could have done it at any time, but I had to pick between using my savings for a flat deposit or traveling, and I chose logically."

"Where would you have gone?"

I shrug. "Pacific probably. Australia, Thailand." I lick my lips as I glance up at him. "New Zealand."

Jackson laughs and throws his arm around me tugging him to his side. "I'll take you to New Zealand don't worry, pretty girl. I won't be able to keep you away when my mother meets you. She's already nagging me to put you on the phone, so if you get a random friend request it will most likely be her."

"I can talk to her, if you'd like me to," I say quietly. God, what must she think of me? The random girl her son hooked up with on the other side of the world.

"Here, let's send her a picture." He pulls his phone out of his pocket and tilts his face closer to mine. My glasses bump his jaw but it doesn't stop the wide grin that breaks out on his face as we smile into the camera.

He presses some buttons on the screen.

"Send her the ultrasound too," I say, digging it out of my bag.

He smiles wider. "Come here." I'm tugged back under his arm as I hold the ultrasound up to our faces.

I glance at the photo. It's the first one of the three of us.

12

JACKSON

I was excited when Tony messaged me to meet up for a drink. I genuinely miss the guy. He's a little bit of home that I can cling onto. I've not been the best of friends to him, especially after moving to LA. I don't really think I've really kept in contact with any of my old school friends. I couldn't even tell you what most of their partners' names are, but I've never minded making the effort with Tony.

Except, what I thought would be one drink turned into two, which turned into five. I switched to water an hour ago but Tony is on his sixth beer and his eyes are distinctly red rimmed. I haven't drunk much alcohol since that one beer in Rosie's flat when she told me she was pregnant. It doesn't feel right if she's not allowed to either.

Tony also offered to split a bag with me in the bathroom but I laughed him off. I haven't touched anything harder than whiskey for a while now. At some point, it's less fun and more concerning. Tony makes a show of putting his wallet away but unless his bladder has shrunk, he's been using the pub's porcelain for something other than taking a piss.

"...and you spent ten minutes with a harness up your ass because you didn't want to admit you'd done it wrong." Tony laughs, slapping the table as he finishes recounting the story of our first rig.

I chuckle darkly as I throw a balled up napkin at him. "Laugh it up but I haven't fucked up a harness since."

Tony wipes his eyes before gesturing to the waitress to bring him another drink. In all the years I've known him, I've never seen Tony drink this much. He always used to be a one and done guy, preferring to get eight hours of sleep and an early gym session over a hangover.

I rub my beard, "Hey bro, is everything good with you?"

Tony nods his head frantically. "Yeah, yeah of course. Kaia's back in Wellington, did I tell you?"

I shake my head.

"Yeah, yeah, she's just spending time with her parents."

"Is Masen over there too?"

Tony nods as his next drink is placed in front of him, he takes a few gulps of his beer before setting it down. "She's left me."

I huff out a slow breath. Tony and Kaia have been together since we were kids and I've known her almost as long as I have him. "Ah shit bro. What happened?"

Tony shrugs, waving his hand. "I don't know. We were arguing a lot and I was working away so much. We moved over here so I could work with Marky and the guys, get into some big jobs shooting over here, and she hated it. Missed her folks."

"Tony," I say, not really sure what else there is to say.

"So, you know I'm still here. Still working."

"You don't want to go home?"

Tony shakes his head. "Nah bro, I'm doing the job I love.

I'm doing stunts for jobs we used to watch on the big screen. Every day's an adrenaline rush, y'know."

I nod, knowing the feeling. It's addictive.

"When did this go down?"

Tony shrugs. "A few months maybe."

"And Masen?"

At that Tony's gaze shutters, spinning his nearly empty glass on the table. "He's—" he breaks off. "He's hard to reach sometimes."

My nephew Cody is definitely on the way to becoming a moody teenager, preferring to sit in his room with his video games than hang out with his family. I send him messages when I'm working away but it's only really when I'm in his house that he allows me to give him any attention.

"She wants to get back together."

"She does? That's great right?"

Tony nods, tracing the condensation on his glass. "She wants me to quit."

"Quit?" I lean back in my seat.

He laughs sardonically, "She says it's too dangerous. I've been doing this job for nearly fifteen years, Jackie. I've never been hurt. She wants me to give up everything I've worked for."

I sigh heavily. "There are other jobs, Tony. This is your family."

Tony scoffs. "You left your family for a little bit of fame as soon as you could."

"Hey," I say sharply. "That's not fair."

"Sorry, but it's a bit hard to sympathize with the guy who's got enough in the bank to retire at thirty two and fucks a different girl every weekend. You don't have the same responsibilities I do, and anything you were responsible for you left behind to chase fame."

I could snap back, throw in the fact that my family is currently growing just around the corner from here, but Tony slumps forward, his hands tangling in his hair and it doesn't feel worth it. I had planned to pull out the ultrasound I carry around in my wallet to tell one of my oldest friends my news, but this is no longer the time.

Plus, I don't want to reduce Rosie and the baby to a 'gotcha' moment. Even though I do have responsibilities, *thank you very much.*

"I think we'd best call it a night, bro." I gesture for the bill.

Tony doesn't say anything, still slumped in his chair. I bite back my irritation as he folds his head further on his arms. I love my friend but he's really starting to get on my nerves.

"I'm sorry," he slurs.

"It's okay." I help him out of his chair. "Where are you staying?"

"Marky's spare room." *Jesus.*

"Alright, let's get you in a cab." He doesn't protest as I sling his arm over my shoulder and help lead him out of the pub.

"I'm sorry man." Tony pulls himself unsteadily to his full height, the fresh air hitting him.

"Stop apologizing. I owe you for the help with that harness back then anyway."

Tony snickers as he slumps up against the brick wall. I scan the street but can't spot a black cab so I lean against the wall next to him.

"Listen Tony, if you're not happy about the split, I think you might need to consider it. Marriage is all about compromise, right?" I nudge his shoulder.

"I don't want to give it up," he snaps.

I bite my tongue. He is definitely not in the mood for constructive criticism. "Alright, bro. Whatever makes you happy, man."

I spot a taxi and flag it down, hustling him into the car. "Are you good from here?" I ask.

He nods his head, taking a deep breath.

"We should do this again sometime." He shoots me a half grin.

"We'll see about that, lightweight."

Tony snickers. "Thirty really hits like a train, doesn't it?"

"We're growing up, bro."

"Make it stop," Tony whines playfully as I close the taxi door.

I lean through the open window. "Let me know when you're home safe, yeah? And don't worry too much, it will all work out in the end."

I offer him my hand and he clasps it in his own.

"Thanks Jackie, you're a good one."

I tap the taxi as it pulls off into traffic and watch as it disappears down the road.

Exhaling heavily, I pivot on my heels and pull my phone out of my pocket.

ME

Any chance for a game of Sixth Temple?

ROSIE

Ready for me to beat you?

I chuckle, I want nothing more than to shake off the weird evening side by side with Rosie.

ME

Always

13

ROSIE

"HI PAMMY," I SAY TO THE NURSE BEHIND THE DESK. I'VE BEEN here so often, I know most of the staff by name. She looks up at me with a smile that freezes when she spots the large man lingering behind me. "This is my...friend."

Jackson steps forward holding out a hand. "Jackson, lovely to meet you."

"Uh, uh," Pammy stutters. "Sign here please." She hands over the sign in sheet and I scribble both our names down. She leans over the counter, resting on her arms and thrusting her chest out, her low cut blouse straining at the action.

She opens her mouth to speak but I cut her off.

"How is she today?" I ask Pammy, dragging her gaze away from Jackson.

"Oh uh," Pammy stammers, suddenly remembering how to be professional. "She's having a good day." She offers me a small smile before her gaze darts back to Jackson like a ping pong ball.

"Great, I know the way." I clasp Jackson's arm and tug him down the hall.

"What's the rush, pretty girl?" he asks from behind, whispering in my ear. "She was only being friendly."

"I don't usually shove my tits in someone's face when I'm being friendly."

"You can do that to me if you like, *friend*." He isn't going to let me let that go.

I roll my eyes as I walk down the carpeted hallway. I wasn't jealous. I just don't want the father of my child to be harassed by perfectly 'friendly' nurses.

He's teasing but we have become friends of sorts in the past few weeks. He texts me almost daily and he's been at my house every Saturday night and even a few weekdays if he can get away. He's dragged me to nearly every historic home within driving distance and I follow him around as he tells me facts as he learns them from the audio guides. I never would have imagined that I would be friends with Jackson Harper but I also never imagined I'd be carrying his baby either.

We're just two friends who are expecting a baby in five months time. It doesn't need to be more than friendship, although I'd be lying if I said there wasn't a part of me that ached to feel his mouth on mine again.

We walk past an array of doors, each one propped open as families visit their loved ones. It's still a foreign concept to me, visiting her here instead of the home she lived in for my entire childhood. But once my granddad passed, my parents said she was too vulnerable to live on her own. I thought they meant that she could move in with them, especially since my room has been empty since I moved out nearly ten years ago. But her house was sold and she was moved in here before I even had a chance to shop around for her.

The door is propped open but I don't step inside, staying out of sight around the corner for a breath.

Jackson comes up behind me, his chest lightly pressing against my back. His hand comes to lightly rest on my arms and his head rests lightly on my head. "You okay, pretty girl?"

I tilt my head to look back at him, his cap pulled low over his eyes and his dark curls resting on his shoulders. He looks at me with gentle eyes, that charming sparkle still glinting from the corners.

I nod before gently pushing the door open. "Nanny? It's Rosie."

She's facing away from us, sitting in the wing back flannel armchair overlooking the garden. In her lap is a heap of yarn and a crochet hook clutched in her shaking hands.

"Rosie!" she exclaims and I release the breath that was trapped in my lungs. She looks the same as she did the last time I saw her.

Smiling, I cross the room, falling to my knees at her feet as I take her shaking hands in mine. "How are you Nanny?" I push her gray hair back from her eyes as I take her in. Age spots and wrinkles line her face, but her warm chocolate eyes are the same ones I've looked into my whole life.

"I'm better now you're here, sweetheart." She pulls her hands out of mine and raises her crochet hook, "I went wrong, you have to fix it for me."

Laughing I tug the hook out of her hands. "I will, but first I need you to meet someone."

I glance over my shoulder at Jackson. He's lingered by the door giving us a moment but steps forward at my nod.

"Well, aren't you a treat," Nanny says, her eyes widening. "I see my granddaughter's got my taste in men."

"*Nanny.*"

Jackson laughs as he approaches, taking her hand and

pressing a kiss to the wrinkled back of it. "Lovely to meet you Betty. I'm Jackson. I've heard so much about you."

Nanny clings onto his hand, not letting him go as she turns to me. "Don't tell me you've had a man like that in your bed and you've been talking about your old Nanny."

I blush crimson as Jackson laughs. "Nanny," I hiss. "Stop it."

"So, Jackson, how long have you and my favorite grand-daughter been together?"

My eyes just about pop out of my head. Granted, I've never even brought any friends to see Nanny apart from Anya, and I've never introduced her to any boyfriends before but still. I said *friend,* didn't I?

Jackson opens his mouth to say God knows what, but I interrupt. "We're not *together*, Nanny. We're friends."

Jackson, still holding her hand, leans forward and whispers conspiratorially, "I'm working on it."

Nanny giggles–*giggles*!

"What are you working on there?" Jackson asks, gesturing to the yarn on her lap.

"It's going to be a baby blanket for Glenda next door's great-grandson. I've nearly finished but I've gone wrong somewhere so I had to unravel it all."

She picks it back up with shaking fingers but instead of offering it to me, the person in the room who actually knows how to crochet, she shoves it in Jackson's hands as he takes a seat in the opposite armchair. "You have to pull at the yarn until these rows of stitches come undone."

Jackson studies it intently, before using deft fingers to undo the stitching. "I've got it, like this?"

He offers it to her for approval. "Make sure you don't go too fast or you'll lose count and go too far. Careful! Don't let the yarn tangle."

"Like this?"

"No, no." She snatches the growing messy bundle of yarn from his hands. "Here give that to Rosie, you'll just make it worse."

He raises his hands with an amused grin tugging at his lips. "Maybe I should start off with something simpler."

Nanny reaches into her basket and pulls out a large hook and a ball of chunky green yarn before putting a loop in the end, "Here, hold the hook in your right hand and weave the yarn through your fingers like this…" Turning his hand, she brings the yarn over the inside of his pinky finger and back around his index. "This will help you keep the tension…"

I settle on the end of her bed as Jackson listens intently to his crash course in crocheting. I can't help the smile that pulls at my lips as he patiently listens to her instructions and teases her until she lets out a bit of that girlish giggle I have never heard before.

He's so good with her, she's half in love with him already. I feel my eyes start to water as my hand comes to my stomach. He's going to be such a good dad.

"I don't see you fixing that over there," Nanny barks and I jump to attention with a laugh, unpicking the stitch.

"Betty, you're running a sweatshop over here. How much are you selling these for?"

Nanny laughs again. "Don't be silly, I don't sell them."

"You should consider it, especially with all the free labor you've got. You'd make a fortune."

Nanny waves him off. "I just like making these for my family and my friends. I made Rosie's blanket when she was a little girl."

"I still have it," I say with a smile. Granted, it's in tatters and stored carefully in the drawer where I keep my pajamas, but it's one of my most prized childhood possessions and I've always wanted my child to have one of their own. Glancing at Jackson, I can almost read his mind as he sends me an encouraging wink.

"Nanny, I need to tell you something."

I take a deep breath and stand from the bed, resuming my position on the floor. Jackson's behind me, his knee gently resting against my arm, and I use his strength as I turn to my grandmother. "Nanny, I'm uh...that's to say, we're–"

Nanny glances between us both, her thin brows quirking. "Spit it out, sweetheart."

"I'm pregnant," I say with a rush.

Silence. I bite my lip as I wait for her to say something.

She glances between the two of us before letting out a shocked squeal. "Are you really?" She clutches my hands in hers, bringing them to her chest as she clamps her mouth shut, holding back tears.

"Yeah," I nod, tears brimming in my eyes.

"Here," Jackson says, pulling the sonogram out of his pocket. "We got this a few days ago."

Nanny gasps in delight as she pulls the picture closer to her, a lone tear dropping down her cheek. "Oh my Rosie. A baby."

She tugs me to her and I try not to collapse against her familiar weight. I have to remind myself that she's more fragile now than she was when I was a child but I can't help burying my nose in her neck, her perfume stinging my eyes. She rocks me back and forth gently. "You're going to be an incredible mother, sweetheart."

Pulling me back, she wipes the tears from my cheeks. "This baby is going to be huge," her eyes widen as she glances at Jackson.

Jackson hollers as I bark a wet laugh and wail, "I know!"

"Well, I better get started on your blanket! Oh and a hat and booties and a little jacket."

"She's going to be head to toe in Betty Taylor originals."

Nanny squeals. "It's a girl?"

"Yes," Jackson says firmly.

I roll my eyes. "We don't know yet but he's convinced."

"I have a feeling," Jackson says, "I'm very fond of the Taylor women."

Nanny giggles again before digging through her basket for new colors, "Well I'll do cream for now until we know and then I'll make more in different colors, but if Daddy says girl I'm saying girl too."

Jackson clasps his hands together. "Put me to work Nanny."

My phone buzzes in my pocket, my brow scrunching as I realize it's my old boss calling. "I'll be back," I tell the room. I step outside into the corridor and pull the phone to my ear. "Kathleen?"

"Rosie, my love! How are you?"

Kathleen left the post house to go freelance, and the last I heard from her she was trying to get a short film into a festival.

"I'm good, how are you?"

"Great! Listen, I'm actually crewing up for my next short film. It's a small one, with only a female and non-binary crew. The budget's small and it's definitely more of a passion project, but I wanted to know if you'd be up for editing it?"

"Oh!" I wasn't expecting that at all. I haven't edited a short since my university days, working as an assistant ever since. "When are you filming?"

"We're still prepping at the moment and, as it's low

budget, we're looking to shoot nearer the end of the year, around December."

I do my mental math. I'll be around seven months then. Though it's not like I'd be needed on set or anything, and I do have all the software I need at the flat. Low budget is low budget, but I should really be jumping at the opportunity to make a bit of extra cash before the baby comes.

"I'd love to," I tell her, laughing at the squeal of excitement that echoes down the line.

"Yes, I knew you'd say yes! You're going to love the script. I'll send it over to you. I can't wait to work with you again. It'll be like the good old days."

We reminisce for a few more minutes until she has to run and I return to the room, unable to stop the grin on my face.

"Rosie, help him, he's all fingers and thumbs." Nanny says as she glances up at me.

"How is it going in here?" a nurse asks when she arrives a few hours later to find all three of us in a circle around Nanny's chair, streams of wool piled between us. "I've been hearing all the laughter from down the hall and we all want to know what's so funny." I usually spend a few pleasant hours with Nanny, catching up on our days or knitting quietly. I've never laughed as much as we have today.

"I've been trying to learn, but these two keep distracting me," Jackson complains, lifting his jumble of wool.

Nanny playfully swipes at him with a wrinkled hand. "You keep winding us up."

"Visiting time is nearly over," the nurse says kindly. I tug down on the disappointment in my chest as I press a kiss to Nanny's cheek.

"I'll see you soon, Nanny," I tell her, folding away the knitting.

"Okay sweetheart," she says before turning to Jackson. "It was lovely to meet you, Jackie."

"The pleasure was all mine, Betty." He presses a kiss to her hand.

"Will you come back again?"

"If you'd like me to."

"Well you need to finish this blanket," Nanny says gesturing to her basket of wool.

"I'll get some practice in."

I tug my jacket on and Jackson does the same.

"Enjoy the Strictly results, Nanny," I tell her as I cross to the door.

"Praying for Thatcher." Jackson crosses his fingers and winks at Betty as she laughs.

When we leave the home, the sky is dark and there's a distinct chill in the air.

"So, *friend*," Jackson says as he opens the car door for me. "That was nice."

I roll my eyes but I can't stop the smile tugging at my lips. Yeah, it was really nice.

14

———

JACKSON

"My hero," Rosie teases as I pass her a huge bowl of chocolate covered raisins and peanuts. Since the day I found out how much Rosie loves watching her dancing show, and after meeting Betty, I've been over her flat more days than I've been in my hotel. Granted, some of those days I've been on back-to-back shoots, working late into the night or early in the morning, but every spare second I have I want to spend it with her.

"I don't know how you eat that." I shudder as I lift her sock clad feet and take my place underneath them. She's wearing the hoodie I left a few weeks back that she insists is more comfy than hers, her glasses perched on her nose and the bowl cradled in her arms happily.

"Sweet, salty and fruity," she moans happily and I pretend my dick doesn't perk up at the noise. Covered head to toe, in a jumper that still has what I expect to be tooth-paste stains from yesterday and munching on the worst concoction of food I've ever heard in my life, and she's still the most fuckable woman I've ever met.

"Besides, it's your child that's craving it, not me," she says as she shovels in a mouthful with her fingers.

"My child will never eat a raisin in her life."

Rosie rolls her eyes. "*They* can eat whatever they like as long as it's healthy. Anyway, these are chocolate."

I lean back into the arm of the couch, my arm stretching across the back, tugging on her ear gently. "If you say so."

"Oh, it's starting." She shushes me as if I hadn't stopped speaking before tilting her head to the TV. The familiar trumpets of my new guilty pleasure blare on the screen, and I hide my smile behind my hand as she mimics the music. If I told any of my guy friends that my ideal Saturday night is now watching a group of amateur dancers and criticizing their technique, they'd never invite me out again.

The first couple comes on with a slow American Smooth. I groan. "These dances are so boring, when are they going to start throwing each other around?"

Rosie shushes me. "It's technical, so they've got to keep their form and take it slowly. He's doing really well."

"Look at his arm, his elbow's practically by his hip," I say, taking a handful of her chocolate-raisin-peanut monstrosity. "Terrible form."

A few minutes later as all the judges agree with me, I turn to Rosie with a smug brow. "Told you."

She laughs as she sets the bowl on the side table before readjusting and placing her hands on the small curve of her belly. The bump is still small, but Rosie insists she's rapidly becoming the size of a house.

My eyes drop and my hands follow hers, bracketing her dainty hands with my huge ones. It still blows my mind that there's a person in there, a bit of me and a bit of her, growing toes and fingernails.

"I thought I felt a kick earlier," Rosie says quietly, as she tugs my hands to the side, attempting to get the baby's attention. "But I'm not sure."

"She's going to be a rugby player," I say.

"She can pick that up after she's exited my body, thank you." She glances up with a gasp. "Oh yes, Kat is on."

I sit back reluctantly, returning my hand to her foot and gently pressing on the arches of her feet in the way I know she likes.

The lights on the screen dim as the woman appears from the shadow at the back of the stage. The haunting strings of a violin rise in tempo as her partner appears from behind her. The woman jumps as his arms curl around her, spinning her to face him as the tempo increases. He cradles her body close as their lower bodies fly around the floor.

I open my mouth to crack another joke about form when a whimper from my left has my head jerking to Rosie.

Her cheeks are flushed and her eyes are glued to the screen, her legs crossing slightly in my lap.

Awareness washes over me like a shower, causing my cock to twitch.

"Rosie Taylor," I say, my voice dropping to a purr. Her eyes dart to me, wide and guilty. *Busted.* "Are you liking the dance, pretty girl?"

I trace my hand along the arches of her foot, slowly roaming further up her calf.

"No," she squeaks, her face flushing as she shuffles in place.

"Liar."

She gulps, her eyes flashing back to the screen. The music reverberates around the room, sending a chill down my spine.

I never thought that Saturday night television could set the mood, but I'm very happy it has.

"Hmm. I think you're feeling the heat, baby."

Her wide eyes don't leave mine as a little pink tongue peaks out, wetting her lip. I want to chase it with my own.

She shifts her foot in my lap, accidentally brushing my cock through my jeans. Another gasp escapes her and she jerks her foot away. In a moment of lust filled insanity, I catch it before it goes too far. "This is what you do to me, baby."

I could be making the wrong move, pushing her before she's ready. But the way her eyes darken and her hand clenches the arm of the sofa, her mouth dropping open as if ready for my touch, tells me otherwise. "I'm not..." she mumbles. "It's the hormones."

I'll revisit the disappointment flickering in my chest at the excuse later, but now I shake it off. "I can help with that."

I hold her gaze, my heart pounding in my chest, waiting for her go ahead. I tell myself that if she says no, I'll let her feet go and turn my attention back to the TV, but she doesn't. Instead, she gives me a tiny nod of approval.

Gently peeling each of her socks off until I have her bare skin under my palms, I press a kiss to the arch of her foot, not taking my eyes off hers.

I've never been into feet, but I'd worship hers if she gives me even the slightest hint that she wants me to.

I want this hoodie off. I want to watch her breasts rise and fall with the breaths I can tell she's struggling to take slowly.

Another nod is all I see before I release the groan trapped in my throat. *Thank fuck.*

I gently pull her legs apart, leaving a gorgeous cradle for me to slip into.

I kiss my way along her bare thighs, my tongue tracing

the soft sensitive skin that makes her shiver. I tease her as I dart my tongue to explore her inner thigh before mirroring the motions on the other.

My hands reach her shorts before my lips do and I glance up to see her gorgeous lips between her teeth, her eyes wide behind the black frames. I'm about ready to come in my pants from the sight. I gently tug at the material in question and her nod almost makes her glasses fall off her nose. I reach for her, gently pushing them back up.

"I want you to watch while I feast on you, pretty girl. I want you to see the mess I can make of you." I press the smallest kiss to her nose, knowing that if I catch her mouth, I'll never want to never let go.

The small moan that escapes is enough to bring a smirk to my lips as I return to her shorts, slowly tugging them off, revealing her to me. All that's covering her from me is a thin scrap of lace. I gently trace the floral design, feeling her wetness through the material.

I can't take it anymore. Her scent is intoxicating. I press a lingering kiss to her pussy through the lace and her back arches off the sofa. I tease her through the material, swirling my tongue around her clit until she's whimpering beneath me, pulling away before I grab her thighs and tug her back to my mouth like a starving man. I gently bite her inner thigh as my hands slide under her plump backside, dragging her underwear down her legs and letting it hook over one ankle.

"Stop playing with me Jackson," she whimpers. "Please."

"Anything you want, baby."

I place my hands back on her ass, spreading her wide and tilting her hips to my mouth as I bury my face between her thighs.

Her cry of pleasure is all I hear before her hands come to

my hair, tugging at the strands and making my eyes roll to the back of my head. I never got to do this last time, though thoughts of her tight pussy kept my hand very occupied for the week afterwards, wondering what she would taste like on my tongue. Heaven, is the answer.

I glance up at her, her head tilted back over the arm of the couch and her nipples nearly poking through the thick material of my hoodie. I groan at the sight before sliding one finger inside her tight, wet heat.

I flatten my tongue against her, swiping through her juices like she's my last meal. I crook my finger inside of her and speed up my motions, her body writhing beneath me as her hands clutch at my hair. Keeping my pace, my tongue flicks against her until she comes with a gasp of pleasure, squeezing my finger and flooding my mouth with her taste. I kiss her through it, lapping her up on my tongue as her thick thighs clench around my head.

If I die smothered in this woman, it will be a hell of a way to go.

She takes a shuddering breath as I pull back to sitting, my cock weeping in my boxers.

She looks at me dazed, the orgasm having robbed her of speech. "Thank you," she whispers and I can't help the chuckle that escapes me.

I gaze down at her as I settle between her open thighs. She cups my cheek with her hand, gently brushing her thumb across my bottom lip, still shiny with her.

It takes all my willpower to not grind into her hot pussy, my cock begging for any relief. But instead, I press a kiss to her flushed cheek.

"You're welcome, pretty girl."

I could stay like this forever, her thick thighs wrapped

around me and the big blue eyes gazing at me behind the thick frames of her glasses.

I nearly give in, nearly rip my jumper off her body and feast until we're both groaning in relief, but I see the yawn she tries to hide behind her hand. "Did I wear you out?"

She laughs softly. "Leave me alone. I'm growing a human being."

I wink at her as I pull myself off the sofa. "Do you want me to leave?"

Her eyes widen, "No! We have to finish Strictly."

She falls asleep less than one dance in, a blanket thrown over her lap and her feet in mine. I quietly turn the TV off and pick her up, her head tilting towards my chest as I carry her to her bedroom.

She stirs awake enough to grumble in my arms, "I'm too heavy."

I clutch her to me tighter. She's as light as a feather compared to the weights I can push at the gym. "Never."

I gently deposit her in the bed, her eyes firmly closed. There's nothing I want more than to climb into bed with her, but instead I press a kiss to her forehead and gently pull her glasses off her head. I set them on the bedside table and tiptoe out of the room, gently closing the door behind me.

15

ROSIE

I AM A WEAK, WEAK WOMAN. I SHOULD NEVER HAVE DONE IT, never even hinted to Jackson that I had any sort of urges.

By Sunday evening, I've mentally slapped myself from shame multiple times. Not only did I practically beg him to eat me out, but I immediately fell asleep afterwards. I woke up alone and disorientated in my bed, taking a few minutes to remember falling asleep on the sofa as he massaged my feet. *After* he gave me a mind-blowing orgasm that turned my insides to molten lava.

I should never have gone there with him, blurring the lines that are already so faded.

What was I thinking? Offering my body to him like a cat in heat, over an amateur tango on Saturday night television.

No, I shouldn't have done it. And I will *not* do it again,

There is no need to get Jackson to scratch an itch I've spent many years scratching myself perfectly well.

Which I tell myself every day for the next week.

I tell myself when I'm tossing and turning at night a few days later, the sheets damp with sweat and my nipples scratching against my shirt. In frustration, I jerk upright and dive for the drawer beside my bed.

Pulling out my trusty pink vibrator, I close my eyes, lie back and take a deep breath. Nothing. The vibrations that work for me every time are somehow not soft enough, not hard enough, not *enough*.

I almost knock my lamp off the table as I shove the drawer closed in frustration.

The next day I try again and when the same thing happens I switch to manual mode, my fingers tracing where I'm aching. But they're too soft, too small.

On Thursday, I have a fleeting notion to try the shower head but after I nearly slip on the wet shower floor, I give up that one before I break a leg.

On Friday, I reach a new low and allow myself the most shameful experiment. Curled up on the sofa under a blanket, I use my vibrator in the same place Jackson set me aflame. Remembering his hands on me, the way he teased me, his dirty words buzzing in my ears. My skin tingles as I chase the vibration with my hips but it's still not enough. I take a deep breath of frustration and throw my vibrator to the other end of the sofa.

By Saturday, I'm a mess. My body is buzzing, unable to release any of the tension that's held me in a chokehold for days.

By the time Jackson is due to arrive I've progressed to baking to distract myself and have accidentally made at least three different cakes.

I lay them out on the table on decorative plates and fan out napkins. I assess my array for a few seconds before my senses finally return to me.

Why did I let the man get me off and then laid out a

display of home baked goods as if I'm hosting a weird 'thanks for the orgasm' party?

He buzzes the intercom and I snatch the Victoria sponge cake off the table, put it back in the cake tin and hide it under the sink. The blueberry and vanilla muffins I start haphazardly throwing in a ziplock bag and shoving them in the cutlery drawer.

I've lost my fucking mind.

Jackson knocks on the door and I only have the banana bread left. Banana bread is fine, right? Savory, plain, and unimpressive. The un-sexiest of all the baked goods.

I open the door and nearly swallow my tongue. How can this man look like a wet dream when he's literally dressed in a t-shirt and jeans?

"Hi," I say, adjusting my glasses.

"Hi, pretty girl," he steps inside with a smile.

"How—" I swallow against my dry throat. "How was your week?"

Jackson sighs. "Long. I've been waiting all week for this."

I gulp.

"I can't wait to see Thatcher take on the American Jive."

An awkward laugh bubbles out of me. Of course. He's talking about the show. *Get a grip, Rosie.*

We've had an easy repertoire the last few months, though we haven't been able to see each other this week thanks to his busy schedule. I usually welcome him like a typical human would and not a walking lust ball that over bakes sweet treats and hides the evidence.

Thankfully, Jackson is acting like normal, wandering into the living room and taking a seat on the sofa.

I head back to the kitchen, needing to take a minute to gather myself. I move the pot of veggie pasta to the oven to bake and take a few calming breaths.

This is fine. We just need to reestablish some boundaries. The best thing for the baby is for us to remain friends. Just two friends raising a baby together. Just two friends who talk every day and cuddle watching Saturday night television. Just two friends who occasionally share mutually beneficial orgasms...

No, Rosie, I mentally scold myself. *Stop thinking about orgasms!*

"Rosie, can you come in here for a minute?" I jerk, his stern voice making me feel like I've done something naughty that I'm about to be punished for. I swallow, my chest heaving. My brain is officially lust-addled.

As soon as I walk back inside, my confused lust filled lizard brain leaps.

Jackson lounges on the sofa, his big arm along the back rest. He's staring at me, his familiar smirk hardly present, replaced by a heated look in his eyes.

"How was *your* week?" he asks.

Is that what he wanted me in here for?

"Uh—" Torture. "Yeah, it was fine." I rub one sock clad foot against the other like a cricket.

"Hmm," he says, rubbing his beard and drawing my attention back to the mouth that I've been dreaming about for days on end.

"Did you have any fun?"

I blink, "Uh—"

Before I can string more than a sound together, Jackson holds up my small pink vibrator.

My cheeks burn. Humiliation and arousal flood my body, warring for attention. I must have left it there last night. I can't believe I forgot it.

But the image of Jackson, sprawled out on my sofa with that look in his eye, his huge hands clutching my favorite vibrator, will be burned into my mind for the rest of my life. Which will hopefully end within the next thirty seconds.

I shake myself awake and cross the room to him, snatching it out of his hands.

"I don't—" I stumble, shaking my head fruitlessly. "I —uh."

Before I can turn away, Jackson's hand catches my thigh. He sits up straighter, tugging me closer until I'm cradled between his open legs.

My brain switches off, the room closing in. I can't see anything but the hungry look on his face and the crinkle in the corner of his eye.

"What's your vibrator doing out here Rosie, hmm?" he asks, his voice a low purr.

My knees almost buckle. "I tried to use it," I whisper.

"Tried?"

I nod my head slightly, unable to peel my eyes away from his. "It didn't work."

"What didn't work, baby?"

"Nothing," I confess with a whimper. "Nothing has worked."

He lets out another gruff hum, the noise shooting straight between my thighs.

His large hands curve around the back of my legs, inching closer and closer to where I'm aching. Where I have been aching for days.

Time stops as I gaze down into his face, his dark eyes promising what I know he can easily provide.

"Do you need some help, pretty girl?"

My mouth opens and all I can do is nod. Is this really happening?

Effortlessly, he tugs at my thighs until I'm straddling his lap, my legs spread across his thick thighs. His erection presses into me and it takes everything I have to not grind against him but he makes the decision for me, thrusting up into me.

"Tell me," he says, gently tracing his lips across my jaw. "Tell me what you need help with."

I swallow, inhaling his musky scent. "I can't come," I confess breathlessly. "Not without you."

I can't help the moan that escapes as he presses his lips to the juncture of my neck, gently nipping at my flesh.

This time, I don't stop myself from tilting my hips, desperate for some friction.

His large hands cup my ass, pulling me further onto his hard cock as my hands explore his shoulders, tugging him closer as a frenzy overtakes me.

He pulls back, cupping my face in his hands.

"Please," I admit before he can say anything else. "It's the hormones, I can't—I just need some help. It doesn't have to mean anything," I insist.

He licks his lips, eyes searching mine. I almost look away but I'm trapped by the intensity burning in his lidded stare. "You just want this? Just some...help?"

I nod my head desperately, shifting my hips on his lap. I can't think straight, my body blazing and desperate. I'd do anything just to be able to orgasm.

"Okay, baby." He gently rubs his finger against my jaw. "I'll get you there."

I almost tremble in relief, my thighs clenching around his.

"But first," he says, "I want to see you."

I blink in confusion as a slow smirk spreads across his face. "I want you to show me how hard you've been trying, how desperate you've been for something I'm very willing to provide."

I whimper as he lifts his hand, showing me the pink vibrator in his hands.

"Take your clothes off," he orders.

I slowly swallow before nodding, lust buzzing in my veins.

I peel myself off his body and strip my clothes off my body with shaking fingers. An unfamiliar boldness over-takes me and I take a seat on the coffee table opposite him. I don't take my eyes off him as I spread my legs.

He leans forward in his seat, his hands following mine to spread my thighs further, exposing me to his gaze.

I relish the way he swallows, unable to tear his eyes away from me.

Sitting naked before him as he's still fully dressed, I feel powerful, sexy under his gaze. I hold out my hand for the toy.

He hands it over without a word, his hand clenching on my thigh.

I switch it on and hold it to my clit, the familiar buzzing sensation causing my eyes to flutter. Last night, it wasn't enough. But now, lewdly spread in front of this man as he watches, it sends sparks along my skin.

It's still not enough, I know that instantly, but it's close. I move it in small circles, glancing at Jackson through hooded eyes.

His hands creep higher, spreading my legs further apart as he traces his thumb closer to where I'm aching for him.

"Good girl. Look at this pretty pussy, begging for me."

I groan at his words, using my other hand to steady myself as I wobble.

"Is it still not enough, Rosie?"

I shake my head wordlessly.

Without taking his eyes off me, he presses one finger inside me and I moan at the intrusion, my head falling back.

"If you'd have told me that this was happening, that you were waiting for me, you wouldn't have been able to keep me away. I've been thinking about you all week too, baby. In the shower, at night when I can't sleep. I've thought about this. Your greedy pussy, dripping for me."

His words settle over me, setting my skin ablaze. The vibrations and the feel of his fingers is almost enough but just as I'm about to reach that edge I've been climbing to, he pulls out of me.

"Jackson–"

He leans back in his seat, spreading his thighs, and licking his fingers, groaning as he swallows my taste. I'm reaching for his belt before I've even registered the thought.

Wordlessly, I drop to my knees, tugging at his belt until his cock springs free. My mouth waters at the sight, at the drip of precum beaded at his tip. I lean forward and lick him up.

"Rosie," he says, leaning his head back as his hands come to my hair. "Touch that pretty clit for me, baby."

I take him into my throat as I reach my fingers between my thighs, playing with myself the same way I have all week.

With my other hand, I grip his thigh, wordlessly looking up at him and telling him what I want.

"Do you like being on your knees for me? Want me to fuck that pretty mouth while you make yourself come?"

I can barely contain my hum of approval as he starts to pick up speed, using me. My fingers slip in my wetness and I can barely contain myself. Climbing higher and higher, I can't stop the moan that purrs from my chest.

"Jesus, Rosie, I'm—" I tighten my lips around him,

moving faster against him until I feel him spill down my throat, his thighs twitching underneath me.

"Fuck," he groans as I pull off him, keeping his eyes on mine as I swallow and lick my lips.

He pulls me to him once again, my legs straddling him as his fingers replace mine and his tongue sweeps into my mouth. His hand grabs a handful of my ass and he grinds my body on his hand.

"Good girl," he praises, taking a raised nipple in his mouth. His fingers curl inside me, and his thumb flicks at my clit until finally, finally, I come, my body shuddering and shaking as I clench around him.

I fall into his shoulder, barely able to catch my breath as my heart pounds in my chest.

I could sleep here, curled up on his lap like a cat, but the blaring of the smoke alarm causes me to jump out of my skin.

"The pasta!" I gasp, clattering off his lap, snatching the first item of clothing I find on the floor and tugging it over my head as I sprint to the kitchen.

I open the window and start fanning the smoke away from the alarm before turning the oven off and pulling out the charred remnants of pasta.

"Fuck," I hiss as I dump it on the side. The perfectly timed crispy brown is now a dark charcoal.

"Is it salvageable?" Jackson asks from behind me. I glance at him over my shoulder. He's pulled his jeans back on but left his belt unbuckled letting them hang loose around his sculpted hips.

"No," I say, turning back to the alarm that is still ringing through the flat. I attempt to fan it again but he reaches up and easily presses the button that I usually use a broom handle to hit.

"Thanks," I mumble as I try to dissipate the smoke. It's mostly gone now but I need to do something. I've never burnt dinner before, never been so *distracted.*

"Can you pass me a spoon please?" I ask, not looking at him. "I'll see if there's anything to save." I poke at the charred remains of dinner.

"Rosie," Jackson says, "Why are there muffins in your cutlery drawer?"

16

JACKSON

The phrase "just hormones" is probably going to be ingrained behind my eyeballs soon.

It's all I can think about, mostly because Rosie insists upon repeating it after every time we hook up. Which has thankfully happened more than a few times.

Our weekly Saturday night Strictly session has been pretty effortlessly replaced with Saturday night orgasms and I would have no complaints if it wasn't for the doubt in the back of my mind that I'm just here to scratch an itch.

So far we've done almost everything apart from kissing. And penetration. I want nothing more than to go further but I'm trying to hold the line for as long as I can. I can't let myself be consumed with her when all she wants to do is keep things casual. I can't go that final step until the day she admits she wants everything, not just the occasional hit of oxytocin.

But, if it means I get to spend time with her, then I'll legally change my name to 'hormones' and be with her every minute of the day.

The shoot is ramping up, with a cluster of intense

shooting before it starts to taper off closer to Christmas. I don't usually mind. I'd rather be working hard for days, weeks at a time with barely any time to sleep in between. It keeps my energy up, keeps my mind focused. No distractions, no plans, just the character I've stepped into and my responsibility to the team.

It's harder now though with Rosie and a baby on the way. Every minute I'm not reciting lines to the camera or throwing fake punches, I'm reading baby books in my trailer or driving across London to get a few stolen hours with her.

I've even downloaded an app on my phone so I can track how big Smudge is getting. She's currently a bell pepper. We're still a few weeks away from finding out the gender but I just know she's a girl. A little mini Rosie.

"That's a wrap guys," Shaun calls and I let out my breath, stretching my neck. I can't wait to get out of this costume. I had hoped I'd left the skin tight lycra days behind me, but the scene is a heist so I'm kitted out like catwoman. Sure, on the screen it looks cool, but in real life surrounded by a bunch of guys in North Face jackets and lighting rigs, I feel like a giant tool.

Eric appears at my shoulder. "Ready?"

I send him a nod and follow him. It's easy to feel like a child when I'm escorted at all times, but I also respect that that's the way it is. Me getting lost in the backlot or running late to set would cost a lot of people wages and time. It's not worth the hassle of fighting it. And hey, I love my job. I'm riding whatever waves are put in front of me.

Plus, it's kind of sweet how Eric puffs up his chest when he escorts me, as if he's my personal bodyguard protecting me from a rogue craft trolley.

"You up to much tonight, man?" I ask Eric as we cross the row of trailers.

He blinks at me. "Uh, yeah me and my boyfriend are heading into the city to go see a comedy gig."

"Oh nice, who you seeing?"

"Thatcher Price."

I stop with a gasp and tug at his arm. "You're kidding. I didn't know he was doing shows! How is he doing that whilst on Strictly?"

Eric's brows furrow. "Uh—I," he fumbles when we get to my trailer.

"If you speak to him," I throw over my shoulder. "Tell him I'm a big fan."

I check my phone and text Rosie the news. I'm about to invite her to go see Thatcher with me, but then I remember. *Just hormones.*

We've been to at least three National Trust sites in the last few months and that wasn't hormones or a date. Just two friends, hanging out and looking at old shit. We can upgrade that to a gig, right?

No matter how many times I try to convince her to go on a real date, she bats me down. Combined with my new official position as sex assistant, it's enough to give my ego a bruise.

It's as I'm getting dressed that I get her reply.

ROSIE

LOL, maybe we should go see it

If you wanted to I mean

We don't have to though

Never mind, ignore me

Hope Eric has a good time!!

I snort. Seems like someone's been overthinking. At least it's not just me.

"Hey Eric," I say as I leave the trailer, "Would it be cool if me and my girl come along tonight?"

He blinks at me. "You want my tickets?"

"No," I scoff. "No, God, those are your tickets. I'm thinking we'll do our own thing, but you might not want your boss showing up on date night."

"Oh," Eric says. "Well, yeah, that's fine I guess."

"Amazing." I grin, rubbing my hands together. "Now, how do I get tickets?"

An hour later I'm knocking on Rosie's door, dressed in dark jeans and a jacket.

She answers the door still in her work gear, her shirt baggy enough to hide the bump that she still swears is there and that I'm starting to silently agree with but would never admit to.

"Oh, hey."

"Ready?" I ask, grinning.

Her brows scrunch behind her glasses.

"The gig. You invited me, remember?"

A blush covers her cheeks as she glances at her feet.

"I'm teasing, pretty girl," I say, nudging her chin up with my knuckle. "I got us tickets. Well, my assistant Eric got us tickets. Come on, it starts in an hour."

She narrows her eyes at me suspiciously.

"Come on, I want to go see Thatcher. Hopefully he tells me his secrets to the American Smooth."

"Oh my God, do not ask him that." She turns around and heads to her bedroom. "Let me get changed."

I could follow her into her room, wrap my arms around her, press my lips to her neck and feel her soft curves in my hands. But no, it's just hormones.

I rub my hands across my face as I linger in the kitchen. I need to focus. I'm not here to seduce her, I'm here to be the supportive co-parent. It would be messy to get any more involved.

But as she steps into the kitchen wearing a blue dress and black knee high boots, it's easy to forget that.

It's not a date, I remind myself. *Just hormones.*

It's just hormones, I say when she takes my hand as I help her out of the car, and she smiles up at me.

It's just hormones, I say when I leave my hand on her leg in the cab and she crosses her legs, trapping my hand between her gorgeous thighs.

It's just hormones, I say when she laughs at Thatcher's joke and leans into my shoulder.

It's just hormones, I say when I put my arm around her as we leave and I feel her chilly fingers under the hem of my shirt, tracing the slice of my skin above my jeans.

It's just hormones, I tell her as I bury my head in her neck and finally lift her skirt as soon as we get back to her place.

It's just hormones, I tell myself.

Fuck.

17

ROSIE

I'M CHOPPING PEPPERS WHEN MY MOTHER RINGS. I WIPE MY hands on a towel and place it on speakerphone

"Hello," I answer. "Sorry, I'm hands-free while I cook."

"What are you making?"

"Risotto."

"Just for you?"

"I'm making a big batch," I tell her, stirring the rice in my cast iron pot and not sure how to tell her that I'm cooking for my six foot five baby daddy who eats enough for three people. The bright orange casserole pot is a knock-off of the Le Creuset that Cleo got one year. I asked for one for myself the year after and got this instead. I can't complain though. She uses hers for decoration, but I use mine nearly every week. I'd end up using a real one so much that it would lose its color or scratch the base.

"You know you have to double the recipe for that?" Mum reprimands. "You need to add protein. You always need to add protein to your diet, you can't survive on just vegetables."

"Yes, I know I've got tofu."

"You should just use chicken, it's much nicer with real meat."

I sigh but continue chopping. I've been a vegetarian for almost nine years now, but we have this argument every time.

"I don't have chicken, I have tofu," I say patiently.

Mum huffs down the line, so I divert before she can turn it into another lecture about how every meal needs meat, veg and carbs.

"Are you up to anything nice this weekend?"

"We're in the city for the day," she says.

"Oh," I say, surprised. They hardly ever come to London, preferring the countryside and their small town. Dad gets stressed driving through the city but refuses to take a train, so it's typically a rare occurrence. "You should have said, I would have come and met you somewhere."

"It was a last minute decision."

"Is Cleo with you?" I ask.

"Hmm?" she answers distractedly. I can hear my Dad's low voice on the other side of the line as her attention is pulled away.

"I said, is Cleo with you?"

I tip my peppers into the pot and adjust the heat as I hear a low mumble in the background. "I'll let you go, Mum," I raise my voice to be heard over her other conversation.

I don't get a reply before the phone line goes dead.

I nod my head. Sounds about right. I still haven't told her about the baby, but whenever we have one sided conversations like this I remind myself why I haven't.

I lose myself in my cooking, Michael Kiwanuka's voice serenading me through my speaker. When I'm nearly finished, I hear the buzz of the intercom.

Jackson's early. I quickly down my tools and cross to the phone, letting him up without waiting for a reply.

I quickly turn the burners off and wipe my hands on my towel just as a knock sounds at the door.

I fix my frazzled hair, which has escaped the messy bun I threw it up in, before swinging the door open with a smile.

A smile that drops at the sight of my parents and sister standing at the door with expectant faces.

"Well?" Mum asks, with a quirked brow as I freeze on the doorstep. "Are you letting us in or making us stand here like solicitors?"

Wordlessly, I step backwards and allow them in. We're not a hugging family so I hold onto the door for longer than necessary just for something to do with my hands.

"What are you doing here?" I ask.

"We couldn't decide on a restaurant so decided risotto sounded nice. Don't worry, I bought some chicken from the shop that you can add in."

What?

I'm so stunned by the presence of my family in the flat that they've never been to before to even compute the words.

"Uhm, I—"

"Where do you keep your chopping boards?" Mum asks, rummaging through the cupboards as if they aren't propped up on the side.

I turn helplessly to my dad, hoping he'll help me make sense of the situation, but he's already pulled out a seat at the head of the table and is thumbing through his phone.

My attention is pulled to Cleo, who's wandering closer to the living room, her silky blonde hair swinging behind her.

I rush after her, cutting her off. "What are you doing here?"

She sends me a saccharine smile between full lips, as if we haven't avoided being in the same room for the last ten months. "Why so stressy, Rosa-pee? You're so jumpy." The nickname grates over my skin the same way it has since I was eight years old.

Cleo had let me join her birthday sleepover with all her friends. We had fun, watching films and stuffing our faces with chocolate. Until we woke up the next morning and Cleo poured her water bottle on my sleeping bag and told the other girls I'd had an accident in my sleep. I had spent the rest of the day locked myself in my room crying and the nickname stuck.

I brush away the memory to focus on the more pressing matters. Like getting rid of all the evidence of Jackson or the baby that I possibly can.

"Cleo, come look at this," Mum calls. I dread to think what she's found that they can comment on in the kitchen, but I know more trouble can be found in every other room in the flat. As soon as Cleo swans back to the kitchen, I fly around the room grabbing every baby book, spare item of Jackson's clothes and the pillow he's taken to sleeping on when it's too late to drive back to his hotel and hide them in my bedroom wardrobe.

If only every time I cleaned I was this frantic. I could actually get quite a lot done.

When I'm sure every item of baby paraphernalia or male belongings are out of sight, I return to the kitchen. My mother has taken over my cooking and my nearly perfect risotto now has large chunks of unseasoned, cooked chicken floating on the top.

I take a deep breath even as my stomach lurches, and I shakily take a seat at the table.

"So, what have you been doing today?" I ask my dad, desperate to fill the tense silence.

"Hmm?" he asks distractedly, lifting his eyes from his screen.

"By all means Rosalie, sit down, relax. I'll do all the work shall I?" Mum snaps from the stove top.

My stomach sinks as I rise to my feet, my once organized kitchen and nearly finished meal now chaotic and busy. "I can do it," I say, sliding next to her and attempting to take the spoon out of her hand.

"It's fine, you get the drinks."

I press my lips together and head to the fridge, removing the drinks and bringing four to the table.

"No alcohol?" Cleo asks, in a sugary sweet voice that makes my skin crawl.

I shake my head. "Haven't been to the shop for a while."

Dad sighs heavily as he takes a sip of his Coke. "It's fine."

I grit my teeth but ignore them, taking a sip of my drink and attempting to calm my racing heart. How have I lost control of the situation so quickly? I'm not used to them descending on me like this, they've never even been here before. I wouldn't even be sure that they knew my address if it wasn't for the fact they had to forward on letters that arrived home by mistake.

My phone buzzes on the counter and I nearly choke on my drink as I dart towards it before my mum–or God forbid, *Cleo*–picks it up for me.

I swipe it off the side and escape to my bedroom before answering.

"Hello," I breathe into the phone.

"Hey pretty girl, you okay?"

I take a full breath for the first time since my parents barged into my house. "Uh—"

"What's up?" Jackson asks, on full alert.

"My family is here."

"Oh," he says, surprised. "I didn't know they were coming over."

"Neither did I," I mutter.

"You need some backup?"

I take a deep breath. Backup sounds really nice right about now, but I can't ask him to do that. He's already done enough for me. I can't ask him to rush to my aid when all that's happened is an impromptu dinner with my stressful family.

"No, no, it's fine. Just thrown me off a little. I can let you know when they leave."

He hums on the other line. "Okay pretty girl. But you let me know if you need me. Send me a codeword or something. Oh, text me 'Glitterball' and I'll rush right over."

"Can't it be something like SOS? It's a classic for a reason."

Jackson scoffs. "Don't be so basic, Rosie. We've got our own secret code. It's perfect."

I laugh, feeling lighter than I have since I opened the door. I'll get through this and they'll leave soon. Plus, now I have backup on standby. I've got this.

"Okay, I'll text you."

"Good girl," he says in a low voice and I have to squeeze my thighs together. Not now, I scold my horny inner self. This is *so* not the time.

"I'll call you back when they're gone."

"Good luck."

I hang up the phone and straighten my spine. I once read that if you stand in a superhero pose for a few seconds, it tricks your brain into thinking you're confident. So I stand there like Wonder Woman and take a few deep breaths before returning to the kitchen.

My family are sat at the table, each with a bowl of risotto in front of them.

"Who was that?" Cleo asks innocently.

Before I can come up with a lie, Mum says, "We didn't know how long you'd be so didn't want to waste it."

"Thanks," I mutter, before spooning some of the risotto into my bowl. This was supposed to be a week's worth of lunch but there's probably only one portion left. Plus, since partially cooked, processed chicken was added, I don't even know if I can have it. Never mind the vegetarian in me, the baby in me is almost certainly not allowed processed meat.

Maybe I can eat around it? I think miserably as I sit at my table. Not wanting to bring attention to the culinary dilemma I'm facing, I stir my food around in my bowl.

"So," Cleo starts and I glance at her warily. It's always tense the moment before she opens her mouth. I never know what she's going to say but I brace anyway. "How have you been Rosie?" She asks the question so earnestly that I'm shocked for a second.

"Uh, good. I've been good, you know, just working."

"Are you seeing anyone?"

I furrow my brow. "No." My voice is firm even if I'm not as convinced myself. I'm seeing Jackson often and in a lot of different positions.

Oh, and I'm having his baby in four months.

"Rosalie, there's far too much butter in this, no wonder it looks like you've gone up a size," Mum scolds, barely looking up from her dish.

I suck in a breath as Cleo grins into her drink.

"This table is wobbly," Dad announces, shaking the table and causing the bowls to rattle on the wood. "You should fix these things before they get too loose, it's a hazard."

"I can't believe you can even fit a six person table in this kitchen," Cleo says, leaning back in her chair and glancing around. "It's so...quaint."

My phone buzzes in my pocket, and I pull it out under the table.

JACKSON

Proof of life please

I can't help the smile that pulls at my lips.
I type before I can help myself.

ME

glitterba

Before I can finish typing, Mum snaps, "Rosalie, get off the phone at the dinner table."

My thumb nudges the screen as I hasten to lock it.

I turn back to my food, pushing it around my plate.

Then, the handle turns on the front door and Jackson Harper walks into my kitchen with a smile.

"Hello, Taylors."

18

———

JACKSON

It's a good thing dinner is already served because you could cut the tension in this room with a knife.

Four shocked faces stare back at me and I let my gaze brush over the three strangers until I reach Rosie.

"Smells delicious," I say with a wink. That gets Rosie on her feet.

She rushes over to me. "What are you doing here?" she asks in a low voice.

"You say Glitterball, I come running." Well, I received a *glitterbalddghts*, which I interpreted to mean *dear God come and help me now*. I smirk as Rosie takes a deep breath, curving into me slightly as if I'm holding an umbrella that can shield her from her guests. "You good, pretty girl?" I whisper.

She nods. "Better now,"

I gently clasp her shoulders and step around her. "Jackson," I say, extending my hand to her father. He's tall and slim, with Rosie's blue eyes behind his glasses. He warily clasps my hand in his.

"Rosie didn't tell us you were coming." Rosie's mother

stands with a simpering smile. *Rosie didn't know* you *were coming*, I think. "I'm Andrea."

Andrea is slim with neat blonde hair around her shoulders and looks almost nothing like Rosie. I gently place a kiss on each of her cheeks and flash her a winning smile. "We all hate an unexpected surprise."

Andrea stares at me. "Has anyone ever told you you look *just like* that guy from those superhero movies?"

"Once or twice," I shoot her one of my friendly camera smiles. It's always a little awkward meeting people who recognize me but can't place me. That split second when they can't figure out if they've seen me on TV or if we go to the same gym. But, then again, I feel like I already know enough about this woman myself.

"Same person," Rosie rushes out from my side, her cheeks pink. Andrea gapes at me but Rosie drags my attention to the other people gathered around the table. "This is my Dad, Terry and my sister, Cleo."

Her sister, Cleo, stands and angles towards me with a smile that I assume is supposed to be seductive. Despite her conventional good looks and heavy makeup, she's got nothing on Rosie.

I cut her off with a friendly wave before crossing back to the kitchen counter where Rosie is dishing up a bowl of risotto.

I take a dramatic sniff. "Smells lovely." I spot little white chunks swimming in the stew and lower my voice. "Updating the recipe?"

Rosie's shoulders stiffen as she whispers, "Mum brought some cooked chicken to add."

I frown at her but she shakes me off and takes my bowl back to the table and sets it beside her seat. Unfortunately, it sets me right next to the sister, who brushes her hair back in such an exaggerated motion that I think she might topple off her chair.

"So *Jackson*," she says, resting her hand on her head and leaning closer to me. "How do you know Rosa-pee?"

The way she says the nickname sets my teeth on edge, a little malicious glint in her eye as she enunciates the 'pee'. I lean back, resting my arm lightly along the back of Rosie's chair.

"Mutual friends," I say with a tight smile. "What are you guys doing down this way? It's nice of you to come and visit your daughter." I'm being a dick but I don't care.

Rosie straightens in her seat and I gently tug a strand of her hair before trailing my hand along her shoulder.

"No, we were at Cleo's launch event," Andrea says sitting up straighter in her seat. "She wore such beautiful a dress, you should have seen it. Everyone there was saying that pink is just her color."

I nod my head politely.

"Her post got *a quarter of a million* likes." Andrea emphasizes it like I should be impressed.

I'm not.

"Yeah, I saw it," Rosie says quietly, scooping up a spoonful.

"Is it true you're dating Ashley Peters?" Cleo asks, leaning her head on her hands and tilting her body towards me, fluttering her false eyelashes.

I feel Rosie freeze up next to me and I restrain myself from tugging her into my lap and claiming her in front of her entire family. "No," I say firmly, angling away from her and closer to Rosie.

Cleo shares a look with her mother. I've spent enough years watching my sisters and mother communicate with their eyes that I know something passed between them.

"How are you finding London?" Andrea asks me brightly. "Cleo can always take you on a tour. There's an amazing restaurant in Kensington–"

My blood boils under my veins. Why do they think I'm here? Do they think I spiritually connected with Cleo from LA and something tugged me to a random flat in Clapham so I could sit here at a dinner table where none of the occupants were invited?

I hope that whatever delusions these guys have misses our kid in the gene pool. I grimace. "No, thank you."

I curl my fingers around the back of Rosie's chair, almost ready to pick it up and carry her out of here.

Cleo flicks her hair over her shoulder and rests her hand close to my arm. Before she gets any ideas I pull my hand under the table.

"If you change your mind, I can give you my number." Cleo purrs. "Or you can DM me, I won't let you get lost. I get so many messages it's hard to keep track sometimes, you know how it is."

Rosie's fork clatters against her bowl and I watch her shoulders hunch inwards. I remove my hand from the back of her chair and drape my arm over her lap instead, gripping her thigh and running my thumb along her jeans. It will be a cold day in hell when I willingly message that girl. Rosie's cold hand gently rests over my fingers and I try to take a calming breath.

Changing tactics, I turn to Rosie's father. "Terry, Rosie tells me you're retired." Terry blinks in surprise, but I shoulder on. "Picked up any hobbies?" Please have some hobbies, Terry. Please.

"Well yes...I've got a 8700 Vintage Model Train set set up in the—."

"He spends all his time in the garage," Andrea interrupts, rolling her eyes. "It's like I haven't even got a husband anymore. He's gone full granddad."

Rosie tenses under my hand.

"Good timing," Cleo says, with a sinister smile. "Isn't that right Rosa-pee?"

The room stills, with all heads turning to Rosie.

What. The. *Fuck?* How did she find out?

"What are you talking about?" Andrea asks.

Rosie shifts underneath me pushing my hand away. I take the hint and return to my seat. I refuse to look at Cleo, keeping all my focus on the woman next to me.

She takes a deep breath and faces her parents, angling her body away from her sister. "I'm pregnant."

She releases it in a rushed breath, shoving her shoulders back and sitting up straighter.

When I told my mum, she shrieked and cried and I couldn't get her to shut up. When Rosie tells hers...nothing.

Andrea's mouth hangs open as she processes.

"How did you find out?" Rosie asks her sister, barely turning her head to address her.

"Nanny's care home rang to congratulate *me*," she snickers, as if this is all one big joke. "She must have gotten confused, or maybe she just forgot. You know what she's like nowadays." She shrugs her shoulders as she flips her hair again.

I grind my teeth at the comment.

Terry clears his throat, his eyes shining. Before he can say anything, Andrea barks, "Are you serious?"

Rosie flinches ever so slightly but doesn't reply.

"How could you be so—so irresponsible?" Andrea snaps, "Are you going to *keep it*?"

"Yes," Rosie says sharply. "Yes, I'm keeping my baby."

I clench my jaw, wanting more than anything to jump in and bulldoze, but also wanting Rosie to lead this.

"Plus, that window has passed. I'm due in February."

"*February*," Andrea shrieks and I wince as the sound pierces my eardrums. "It's October! This is ridiculous, you're having a baby in *five months* and you didn't even tell your own mother? I can't believe this, Rosalie. Why didn't you say anything?"

Rosie shifts ready to open her reply but her mother cuts her off.

"How have you let this happen? Are you going to raise it here? In a one bedroom flat that you're renting?"

"You're acting like that's never been done before."

"You're not even married for God's sake, what were you *thinking*?" Andrea asks, her voice pitching further upwards. "Who's the father?"

"Don't be surprised if it's a turkey baster and a man in a van," Cleo giggles behind her hand.

"That's enough," I bellow, rising to my feet.

The chair slides back with a screech as four pairs of eyes jump to mine in surprise. "I've had enough of this. I appreciate this is a shock which is why we were going to share our news in our own time." I glare at Cleo, "But if you can't process this news respectfully and quietly, I'm going to have to ask you to leave."

"*You're* the father?" Cleo sputters in disbelief.

I glare at her, almost ready to say *duh*. Are these people *well*? "Yes, and it's the best thing to ever happen to me."

I cross to the door holding it open and gesturing for them to make use of it.

I watch in stony silence as they slowly rise to their feet.

"Well," Andrea says, throwing her hands up. "It's just a shock is all."

"Process it on your own time and then get back to us." I send her a smile that doesn't reach my eyes.

I hold it open as Andrea scurries past. I step further away from the door as Cleo attempts to brush past me. This woman makes my skin crawl. How has Rosie put up with her for her whole life?

Out of the corner of my eye I see Rosie's dad pulling her into an awkward hug. I glance away respectfully but honestly he sat there and let himself get steamrolled by his wife and daughter, without so much as moving a muscle to step in to shield his youngest. I know for a fact that I will never stand by and allow that to happen to *my* daughter. Ever.

He approaches, offering me a handshake which I warily accept. "Thank you," he says, avoiding eye contact before adding a quiet, "and congratulations."

I nod my head once, not trusting myself to open my mouth.

He leaves and I close the door behind him, resting my hands on the wood and dropping my head

"I'm sorry Rosie," I say, turning finally. "I just couldn't sit by and let—"

Warm lips land on mine and it only takes a second for my reflexes to kick in before I circle my arms around Rosie, tugging her to me.

I almost groan as her curious tongue slides past my lips, widening them further. Her small hands cross my shoulders and tug at my hair, sending lightning shooting down my spine.

"Rosie," I mumble as she presses kisses along my jaw. "Slow down."

"I don't want to," she mutters into my skin.

"I'm sorry, I know it's not my plac–"

"Don't say sorry," she whispers against my lips, pulling back to look in my eyes. "Don't say sorry for that. No one's ever stood up for me like that before." She blinks rapidly, as she runs her fingers across my jaw. "So, don't be sorry."

Her lips find mine again and I sink into her, pulling her closer as if I can meld her body to mine. I've not kissed her since that first night, at the wedding, and I want to kick myself for not chasing after her sooner, not kissing her sooner. How have I lived thirty two years on this planet without this woman? Her breasts crush against my chest, and I slip my hand under the hem of her jeans, clutching her ass.

She tugs me backwards until her back hits the counter, and it's second nature to lift her and place her on top of it.

She moans breathlessly as I grind into her pussy, my cock harder than a steel pipe.

My hands explore her, running along her back and around to her throat. Her pulse jumps wildly under my hand, and I pull my lips away from her lips to press a kiss to the jumping point.

"Are you sure?" I mumble into her neck.

"Please, Jackson."

I clasp her jaw with my hands and pull back to look at her. With her cheeks flushed and lips swollen, she looks ready to be fucked.

"Rosie." I swipe my thumb across her swollen lip and watch as her eyes darken. I swallow harshly. "I want this to be real," I confess, unable to hide how desperately I want her. All of her.

"You do?" she asks, licking her lips.

"Hmm," I rumble, sliding my lips across her jaw and to the soft juncture of her neck. "I want us to be us."

I'm glad I'm not looking at her. Buried in her warm skin, I can safely imagine that she's going to agree with me.

"Yes," she says breathlessly. I lift my head gazing into her eyes.

"Yes?"

"Yes," she says, a smile pulling at her lips. "I want it to be real too."

"You really mean that?"

"Yes, Jackson, I mean that. I think a part of me wanted that the whole time but I thought *you* wanted to keep it casual." She lifts her hand to my cheek, her soft fingers brushing against my lips.

"There's nothing casual about us baby." I nibble on her fingers before pulling away from her with a playful groan. "Hold on, so you're saying this whole time, you've been pretending to be overcome with pregnancy hormones just to get into bed with me?"

She rolls her eyes with a laugh. "Yes, yes okay? Now, can we please get to the fucking part."

I gasp. "Rosie Taylor, who are you right now?"

I swallow her laugh on my tongue as I grind my hips into hers. I love the way her eyes flutter at the friction and I let out a low growl as I eat up her sigh.

"Fuck me now please," she whimpers.

Jesus.

"You got it, pretty girl."

19

ROSIE

The kitchen is a disaster, my life just blew up in front of my face and I didn't get to eat my risotto. But all I care about is the man in front of me and the desperate urge to feel him inside me.

I lick into his lips with abandon. It's messy and unrestrained and I can't help myself. I want to taste all of him, feel all of him.

His warm hands explore my skin, curving around my backside and tugging me closer to him as if I can mold myself to his body.

His erection presses between my thighs and my eyes nearly roll back, the countertop beneath us as dangerous as a balcony at the edge of a garden.

My glasses bump against his nose and he huffs a laugh against my mouth. He pulls back just enough to gently peel them off my nose and place them carefully to the side. I blink as my eyes readjust and I take in his face. It's like looking at him in focus, the kitchen a blur behind him. It's just him and me. His eyes burn into mine as I brush my hand through the hair falling in front of his face.

The moment he stood up for me, defended me without me even having to ask, the thin control I was holding on my feelings for this man snapped like an elastic band. We're not just friends, we haven't been for a while, we're so much more than that. I *want* to be more than that.

With a low growl he claims me again, slanting his mouth over mine and stealing my breath. I can't help the moan that escapes as he presses his lips to mine, widening my mouth as his wicked tongue takes whatever I can give.

I shift just enough to free his shirt from his belt, tugging it up and off his chest.

I take a shaky breath as my hands trace his chest. Solid and strong, I slide my hands along his tight stomach, curling my fingers through the hair on his chest. I've seen him enough to have memorized his shape, every tattoo and muscle covering his chest and arms, but it feels different now. It's more.

"You're killing me baby," he groans. "But I want to fuck you in your bed. I want to take my time with you, worship you, wake up with you in my arms. Can I do that, Rosie? Please?"

I think I say yes, or at least nod my head. Whatever I say is lost as I wrap my legs around his waist. My stomach swoops as he carries me out of the kitchen.

"I'm too heavy," I mumble against his lips, but his arms don't even shake beneath me as he effortlessly holds my weight.

"Never," Jackson promises as he nudges open the bedroom door. "If there comes a day I can't carry you, I need to get back in the gym." He gently lowers me onto the bed, controlling the movement, and I nearly swoon. "Or because I'm too old and my back doesn't work the same anymore."

I giggle against his lips. "You won't want to have sex with me when we're both old."

"Baby, I'll be desperate to fuck you every day for the rest of my life."

I bite my lip at the rush his words shoot through me. I never would have imagined this man would be here, saying these words to me.

He helps me wiggle my jeans off before he lowers himself between the cradle of my thighs and all I can concentrate on is him.

I trace my hands down his chest until his erection is in my hand, thick and hot and heavy.

"I need you inside me," I say as I stroke him, directing him between my thighs.

He buries his head in my neck with a groan and my pulse flutters under his lips.

His fingers find my clit and I'm almost embarrassed at the sound of my wetness.

"I'll get a condom," he says, making to move off me.

"Wait," I whisper. "We don't have to." I feel his cock twitch in my hand and can't resist stroking it.

"Rosie, are you sure?" he breathes.

"We can't unbutter the bread," I say, echoing his words from months ago and he swallows my laugh with grinning lips.

"I'm clean. I haven't been with anyone since you."

I nod, desperately. "Please, Jackson, I want to feel you inside me."

"Is that right?" he purrs, his lips teasing mine. "You want to be full of my come? You want to feel it dripping out of your tight pussy?"

I whimper with need, trying to spread my legs further.

"Yes," I moan. "Fill me up, Jackson. *Please.*"

He lifts up on his knees, staring down at me with a reverence that makes me feel like a goddess.

"Is it okay?" he asks, his hands traveling my body and gently feeling the curve of my stomach as he helps pull my shirt over my head.

I nod, biting my lip. "I uh, I looked into it."

He looks at me with a grin. "Looked into what, pretty girl?"

I roll my eyes and attempt to hide the flush in my cheeks. "After the first time, I wanted to know if it's okay for you to use *that*." I tilt my head towards his impressive length.

"*Use that*," he repeats, his smirk growing.

"You know how big you are."

He opens his mouth, his eyes lit up, ready to say something funny.

"Can you just fuck me already?" I ask as an incredulous laugh bubbles out of me.

He chuckles as he uses his fingers to spread me before him like a feast. "I love the sound of you begging, pretty girl."

He gently teases the tip of his cock to my clit and I bite back a moan. He nudges his tip at my entrance and suddenly I'm so full I lose my breath. This is better than the first time, better than the 'hormonal' hook ups we've had the last few weeks.

This is *more*.

His thumb lightly plays with my clit as he thrusts inside me and my back arches off the bed.

"Play with those pretty tits for me, Rosie."

I do as he asks, rolling my sensitive nipples between my fingers as he rocks into me, gripping my thighs.

The feel of his hips pistoning into mine, his delicious length hitting just the right spot, his thumb on my clit, and his hands gripping my waist is almost too much. I run my hands along his chest, my nails lightly scratching at his skin.

I want him closer, so I reach my hands up and tug at his shoulders until his body is bracketing mine and his cock is pulsing inside me. The new angle lets me tilt my head up to his, pressing my lips to his and panting into his mouth as he hooks my leg over his hip.

"Fuck, baby, you're so beautiful," he says, his hand reaching up to play with my nipple. His thumb flicks against the bud before he reaches between us and thumbs at my clit. I can't hold back any longer, my legs shaking around him as I come.

He works me through it, rubbing my clit with his hand, his hips pumping into mine. He throws his head back as he comes, his Adam's apple bobbing as he tenses.

Jackson collapses, careful to keep his weight off me.

We breath together for a few seconds, his arms bracketing me so he doesn't crush me with his weight.

"I think I just got pregnant again," I say in his ear and he laughs before capturing my lips in his.

"I think so too."

I smile into his kiss as he thrusts his rapidly re-hardening cock inside me.

20

———

JACKSON

"Thank you," Rosie says quietly as we lie tangled in the sheets. "For coming."

I can't help the smirk that tugs at my lips and she groans into her hands. "You have the humor of a teenage boy."

"I didn't even say anything!" I insist, leaning up on my elbow so I can peer down at her.

I rest my hand gently on her belly, my hand spanning the gentle curve. "I'll always be here for you, Rosie, you just need to say the word."

"Glitterball," she grins.

"Glitterball." I nod seriously.

She laughs and that's when I feel it.

A flicker against the palm of my hand.

We both freeze. "Was that—?"

Rosie gapes at me. "Yeah." Her hands come to mine, tugging it to the side gently. "I've been feeling these flutters for a few weeks but that's the biggest one yet."

I waste no time shifting down the bed until I'm level with her belly button. "Hey, baby girl," I whisper against Rosie's belly, pressing a kiss to the spot the baby just kicked.

"Hello." I tap on her belly when there's no movement. "Wake up."

Rosie laughs above me. "Oh my God, you're going to annoy her awake."

"She better get used to it," I say, shooting Rosie a wink. "I'm planning to annoy the both of you for the rest of our lives."

I almost jump out of my skin as I feel the tiny impenetrable flutter.

"She likes your voice," Rosie says with a shining smile, stroking her stomach.

"I think she likes your laugh," I slide closer and press a kiss to her lips.

"Say something else," Rosie breathes against my mouth.

Without needing to be asked twice I shuffle back down the bed, resuming my position. "Laugh again."

Rosie giggles. "Fuck off."

"Did you hear that Smudge? Your mummy just told me to fuck off." I press my ear to her belly. "Smudge says you're a bad influence."

"You're going to gang up on me, aren't you?"

We stay like that for what feels like hours, until Smudge stops doing acrobatics and Rosie snuggles into my arms.

"Do you want to talk about it?" I ask, running my fingers across her back.

She turns her head slightly, burrowing further into my side. "There's not much to say."

"Is it always like that with them?"

She nods. "Cleo is...Cleo. I think she always knows exactly what to say to make me feel–" She breaks off.

I kiss her temple. "It was so wrong of her to blurt it out like that, baby. She had no right."

Rosie hums but doesn't continue, instead pressing a kiss

to my skin and snuggling closer, running her hands across my torso.

"What does this one mean?" she asks, lightly tapping the tattoo on my chest.

"It's Taranaki Maunga, a mountain a few hours north of Wellington. My dad and I used to hike it every summer. There's a bunch of tracks and we were planning on doing all of them." I tighten my arm around her, unable to voice that we never managed to finish it.

"Are there any easy ones left?" Rosie asks, tracing the ink. "I could give it a go, though you'd probably have to pull me along."

I grin pressing a kiss to her hair, "I'll carry you if I have to."

The room darkens around us and Rosie's breathing slows until I'm almost sure she's fallen asleep.

"Will you stay?" Rosie mumbles into my chest.

I gently tilt her head back. "I don't know if I've made myself clear enough, pretty girl. I'm here now, and I'm not going anywhere."

Her eyes flutter closed and I press a kiss to her nose, tugging her closer to me and inhaling her berry shampoo.

THE NEXT MORNING, I wake to an empty bed. I lie still for a second, listening. The apartment is so small that I can already hear Rosie clattering around in the kitchen.

I contemplate stepping into my jeans but it's barely eight am and all I want is my woman back in bed with me.

Rosie's back is to me, her hands in the soapy kitchen sink. I gently approach her, wrapping my arms around her. She relaxes into me, her head resting on my shoulder.

"Come back to bed," I murmur into her neck and press a kiss to her skin.

"I woke up hours ago with Smudge doing flips on my bladder and then I couldn't get back to sleep."

I cup her belly, and lightly nip her ear, loving the fact that she's adopted the nickname. "Come back to bed now."

She turns in my arms, leaning up to kiss me. "If you insist."

Her phone vibrates on the counter and she freezes in my arms. She steps out of the circle of my arms to pick up her phone.

I pretend that I'm not curious and start drying the dishes on the rack. Out of the corner of my eye, I see Rosie slump slightly before she puts the phone face down.

"Your parents?"

She readjusts her glasses as she steps around me, "Uh, no. It was just a message in the work chat."

She starts fluttering around the kitchen, moving items from one counter to the other. I gently grab her hand and pull her to a stop, wrapping my arms around her as she buries her head in my chest.

"They'll come around."

"I doubt it," she mumbles.

I acted on instinct last night. I've picked up on all the hints that Rosie's accidentally dropped over the last few months, but she's never outright said that her family's actions affect her. Always just shrugging it off and changing the subject.

"Hey," I say, tilting her chin up. It breaks my heart seeing her big blue eyes water. "I'll be here, no matter what."

I haven't made the career I have, had the life I have, without cutting out the people that don't want to be in it. I got lucky with my family, lucky that I've never had to question their loyalty to me.

She nods her head. "I just don't know why they don't like me."

Ice shoots through my veins as I tuck her closer to me, wrapping my arms around her and swaying her in place.

"They do like you baby, they just show it in a very weird way." I kiss her head. "Whereas I show you I like you in a very obvious, natural way."

She chuckles against my chest, bringing a smile to my face.

Her hands trace along my spine, making me shiver and I pull her face back with my hands.

"Just to be clear," I say, very seriously. "I like you very much." Kiss. "I like our baby very much." Kiss. "And I'd very much like to never hear the words 'just hormones' again."

Her grin tugs at her cheeks. "You're not going to let that go are you?"

I shake my head. "My ego has taken a beating, I'll tell you."

"Well." Her hands come to my wrists. "Just to be clear. I like you very much too."

I let out a dramatic sigh of relief and swallow her laugh with a kiss. "Now, can I please go fuck my girlfriend?"

"Girlfriend, huh?"

"Glad you've caught up."

She laughs as I tug her back toward the bedroom, where I show her just how much I like her.

21

ROSIE

It's been two weeks since my disastrous family reunion and I still haven't heard from my parents. Jackson and I have spent nearly every second not at work locked in my flat and when he suggested we go for a walk before our twenty week scan this afternoon, this was the only place I wanted to go.

I love this time of year and there's nowhere better to spend it than in Richmond Park. The air is crisp and mild, and rust colored leaves crunch underfoot. Unlike Hyde Park which is always packed with crowds, we've barely seen a soul in the hour since we made it here.

We've been meandering through the lanes, but I've been discreetly shepherding Jackson to the coffee hut in the center of the park that sells the best hot chocolate.

Anya and I discovered it last year when we were in the throes of wedding planning and staying in her London house. We'd spend days sipping from reusable mugs as I teased her about her new jet setting lifestyle.

"Okay, so you're being pulled two meters by one arm?" I ask, interrupting Jackson as he explains the stunt he'll be working on this week.

He shakes his head. "That's how it will look on camera, but I'll be in a full rig to avoid any injury."

I bite my lip and concentrate on the leaves crunching underfoot.

"Are you worried, girlfriend?" Jackson grins down at me with a wink.

I roll my eyes but can't stop the way my heart lightens. He's called me girlfriend almost as much as pretty girl in the past week and I feel like giggling like a schoolgirl every time. I've had a few boyfriends over the years, but none of them claimed me in the way Jackson has.

"It just sounds crazy," I burst out. "It seems like every week you're getting thrown into a table or suspended in midair or plunged underwater in a car crash—"

"That's not for a few weeks yet."

I cut my eyes to his. "It's just a lot, is all. Have you ever thought of doing a courthouse drama? Ooh, or animation! That's literally just you in a padded room."

Jackson frees my hand so he can wrap his arm around my shoulder and tug me closer to his side. "What can I say, pretty girl, your boyfriend is a daredevil."

"Adrenaline junkie more like," I mutter as he plants a kiss to my temple.

"Look, I've got a good team around me and they've never steered me wrong. I've done hundreds of these stunts over the years. You should have seen some of the stuff they had me doing for Starseeker."

"Like that fight scene where you smashed through a window and fell three stories in Starseeker's Vengeance? I remember."

He gasps and I feel my cheeks burn. "Rosie Taylor, you didn't tell me you've seen them."

I glance up at him and the bright grin pulling at his

cheeks. "Oh, you mean the most successful superhero franchise of the last twenty years? I might have caught a few."

He tilts his head back as he chuckles. "I was given the suit as a wrap gift." He wiggles his eyebrows. "I can try it on for you if you like."

I laugh. "You can try it on, but the lycra didn't really do it for me."

"You didn't like my lycra?" he asks in mock horror. "What about the bulge that they had to fix in post?"

I snort, imagining the poor VFX person who would have spent hours minimizing Jackson's sizable bulge so as to not scar any kids for life.

"All I'm saying is you need to be careful." I press my hand against my bump underneath my jacket. Smudge has been much more active since Jackson felt her for the first time. She's really making herself known. It's been really hard to not call the baby 'she' before our gender scan but Jackson's unwavering certainty is contagious. It doesn't matter to me either way. I wouldn't mind a mini-Jackson.

Jackson stops in his tracks, turning me to face him. "Are you really worried about this?" he asks, concern and apprehension clear in his dark eyes

"I'm not *not* concerned. I know you're a professional and have been doing this for a long time, but I just can't help but worry." I shrug. "Sue me."

Jackson steps closer, his hand tugging at my jacket and lightly stroking my bump. "I know what I'm doing, pretty girl." He cups my chin and swipes his thumb against my lip. "Trust me."

I take a deep breath. "I do trust you."

He takes my lips in his and my worry burns away as he swipes his tongue against mine.

My toes curl in my boots as I rise up to meet his lips.

He pulls away with a final peck, "We should head back to the car if we want to make this appointment."

"Let me get my hot chocolate first," I laugh. "I can't leave without it. Anya and I always get it with all the trimmings and it's the best one in the city."

We fall back into step as we head towards the hut, fingers entwined. It's the middle of the week so the park is quiet but Jackson hangs back while I order to not draw attention. It's only when we each have a cup of gooey goodness in hands that he pounces.

"Have you spoken to her recently?" Jackson asks. "Anya?"

My gut twists and I cradle my bump. "Uhh," I say, thinking. "A few times here and there. She's still on her honeymoon. They were in the Maldives last I heard from them."

"Hmm," he says.

"What?"

"Nothing!" Jackson insists. "Have you told her yet?"

"Told who what?" I take a sip of my drink, the whipped cream sticking to my lip.

"Rosie," he chides gently.

"I will tell her," I insist, Cleo's smug face and my mother's sharp criticism echoing in my ears. "She's on her honeymoon, Jackson."

He sighs. "She'll be home soon right?"

I nod. "And I'll tell her as soon as she does." She'll probably be able to tell as soon as she sees how big my boobs have gotten.

"Have you heard from your mum?"

I shake my head. I sent her a text the day after she left the flat and asked her when she was free to chat, but she left me on read.

Jackson is quiet beside me as he sips his drink. "You were right, pretty girl. This shit is delicious."

I pull him to a stop and kiss the whipped cream off his lip. "I told you. I'd come here every day if I could."

"Why don't you?"

I shoot him a look, "We drove here Jackson. A two hour walk for a daily hot chocolate would be ridiculous."

"You don't want to move over here?" he asks, grasping my hand in mine.

I snort. "How am I going to afford a flat in Richmond? The rent here alone is more than my entire salary." Plus, when the baby gets here, any left over cash will be spent on her.

My mother's jibe rings in my ear. It was already a push to rent a one bed on one salary in the city, so I don't know what I'm going to do when I have to factor in childcare costs. That's not to mention if my job will even still exist when I return from maternity leave. I've already started meeting with Kathleen and the production team for the short film, but even with the extra hours, the pay will barely cover one month's rent.

I could leave the city, move out into a cheaper area, but then I'd have to quit my job or find a new one. And the opportunities outside London in the film industry are limited. I could get a job doing something else. Admin or cleaning or baking, maybe. Though how would I look after the baby if I'm waking up at five am to open up a bakery? I'd be late sometimes and the customers would get angry and would stop coming and then the bakery would have to close and—

"Where's that head gone?" Jackson asks, after what I realize is a long silence while I worry about the turnover of my imaginary bakery.

I shoot him what I hope is a reassuring smile. "Just thinking."

"Hold up, is that"—Jackson says, ducking his head and peering through some trees—"Pip?"

I whip my head, expecting to see my glamorous friend strolling across the green but instead I can't help the laugh that escapes as I come face to face with a parked taxi with Pip Covington's face plastered to the side of it.

"It is." I drag Jackson closer. The whole cab is bright lilac, complementing Pip's purple gown as she holds a bottle of *Poise Perfect*. It's one of those perfume ads that are designed to confuse you and simultaneously arouse you enough to want to buy a scent that you've never smelled before. I'm sold.

"Look, we're matching," I laugh tugging at my purple sweater. "Can you take a picture of me?"

I hand him my phone and turn, shooting a goofy smile to the camera as I point at the taxi.

"Don't get my bump in it," I say through my teeth.

"Looks good, pretty girl." He shoots me a smile as he hands me back my phone.

I waste no time pulling up Pip's name.

ME

Look what I found!

It's surprising how close I've become to Danny's sister and her best friend, Cassie, considering Anya and I used to scream sing Cassandra's debut album all throughout university and would see Pip plastered on the cover of fashion magazines. But as soon as Anya introduced us after she and Danny finally agreed to make a real go of their relationship, we all just clicked. It's nice to know I have friends on the other side of the screen, even if they do spend their time jet setting across the world.

Jackson and I walk back to the car as I see the bubbles appear by her name. Anxiety curls in my gut the longer it takes her to reply. Maybe we're not as close as I thought we were and now she just thinks I'm a weirdo. A minute goes by and I check my phone for the message but nothing has come through. I'm about to put my phone away when the bubbles reappear and a message finally pops up.

PIP

Imagine the poor driver having to drive that around all day

I snicker as I tuck my phone back in my pocket.

"You ready for this?" Jackson asks, taking my hand in his as we heads towards the hospital.

I place a kiss to his knuckles. "I'm ready."

22

JACKSON

The two flights of stairs up to Rosie's apartment feels like two thousand.

I take a deep breath and heave my body up each step, clinging onto the banister like I might fall back down. When I finally drag myself to her front door, I take a second to sag against the frame.

Get it together, I tell myself.

Pushing myself upright, I knock gently on the door and fix what I hope is a pleasant smile on my face.

"Hey," she greets me with a wide smile. "I thought that was you shuffling about."

"Hi, pretty girl..." My body shudders as I tilt down and press a kiss to her forehead. I would give anything to kiss her lips but she's far too short for me to get away with the motion without giving away just how much pain I'm in.

"Tea?" she offers, turning her back on me and moving to the kettle.

I gingerly rest my back against the counter opposite, toeing out of my shoes. "Yes please."

If I can just angle my shoe onto the lip of the other one, I should be able to slide my foot out without any bending required. My shoe slips off the other and I almost lose my balance completely.

"What's wrong with you?" Rosie asks suspiciously, watching me flail about like I've forgotten how humans take their shoes off.

"Nothing." I brush her off. "Is it okay if I take a shower? It's been a long day."

Her eyes narrow behind her glasses. "Sure. I can make a start on dinner."

"Thanks," I mumble as I awkwardly shuffle out of the kitchen.

Just as I'm about to cross the threshold, Rosie stops me with a hand on my arm. "Are you sure you're okay? You look...stiff."

I force myself to bark a laugh and shoot her a wink. "Later, pretty girl." Well, I mean at this point it will be a miracle if I can get my boots off, so we'll have to reassess that later.

She rolls her eyes but bites her lip anxiously.

"I'll be fine after a shower," I reassure her and attempt to widen my stride on the way to the bathroom.

As soon as the door closes behind me, I sag against it, my energy depleted.

Thankfully, I'm wearing a shirt so it only takes a few tugs with shaking fingers to undo the buttons and pull it off my shoulders.

I turn the shower on and steam fills the room almost immediately. I glance in the mirror, turning my back and peering over my shoulder to see the angry red mark that's likely going to turn into a pretty nasty bruise spreading across my side. Rosie's biggest concern was my arm being yanked from its socket, but we didn't really consider what would happen when I was thrown onto a mat so forcefully I had the wind knocked out of me and a medic going on about bruised ribs. I've had worse, walked off worse, but production still insisted they rearrange the schedule to give me a few days rest. Normally, a few days off would be a blessing but this one comes with resentment from the higher ups for adding days to the schedule.

Gritting my teeth, I sit on the closed toilet seat and fumble with my boots until they're finally off. I'll probably burn them. Jandals only from now on.

Once I've got my jeans and boxers off, I think the worst is over, until I have to step over the lip of the bathtub.

I grit my teeth. I can't wait for a walk in, six nozzle shower head with a bench seat and heated flooring.

I cling onto the white porcelain as I swing my body over into the water. If I slip, I honestly don't think I'll get back up.

I hang my head, letting the warm water pound my body and soothe my muscles. With each drop that hits my skin, I will for it to heal me. I'll get out of this shower refreshed and healthy, and ready to tease Rosie until she blushes, and tumble her beneath her sheets. I just need five more minutes.

Maybe ten.

"Jackson," Rosie's voice calls from the other side of the door.

"Just a minute," I call back.

"Too late, I'm coming in. I hope you're in the shower and not on the toilet. We've been moving very quickly, but I think it's still too soon for that."

My laugh bursts out breathlessly, causing my ribs to clench and pain to shoot down my side.

The shower curtain pulls back gently and her big eyes

peer at me. "I'm going to ask you one more time. Are you okay?"

I suck in a breath. "I've been better."

"Eric just dropped some painkillers off," Rosie says quietly. "Why didn't you say anything?"

I shrug and attempt to hide the wince at the motion.

She quirks her brow. She's definitely got the Mum look down. Smudge and I are never going to get away with anything.

"Are you washing your hair?"

"I uh—tried, but I couldn't lift my arms."

She sucks in a breath and her eyes widen. "Jackson," she whispers before tugging the curtain back further.

I watch as she takes her glasses off and places them on the counter next to a box of pills. Her t-shirt comes next and my eyes instinctively drop to her heavy breasts, the swell of our daughter underneath them. A few days ago we found out we were having a little girl and today I thought I'd broken my back. My heart shudders at the thought of just how badly today could have gone.

My mind runs and I barely notice until she climbs in next to me. "Rosie, what—"

"Shh," she says, running her cool hands over my skin. The contrast of the hot shower and her cool hands are soothing and I let her explore my back, only wincing when she reaches the tender spot.

"Here?" she mumbles. I can only nod, my eyes shut tightly.

"I'll be okay. The medic said I just need to rest."

She brushes my damp hair away from my face and nods. "It's okay."

She reaches behind me for the shampoo, gently combing it through my hair. Her nails scratch at my scalp

and I let my eyes drift shut, enjoying the motion. She lifts
the shower head out of the holder and uses it on my hair so
I don't have to move too much.

"This shower is way too small for you," Rosie says, as if
the thought has just occurred to her.

I chuckle. "Baby, this whole apartment is too small
for me."

"It's a normal size apartment," she defends. "You're just
oversized."

My arms are loose enough now to curve my arms
around her, pulling her wet, naked body to mine. "Nowhere
else I'd rather be."

She curls her arms around my neck and gently cuddles
into me. I can tell she's avoiding putting all her weight
on me.

"Come on, we can get out now," she says into my neck.

My dick pokes against her skin and I let out a low
breath.

Her head shoots up. "Did that hurt?"

"No," I sigh, "I'm horny now but realistically there's just
no way."

She laughs breathlessly. "Down, boy."

She delicately steps out of the shower before my brain
catches up to offer her a hand, and when she turns to help
me out, I shoo her away and copy her movements. "This
feels backwards."

She snickers as she wraps a fluffy towel around herself
and then grabs one for me, helping me into it and wrapping
me up. I'm six foot five, two hundred pounds and she's wrapping me up in a pink fluffy towel. "You're always looking
after me. Let me look after you for once."

I can't argue with that.

I follow her into the bedroom where she pulls out

boxers from the drawer I've taken to leaving my clothes in. I pull them on quickly, not willing to bend over more than necessary.

"Lie down," she tells me, gently pushing at my arm until I'm sitting on the end of the bed.

I send her a bemused smile as I do what I'm told, allowing myself to be tucked in. "Are you going to get in with me?"

She ignores me. "I'll get your meds. Stay here."

I drum my fingers on the bed and stare up at the ceiling. I hope she doesn't take too long. I love her bedroom but it's very much a room for sleeping, with the bed, wardrobe and dresser almost filling the room. She's already measured the space to the side of the bed for Smudge's bassinet, but there's barely enough space to swing a cat in here. I'm debating getting up and grabbing my phone from the bathroom to see if the email I'm waiting on has arrived, when I hear a faint curse and rustling from the direction of the living room.

"Rosie?" I call through the open door. "Can I get up now? I'm feeling much better."

Just as I'm about to stand up, she rounds the doorway with the TV from the living room cradled in her arms.

"Ah," I drawl. "My meds." I pull the blanket away from my body, ready to rise to my feet to grab it from her before she hurts herself, but she shoots me a glare from the over the top.

"Don't move." She gently places the TV on the top of my legs, trapping me unless I want to do some acrobatics which my ribs will not allow.

She spins on her heels and leaves again, whilst I attempt to slide the TV off my body without it crashing to the floor.

Rosie reappears with the pills and a glass of water, standing over me until I dutifully swallow.

She picks the TV up with ease but I still try to slide out of the bed. "Let me help you with that."

"Jackson, if you try and get out of that bed one more time, I will tie you to it."

"Promise?"

She snorts as she slides the TV onto the dresser untangling the wires and plugging them into the socket on the wall.

"Here." She hands me the remote as she slides onto the bed beside me.

I grab the remote and her hand, tugging her closer until I can press a kiss to her lips. "Thank you, baby."

"You're welcome."

I flick through the channels as she burrows into my side. "Do you feel better?"

The pain in my side still hurts, although lying down has eased it slightly, but my heart is bursting at the way she takes care of me. I kiss her forehead. "Much better."

23

ROSIE

THE LAST PLACE I WANTED TO BE WAS THE PUB WITH A GROUP of men talking about my baby daddy.

Yet that was where I currently was, nursing a Diet Coke outside a crowded pub in Soho. After telling Gareth about my maternity leave today I thought it was safer to not rock the boat any more than necessary and agreed to the monthly after work drinks that I have literally never attended before.

Crowds of corporate professionals spill out onto the streets, backpacks and briefcases resting by their feet. Getting a table between the hours of four and eight on a weeknight is next to impossible, so we're huddled on the street corner wearing coats. I stick my hand in my pocket, shifting back and forth on my feet. I spend my days sitting down and my back aches from my desk chair but standing for an hour in the frigid air also causes pain to shoot down my spine. There's no winning and I shift uncomfortably as I try to drink my drink as fast as I can.

I should hold on at least until someone buys the next round, but judging from the half full pint glasses in everyone's hands, I know that won't be for a while. I'm just about ready to make my excuses and leave.

"—Jackson Harper needs to come back to the universe—"

I tune back into the conversation when I hear his name, my heart flipping at the sound. After he came home with a bruise the size of my arm, I forced him to rest in bed for a few days until I was confident he wasn't in pain with every movement. It was almost impossible to let him walk out the door and go back to work, but he assured me that he was perfectly fine.

He's been shooting away for the last few days and isn't expected to be home for another week. Home. I've been so used to him being in my flat, lounging on my sofa or curled around me in bed, that it only feels like home because he's there. I'm almost convinced Smudge knows he's not there and that's why she's keeping me up. I've had to create a Jackson sized form out of pillows just so I can fall asleep and I like to think it's tricking Smudge into thinking he's there.

"Nah, he's done now. He's doing some action film with Christian Denny, I think."

I blink, remembering the men around me have no idea that the guy they're talking about has been sleeping in my bed for the last few months and that his baby is currently growing inside me.

"Is it Christian Denny? No way is he directing another action film. He's been doing those girly melodramas. No explosions or anything."

I roll my eyes. How have I somehow managed to work with a group of people who's enjoyment of media is limited to explosions and CGI?

"I'm looking it up," Kevin says, pulling his phone out.

I take another sip of my drink before Kevin's incredulous laugh grabs my attention.

I look up to find him already looking at me, his confused gaze drifting between me and the phone.

My spine straightens, tension radiating through my body. What? I squint at him. I'm ready to make my excuses. My drink is nearly finished and I'm about done with this day.

Kevin looks back at his phone and nudges Conor next to him, showing him the screen. Conor's eyes widen before he too glances at me like I've just announced I'm running for Prime Minister.

Enough of this. "What?" I ask sharply.

Kevin laughs, his eyes darkening with glee before he meaningfully glances at my stomach.

"You've been keeping that quiet."

I freeze. What?

I blink, my mouth dropping open. Conor passes the phone onto Lee until there's a circle of guys staring at me like I've just taken all my clothes off in the middle of the street.

"Jackson Harper, Rosie? How the hell did *you* pull that off?" Lee gapes at me.

My stomach drops. "Give me that." I grab the phone out of his limp hand as snickers erupt around me.

It's an article.

JACKSON HARPER EXPECTING BABY WITH INFLU-ENCER CLEO TAYLOR'S SISTER, ROSALIE

What? The word reverberates around my skull as my fingers tremble. I click on the article but what I see nearly makes me drop the phone.

I shove it and my empty glass into Lee's hands before stumbling away.

"Wait Rosie, where did you even meet him?"

"Can you get me an autograph?"

I don't hear them as I fumble in my bag for my phone. Tugging it free, I almost collapse against a wall as I click on the video.

"Get ready with me as I tell you the story about how my sister Rosie got knocked up by Jackson Harper. Yeah, that one..."

Cleo.

Cleo posted this? I can barely concentrate on the words coming out of her mouth, barely recognizing the background of my parents bathroom as she goes through a ten step makeup routine while she tells *millions* of people about my baby.

I barely have time to hunch over before I vomit on the street. I've hardly thrown up now that I'm halfway through my second trimester, so I've almost forgotten the feeling. People dart away from me making disgusted noises and my throat convulses as I heave.

Is this what rock bottom feels like? I wipe my mouth with shaking hands and push myself to stand.

I need to get home.

I stumble toward the road, hailing a black cab. I fumble with the handle before sliding into the car, the cracked windows sending a frosty breeze across my shaking fingers as I grip my phone in my hand.

"Where to, love?" the driver asks, his cockney accent thick.

I rattle off my address, taking a deep breath to quell the nausea swirling in my stomach.

I feel the driver glance at me, but I rest my forehead on the window trying to cool my heated blood.

It's okay, I just need to get home.

The street lights blur behind my vision and my eyes itch. Stupid contacts. I wish I was wearing my glasses.

With shaking hands, I bring my phone back up and search the internet for Jackson's name.

Why would she do this?

She's always hated me. Always relished in humiliating me, but this?

I cradle my belly with my hand.

I'm sorry, Smudge.

I take a calming breath and close the app, switching to Jackson's contact. I don't want to bother him at work. He hasn't messaged me yet but surely he knows. *Everyone* knows.

I feel like people can tell which taxi I'm in, gaping at me as I crawl past them in bumper-to-bumper traffic.

I click on his name and raise the phone to my ear.

"Hey it's me, leave a message and I'll get back to you."

I hang up before I leave a message. What would I even say? '*Hi, hope your day is going well. My evil sister leaked the baby news to the whole world and made me out to be a fame chasing gold digger, so I'm feeling a little upset.*'

I send him a text instead.

ME

Call me when you can x

I put my phone down and gaze out the window, the busy flashing lights of central London giving way to urban side streets and local shops.

I dial another number.

"Hello?" my mother says.

"Mum." I hate the way my voice breaks.

"Rosalie? Look, I know what you're going to say, and I really think I should stay out of it."

I blink. "What?"

"Whatever this is, it's between you girls. I don't know why you always put me in the middle."

"Mum, she doxxed me!"

She scoffs. "I don't even know what that means."

"Mum, she's spreading lies about me, about Jackson, about my *baby*. Your *grandchild*."

She pauses. "She's only trying to help."

"Help?" I laugh incredulously. "You think what she's done is *helping*? Have you seen what people have been saying about me?"

"I don't want to know, Rose. You girls need to sort this out between yourselves."

I pull the phone away from my ear. She hung up on me.

I drop my phone in my lap and press my hands to my eyes. I take a deep breath. I cannot cry in the back of this cab. I'm nearly home. I just have to hold on a few more minutes.

I sniff and fold my arms, gazing out the window.

The cab slowly starts to move down familiar streets, and I tell myself it's only a few more minutes until I'm inside my flat, buried under my blankets and hidden from the rest of the world.

"I might have to drop you off up the road, love," the driver says, gesturing to the road ahead of him. "Looks like the pub's got a party on or something."

My stomach drops as I spot the crowd gathered further up the road from the pub, outside the door to my flat.

"Keep driving," I say brokenly.

The driver listens, barely slowing to a crawl as he passes the small crowd gathered outside my garden gate.

What. The. Fuck.

People are here? Outside my house?

With shaking fingers, I pick up my phone again.

She lives in London?? One comment reads.

Yeah, Clapham, next to The Old Crown pub.

Making the most of JII being over here.

There's no way he'd move from LA just for some fat bitch.

What. The. Fuck.

Why would they even need my address? In what world does a story like this warrant people coming to my *house*?

My breath starts to come in shallowly as my vision blurs.

"Are you alright, love?" the driver asks.

I nod my head. Or at least I think I do. It could be that my neck has lost all support and it's trying to remove itself from my spine.

My phone vibrates in my hand and I pick it up without thinking.

"Hello?" I say shakily.

"Rosie? Are you okay?" My best friend squeals in my ear, her familiar tone causing the tears to finally flow.

"Hey," I say weakly. "I don't know what to do."

"Rose, oh my God. Okay, where are you?"

"I uh—I can't go home, there's people there. Annie, there's people outside my house."

Anya swears and I hear her voice muffled like she's pulled the phone away from her face.

"I don't...I don't know what to do. What do I do?" I clench my fists to stop my fingers from shaking.

"Okay Rosie, listen to me, are you walking?"

"No, I'm in a taxi."

"Alright babe, you'll go straight to ours. Do you still have your key?"

"Uh," I say, swallowing thickly. I've had the key to Anya

and Danny's townhouse since they left before the wedding. Ostensibly it was to take care of the one plant Anya decided to keep, but it died before she ever left the country so I haven't visited once. "Yeah, yeah I have it."

"Okay, give the driver the address and head there."

"Jackson–"

"He can meet you there."

"He's on set, he won't even be back in the city until the weekend."

"We'll let him know where you are, don't worry," Anya reassures me. "Listen to me, Rosie. This is just a crisis and we love a crisis, don't we?"

"Yeah," I mumble, "I usually like your crises though, it's never been me."

Anya laughs down the line. "There, so this was a long time coming. And babe you know how to make a splash."

I laugh weakly, sniffing loudly.

"Hang on," I say into the phone, "Uhm excuse me, can you take me to Richmond." I rattle off Anya's address.

"Sure thing love, I'll get you there."

"Thanks," I say before wiping my eyes and curling back to my phone. "I wanted to tell you Annie."

Anya laughs, "Hold that thought, we will be talking about this in detail as soon as I know you're not just driving around South London crying your eyes out."

I laugh again. "Okay."

"Can I say that I fucking hate your sister?" she bursts out.

"Annie," I say weakly.

"I hated her since the day she commented that you looked frumpy in your nineteenth birthday dress. Do you remember that? I do. I'll never forget it. I thought that girl was either blind, dumb or jealous because you looked like a smokeshow in that dress and then you never wore it again."

"I still have it."

"It would be a crime to get rid of it. Leave me alone in a room with her, and I tell you she won't have that smug grin for one more minute."

I take a breath. "I can't talk about her, Anya, I can't think about her right now."

"Okay, okay fine, this is a discussion for another time. But I just want it acknowledged that I hate that bitch."

"Acknowledged," I say weakly.

"Babe, I have to go but text me as soon as you're inside the house. The guest room is all set up so text me and leave your phone in the living room. Don't look at it, don't think about it, just go to bed okay?"

"Okay," I say nodding. "I will."

"I love you."

"I love you too."

"Is this the place?" the driver asks, pulling up in front of Anya's house.

"Yes, thank you." I fumble for my purse.

"Don't worry about it love, you just get inside safely, okay?"

If I hadn't spent the last thirty minutes of my life sobbing, I would probably burst into tears again. "Thank you," I say shakily, shoving cash under the glass separator. "Have a nice night."

I stumble out of the cab and up the path, fumbling with Anya's key in the lock and disabling the alarm.

I don't even take in my surroundings as I send her a thank you text and toe out of my shoes, crawling into the guest bed and crawling under the covers before the tears start again. I barely have the energy to take my contacts out before I fall asleep cradling my belly and pray that I'll wake up from my nightmare.

24

JACKSON

I LOVE MY JOB, I TELL MYSELF AS I NOD SERIOUSLY AT WHAT THE director is telling me. Standing in a semi-circle, I listen carefully as he, Marky, and a pile of other professionals give me instructions for the most exciting stunt I've done yet. My side barely twinges anymore after I spent days being fussed over by Rosie.

The smell of chlorine is thick in the air, despite the towering rigs and bodies surrounding the pool.

Out of the corner of my eye, I can see a car being lowered into the water.

"Okay, Jackson, we're going to take you down with Tom, our diver. He'll give you the O2 until we call action and then you know what to do."

I nod my head. We've spent countless hours on dry land, going through the motions. My character's car hydroplanes off a bridge and plummets into a raging river, leaving me fighting with the stunt double who's trying to kill me.

I've done underwater, I've done fight scenes, I've done rigs, but I've never done it all at the same time.

We've spent the last two days in meetings and rehearsals and safety briefings, but now I'm ready to get in the water.

"Let's do this," I say, practically rubbing my hands together with glee.

"Great, let's get set up." Sam claps me on the shoulder as we disperse.

I gesture to Eric who's lingering by the door. "Are you ready?" he asks excitedly.

I grin. "You bet it. Can I see my phone real quick?"

He hands it over and I smile as Rosie's face shows on the screen. It's still the selfie she sent me of her with her ice cream and I haven't changed it since.

I pull up her messages.

ME

Hey pretty girl, I'm just heading underwater so won't be able to message for a couple hours. Be good x

I keep the phone clenched in my hand until I'm called over and hand it back to Eric. I don't power it off, so I hope Rosie has the sense not to send anything risque and Eric has the sense to not look at it if she does.

Shaun the 1st AD calls everyone to attention, giving yet another safety briefing. I pay attention the same way I do with the flight attendants on a plane. My heart starts pounding in my chest and I glance at the water.

I slowly lower myself into the pool, my jeans clinging to my lower legs and my shoes filling up with water. Stuart and I slowly swim towards the car rig. Tim hands me the O2 tank, I take a breath and then I go under.

"THAT'S A WRAP, GUYS," Shaun calls to a smattering of applause hours later.

Thank fuck. I need to get out of this water and out of these clothes.

I climb out, shoving my hair out of my eyes. I'm exhausted, and I've needed to piss for about two hours now.

A costume assistant hands me a robe and I thank her as I head towards Eric.

He looks pale and his hair is mussed, as if he's run his hands through it often. "What is it?"

Eric hands me my phone with shaking fingers. "I think something's happened."

I scroll through the first page, thousands of notifications popping up on the screen. I can barely scan any of them. "What's happened?" I bark.

"Uh, I uh, I googled it."

"Googled what?" I ask sharply, as I slide up until I get to Rosie's name.

"You," Eric says weakly as I read Rosie's message.

ROSIE

Call me when you can x

"Did Rosie call?" I say, glaring at Eric, dialing her number and holding the phone to my ear.

"Uh," He nods, his cheeks reddening. "Yeah, but you were underwater."

I shake my head as the call drops. Maybe she's got it turned off. What the fuck is going on?

I try again but it rings before I can dial.

"Rosie?" I answer.

"Jackson mate, where have you been?"

"Dan?" I ask, checking the caller ID. "What the hell is going on?"

An assistant approaches, trying to usher me off set, likely to some dry clothes, but I wave them off as I maneuver closer to the wall.

"God, we've been trying to get to you for ages." Danny says. "You on set?"

"Yeah, ten hours underwater, and messages were not going through." I glare at Eric who's standing wringing his hands. "What's happened?"

"Rosie's okay, she's at our place. We're on our way there now."

"Is she okay? Why is she at your house?" My heart is pounding in my chest and I can feel dread curling under my skin.

I hear Danny blow out a breath. "Her sister. She posted a video online and she's been all over the press all day. Calling Rosie a gold digger, basically implying that she seduced you and impregnated herself."

My heart drops. "What?" I hiss.

"Yeah, she's a real piece of work. Rosie tried to get home, but there were paps outside the flat. Fucking paps man. I don't know who this sister is, but she's obviously got some connections."

"Fuck me," I say, wiping my hand over my face. God, Rosie called me and I didn't answer. She's had this day from hell and I was pissing about in a swimming pool like an idiot.

I run my hand through my hair, tugging on the damp knots.

"She's with you now?"

"We're not with her, but she's at our house. Hang on." I hear him pull the phone away from his ear, talking faintly. "How soon can you get there?"

"A couple hours." I glance at Eric and usher him over. "Thanks for this Dan, I appreciate you."

"Of course, mate. And we will be discussing this. Can't believe you're having a baby with my wife's best friend and I don't even get a text."

I laugh but the noise gets caught in my throat. "You can shout at me later, after I look my girl in the eyes and see she's okay."

"You might get there before us, but Rosie left the door unlocked behind her."

"Thanks, man." I hang up as Eric approaches.

"I'm sorry, Mr Harper, I didn't know how to get you out of the water."

I wave him off. I know he couldn't have done it but I can't help feeling frustrated that he didn't.

"I need a car within ten minutes. I've got to get back to London."

Eric's eyes widen. "But your hotel is booked and all your stuff is still there."

"I don't give a fuck, Eric," I snap. "I need to get back now."

"Is everything alright, Jack?" Shaun approaches.

"I'm going back to London." I move to step past him but he raises his arms.

"Woah, hold on, what's the problem?"

"I just need to get back."

Shaun laughs incredulously. "We need you back on set in ten hours. By the time you make it there you'll only have four hours of sleep before you need to be back."

"I won't be here tomorrow."

I barely spare them all a glance as I storm past them, desperate to get out of this place. The air is thick with chlorine and my water clogged jeans are starting to chafe. I need to get home to Rosie.

"Can you call a car?" I ask Eric before I jump the metal stairs into my trailer, shaking the frame with the force. I quickly strip the damp clothes off, leaving them in a pile on the carpeted floor. I tug on my street clothes before groaning internally, rummaging for a bag and sweeping the clothes inside. My mother would kill me if she knew I left a wet heap of laundry for someone else to deal with. She used to make me re-wear my damp rugby socks if I left them on the floor until I learned my lesson.

I swipe my keys and wallet off the side and check my phone for any messages from Rosie. Nothing.

Clenching my jaw, I swing the door open into the cool night air. Thankfully, Eric wordlessly leads me to the car idling in the lot and I offer a genuine thanks as I slide inside the cool exterior. It's not Eric's fault I'm here when my life is imploding back home.

I settle into the seat, pulling up Rosie's name.

JACKSON

I'm on my way baby.

The car pulls out of the lot and winds through the country back roads. I don't look up from my phone until we start stopping and starting at the traffic in London. I scan post after post mentioning either of our names. It's everywhere. Social media is going crazy and there are more than a few tabloids running the story. Finally, I find the source.

I have never liked Rosie's sister, but the rage I feel when I see her face on the screen, spewing lies about her sister with sickly sweetness disguised as concern, makes my blood boil.

I lock my phone and take a breath as I try to unclench my jaw.

I know enough from the bits and pieces I've gleaned from Rosie to know that her sister is the worst kind of person. My sisters and I had our arguments growing up, but as soon as we hit our teen years, we started to see each other as cordial roommates. The older we got, the more we became friends rather than just siblings. Sure, I occasionally rib them and they do me, but I've never been outwardly cruel. And they've never talked to the public about me. Ever.

Slowly, we start to take familiar corners heading to Danny's house. It's a tall Georgian townhouse on a quiet residential street, a walled gate high enough for privacy.

I thank the driver as I slide out the car, glancing up and down the street for any lurkers. Empty.

I don't know who was outside Rosie's flat, but it's safe to say they didn't track her down to here.

Inside, it's dark. Checking the time on my phone, I figure Danny and Anya aren't here yet.

"Rosie?" I call out into the darkness.

I peer into the rooms downstairs quickly before toeing off my shoes and climbing up the stairs. I feel like a cat burglar, so I hope Rosie doesn't leap out at me with a cricket bat.

"Rosie?" I whisper as I peer into each room.

The guest room door is ajar and I push it further in, my heart stopping. There she is, curled on top of the bed with her jeans still on and a human sized pillow clutched in her arm.

The moonlight from the open curtain bathes her in a glow, and I have to lean on the door to prop myself up. She's okay. I watch the rise and fall of her chest for a few minutes before tiptoeing into the room. I gently approach her, brushing the hair back from her face. She whimpers softly and my heart nearly cracks in two.

"Hey, pretty girl," I whisper, pressing a kiss to her forehead.

"Jackson?" she mumbles, turning towards me.

"I'm here, baby."

"I'm sorry," she says, her eyes closed and voice sluggish.

"You've nothing to be sorry for, Rosie. It's all going to be okay." I press another kiss to her lips, desperate to be close to her. "Let's get you in bed."

She makes a little noise as I flick the button of her jeans and gently tug them off her legs.

She wiggles slightly so I can tug the sheet out from underneath her, pulling it up to her chin.

Her eyes stay closed but I can see the mascara smudged on her cheeks from tears that I wasn't here to wipe away.

I creep into the bathroom until I find a pack of face wipes. Returning to Rosie's side, I cup her chin in my hand as I gently wipe away the streaks.

I rise again but her hand grabs my bicep, tugging me forward.

"Stay," she whispers.

She doesn't have to tell me twice. Shrugging out of my jeans, I round the bed, climbing in and raising my arm so she can burrow into my side, her leg hooked over mine and the gentle swell of her stomach resting against me.

I curl my arm to gently play with her hair and rest my other on her belly. "I'm right here, pretty girl. I'm not going anywhere."

25

———

ROSIE

I WAKE UP IN THE PITCH BLACK WITH SMUDGE PRESSING ON MY bladder. I blink, taking in the dark room, barely illuminated by the moon, and the arm slung over my chest.

Jackson.

I vaguely remember him climbing into bed with me, but I thought it was a dream. The man softly snoring next to me assures me that he's as real as my new reality is.

His warmth blankets me and all I want to do is snuggle further into him, safe from the day I'll have to face as soon as I wake up.

I quietly ease out from under him, awkwardly sliding out of bed so as not to disturb him. His breathing changes but he doesn't wake up, just turns onto his back, showing me a glimpse of his delicious torso underneath the sheet.

I tiptoe to the bathroom, quickly using the toilet and brushing my teeth with a spare toothbrush I find under the sink, since I'm sure I definitely didn't do that before I collapsed on the bed last night.

I idly wonder if I should text Anya to tell her I'm here, but the man currently asleep in the next room leads me to deduce some communication has already been had whilst I slept.

I creep back into the bed, lifting the sheet and sliding beneath it. Jackson reaches for me, tucking me back into his side and pressing a kiss to my hair.

He must be awake but he doesn't say anything and neither do I, and it's only a few seconds before sleep tugs me back under.

When I wake the second time, the weight on the other side of the bed is significantly lighter, and the hand gently shaking my arm is significantly smaller.

I blink one eye open to find Anya lying beside me, head resting in her hand and a smile on her face. "Hi Mumma."

I burrow further into the soft duvet. "Hi." The urge to cry washes over me. I didn't even get a chance to tell my best friend. I waited too long and now I've lost the chance to see her reaction in person, to show her a baby onesie or shout about it on a video call. Remorse clogs in my throat and I can't stop my lip from wobbling.

"So," Anya sighs dramatically. "Is there anything you need to tell me?"

I tug my duvet up to cover my face with a wet laugh.

"Is this my punishment for not telling you about Danny? Because in my defence, that was a six week secret, this is more like six months." The mattress bounces as she burrows under the sheet next to me. "How many times have we spoken and you just didn't mention it? I mean, yeah, I could have asked but I'll be honest, you having a baby with Jackson Harper was never really something I was suspicious of. When did this even happen?"

"At the wedding," I mumble into the duvet, squeezing my eyes shut.

Brightness blinds me as her startled face peers down at me. "At *my* wedding? You mean after?"

"Uhh—"

Anya gasps. "You mean *during* my wedding? *Rosie Taylor.*"

I laugh and cover my face with my hands.

"I can't believe this," Anya cackles. "You got impregnated *at* my wedding. By the best man!"

The bed shakes with the force of Anya's laughter. "Where did you do it? The bathroom? It was occupied for ages, but I did think that was my Aunt Claudette."

"It wasn't the bathroom," I correct.

Anya lifts her hands in front of her ticking off on her fingers. "The cloakroom? Dark, private, comfortable I could see that. There was the honeymoon suite but honestly if you tell me you had sex in that room before I did I will be quite cross at you—"

"The balcony," I mumble quickly.

If Anya's jaw drops any further, she'll have to pick it up off the floor. "Sorry, did you just say the *balcony*?"

I nod, cheeks flushing.

Anya throws her head back with a cackle. "Oh Rosie, you little whore. I'm so proud of you."

"Stop laughing," I giggle, nudging her as if I can push her out of the bed.

"Wait, wait, wait," Anya says, catching her breath and tugging her phone out of her pocket. "We took photos out there, I need a visual."

"Oh my God," I groan. "You do not need a visual."

She shoves her phone in my face, showing me candid pictures of her and Danny laughing as he twirls her in his arms overlooking the same view I stared out at before Jackson found me. "Here?"

I swipe my finger through the pictures until the shadowy alcove can be seen in the background. I point quickly before pulling my hand back under the duvet.

"There?" Anya pinches her fingers on the screen.

"Would you stop zooming in?" I groan.

"I need to know so I can tell my future nibling where they were conceived."

"*Why* would you need to tell her that?"

"It's a girl?" Anya asks, the phone discarded as she turns to me with a wide smile.

I nod shakily, feeling tears well in my eyes as Anya squeals beside me. "We found out at our last appointment. I had a whole plan for how I was going to tell you. I got a little onesie made and everything. I was just waiting until you got home so I didn't drag you off your honeymoon. But I guess I did it anyway."

Anya wraps her arms around me. "Rosie, don't be silly. We wanted to come home as soon as we heard the news." She pauses. "So, you're right. You probably would have dragged me home and then I'd be a divorced woman by now," she jests and I splutter out a laugh. "More importantly–you're having a little girl!"

She squeezes me tightly and I let my head fall on her arm as she presses a kiss to my hair.

"I get first dibs on the name."

"You don't get first dibs on the name," I laugh, pulling back until we're side by side.

"Why not? She was conceived at *my* wedding. She's an honorary bridesmaid."

"You also can't name your bridesmaids."

"I can, if they're conceived at the wedding. It's the rule."

"What rule book is this?"

"It's the 'Best Man Impregnates Maid of Honor at the Wedding: How To Guide.'"

Twelve hours ago, I felt like the sky was falling around me, but lying in a bed with my best friend, it seems to still be up there.

Eventually, Smudge demands another bathroom break so Anya promises to make some tea. I emerge into the living room to find Jackson lounging on one sofa, Danny on the other.

"Get over here, pretty girl," Jackson smiles, his eyes crinkling. His gaze roves me, assessing me from head to toe, lingering on my belly. I approach and he takes my hand in his, tugging me until I'm curled into his side on the sofa. I rest my head on his chest as his hand comes protectively to my stomach. "How are you?"

"Better now." I reach up to press my lips to his.

I glance at Danny sitting in the armchair catty corner. "Congratulations," he says with a smile.

"Thank you," I return the smile. I didn't know what to make of Danny when I first met him. I'd spent days comforting my friend when they broke up in the cloud of a different scandal, but he's always been the kindest person to me. Plus he loves my best friend, so I'm a fan.

Anya appears with a tray of tea. "I've had such a morning already. Did you know this all happened because of us?" She hands Danny a mug.

"Well, freckles, I don't think they would have met otherwise."

"No I mean—"

"Okay," I say, sitting up. "Moving on. When did you guys get back?"

"This morning. We got the first flight out here."

"You really didn't have to."

Danny lifts a hand dismissively. "Don't worry about it. It just gives me an excuse to take her on a second honeymoon."

"Oh God, not another one," Anya sighs with a smile as she settles next to her husband.

Danny keeps his gaze on me. "What's your plan?"

I lean my head on Jackson's bicep with a groan. "I don't have one. I barely have a plan for having a baby let alone such a scandalous one."

The muscle under my head tenses and I glance at Jackson with a weak smile.

"I've already spoken to my lawyers," Jackson tells me, his face unusually serious.

I let out a breath, puffing out my cheeks to distract my eyes from watering. *Lawyers.* "Lawyers?" I ask quietly.

Jackson sighs. "We can issue a cease and desist. It's slander, Rosie."

I bite my lip and stare into the breakfast tea Anya placed in my hands as if I can read the leaves for advice.

"Have you seen my phone?" I ask him, sitting up straighter and glancing around the living room. I barely remember taking my coat off last night, let alone where I left my bag.

Anya quickly jumps to her feet. "I'll get it."

Danny leans forward in his chair, resting his hands on his knees. "It's better to get ahead of it, Rosie. Release a statement or something."

I bristle. "I don't need to release a statement."

Jackson and Danny exchange a glance but before I can snap at them, Anya jogs back into the room. "I think it's dead."

She hands me my phone and the end of a phone charger. I plug it in and place it on the coffee table.

Jackson turns to face me. "Rosie, I think Danny's right. We need to release something. I can get my PR team to—"

He cuts off as my phone vibrates on the table, the screen lighting up.

We all stare at it as dozens of notifications flash on the screen. The room is frozen for a second before I'm moving, snatching up my phone and watching the words as they appear on screen.

Slut

Whore

Golddigger

Maybe it's not his

Her?? Is this a joke?

Hole in the condom. Obviously.

I can't peel my eyes away, my ears ringing and my heart clenching in my chest.

I don't say anything but I see Jackson's hand reaching for the phone. I stand up quickly out of his grasp as I keep reading. Each comment cuts like a knife, but I can't look away.

"Rosie," Anya says gently.

I take a deep breath and turn to my messages. I click on my mum's contact, my dad's, *Cleo's*.

Not a single message.

I throw my phone back on the sofa and step to the window. It's a picturesque street with barely any cars and leafy green trees lining the pavement. It's the kind of street I pictured living on as a teenager, before I realized that I would never in a million years be able to afford the deposit for a house let alone one around here.

Cleo bought a house as soon as she graduated and it was all we talked about for months. I never figured out where she got the money from. Who has that kind of money from a few social media posts? At that point, she only had a few hundred followers, nothing like the hundreds of thousands she has now. It was a few years later that mum let it slip after a few glasses of wine at lunch that she paid most of the deposit.

I couldn't believe it. All of the school trips I missed, the holidays I wasn't invited on because it wasn't discounted, all the hand-me-downs I had to get from my sister, but they somehow had a house deposit for her?

I had to scrimp and save for the deposit on my flat, working all through university and afterwards to save as much as I could and giving up my pipe dream of traveling the world. Suffering through horrendous house shares before I was able to upgrade to my one bed flat, and even that comes with a shitty landlord who takes six weeks to fix any complaint whilst pocketing seventy percent of my income every month.

For my whole life, I've rolled over and taken it, let my sister bully me, let my mother encourage her and let my dad stick his head in the sand and ignore it all.

This is a step too far.

"Okay," I say, straightening my back and caressing my belly. I turn back to the others, to the people who have proved that they've got my back more than my family will ever have. "Let's do it, the statement, the lawyers. We can do it."

26

———

JACKSON

THE FURY RACING THROUGH MY BLOOD HAS ALREADY SUNK deep into my veins and my jaw aches from how tightly clenched it is. I try to get the phone off Rosie again, but she shrugs me off, stepping out of my hold.

Her shoulders tense as she reads, and she throws the phone on the sofa, before glancing at Anya. "Can I use your shower?"

Anya jumps up. "Of course, let me get you a towel."

She escorts Rosie from the room without a backwards glance and I collapse back in my seat, letting my legs sprawl out in front of me and my head rest on the back.

The giggles I'd heard earlier had sent hope shooting through my chest, but the detached look in Rosie's eyes as the notifications poured in broke my heart all over again.

Like I'm defusing a bomb, I gingerly pick up her phone. I don't pry and I'd never read anything she doesn't want me to see, but it's hard to miss the notifications still lighting up the screen.

"This sister," Danny says, running his hand through his hair. "What a piece of work."

"You have no idea," I mutter, putting the phone face down on the coffee table.

I can't decide what's more egregious. The lies the woman has spewed or the fact that she'd make it all up for a few views.

Anya walks back in the room with a stormy expression on her face. "I don't hate women, but I've always hated that witch."

"What did Rosie say?"

Anya shrugs. "Nothing, she just said she wanted some time alone." She lets Danny tug her back until she's perched on the arm of his chair.

My phone rings in my pocket. I pull it out and grimace as my agent's name flashes on the screen.

"Hey, Travis," I say, rolling my eyes at Danny.

He gives me a sympathetic grimace as I rise to my feet.

"Jackson, I've been doing some damage control this end. They've brought in a double to finish the stunt today."

A few months ago, the prospect of not doing my own stunts would have sent my heart sinking, but today I can't even find it in me to care.

"Great," I say, rubbing my hand across my beard. "I don't think I'll be back in tomorrow either."

Travis sighs down the phone. "Look, I didn't want to say it but I have to ask. This story...any truth to it?"

I grind my teeth. "Rosie and I are having a baby. That's it. There is no story."

"Okay, okay," Travis soothes. "I've already spoken with the PR team, so just say the word and we can get a statement out."

I blow out a breath, tugging at my beard.

"I don't think this one is going to blow over, I'll be honest," Travis says carefully.

"Yeah, I don't think so either. Send me the draft but let's get a statement out as soon as possible, please. Thanks."

I hang up with Travis and pull up a text thread with Eric.

ME

Can you swing by this address and let me know if there's anything weird there?

ERIC

Weird how?

ME

Lurkers outside, graffiti, litter. Anything that shouldn't be there.

Eric thumbs up the message so I slide my phone back into my pocket.

I wander back into the lounge to see Anya and Danny whispering together.

"What are you guys doing next Saturday?" Anya asks.

I raise my brows as I reclaim my seat. "Plotting revenge, why?"

Anya shifts in her seat. "Pip and Cassie are coming to London, and they want to go out."

I look for clarification with Danny, and he shrugs with a small smile. "Cavalry are coming."

Anya grins. "We'll go out as a group to dinner. Show a united front."

I consider it. A public outing with Rosie and our friends. Showing that she's not a dirty little secret, and already has her own friendships outside of me. Could work.

Cassie especially is sure to get media attention, the girl can hardly walk out of her front door without an onslaught of paparazzi following her around. She's the biggest name out of all of us. Her most recent tour that lasted over a year and sold out in minutes made sure of that.

"It's Rosie's call."

"What's my call?" Rosie asks, wandering back in the room, cheeks flushed and soft from her shower.

Anya swivels on Danny's lap. "Saturday night with the girls."

She bites her lip. "I don't know."

"You've come out with us all before," Anya points out.

"Yeah, but I wasn't the one people were looking at."

"Come on, you have to get out there eventually."

"I don't have anything to wear."

Anya waves a hand. "Have you met Pip? You'll have something to wear."

"I don't know." She rests her hand on her belly.

"Come on, show off that gorgeous bump. It really suits you, by the way. I can't wait to have my own."

Danny sits up straighter, staring at Anya with stars in his eyes. "Huh?"

"You know, I think I'd look really cute with a belly."

Danny stands up quickly, dislodging Anya with a laugh.

"Okay by me, freckles." He bends at the knee and throws her over his shoulder. "Let's go do that right now."

Anya screeches as he carts her out of the room like a sack of potatoes.

"Saturday, Rosie!"

Rosie giggles as she sits down beside me. I rest my hand on my fist and glance at her, our first moment alone all day.

She peers up at me, mirroring my position. "What do you think?"

"I think I want to show you off, pretty girl, I have for a while now. This just gives me the opportunity."

She sends me a soft smile.

Laughter erupts from down the hall, and she glances towards the sound. "Maybe we should get out of here, give them some space."

"I think that would be the best for my ears."

"I should get back to the flat," she says, sounding like it's the last thing she wants to do.

My heart pounds in my chest. "There's somewhere else I'd like to take you first, if that's okay with you."

This plan is either the stupidest thing I've ever done or the best, and we're about to find out.

More laughter from down the hall and Rosie shoots me a wide eyed grin. "Let's go."

We don't need to take the car, since the journey is less than fifteen minutes on foot and I know how much Rosie likes to walk. But it's too risky this morning, not with every person rounding the corner likely to make her jump.

I hold the car door open for her and help her inside before closing the it behind her. She's quiet on the drive, head resting against the seat. A few turns of the wheel and we're pulling up in front of the building I've visited more than a few times over the last few weeks.

I take a breath as I undo my seat belt.

"Okay, before we do this, I need you to keep an open mind," I tell her.

"Where are we?"

"You'll see."

I round the car and help her out. She turns her body as if to walk down the road but I tug her towards the gate built into the white wall.

"Jackson," she says quietly.

"Open mind," I remind her.

I key in the code and gently tug her through the gate and up the gravel driveway with a cherry blossom tree in the center. I lead her across the path, until we reach the large green door.

I hold my breath as I take the key from my pocket and open the door, gesturing for her to go in first.

She steps inside and freezes. The large entryway has vintage tiles along the floor leading to multiple rooms and a stained glass window above the door causes colorful reflections to glisten along the white walls.

I rub my hands together to expel some energy.

"This is the living room, but there's not much in there yet." I gesture to the room beside me, "Kitchen's this way."

I grab her hand and tug her further through the house. I can't look at her face yet. I need to get this over with first. Let her see everything before she processes it.

All I can do now is pray I've done the right thing.

27

ROSIE

Any minute now I'm going to wake up and the last twenty four hours of my life will have all been a dream. It'll be yesterday and instead of dragging myself to the office, I'll somehow destroy my sister's internet access so she can't upload any video, and I won't find myself in the Victorian townhouse of my dreams with my head somewhere on a different plane.

The kitchen faces the back of the house, and sunlight streams in through the large windows from the covered garden. A huge island takes up the center of the kitchen and I find myself doing a full lap as if it's a roundabout. I have the strongest urge to open all the cupboards and see what's in there, but I clench my fists together to stop myself.

The house is still a blank canvas, half opened boxes propped against walls and a random assortment of furniture. A question lingers in the back of my mind, but I haven't got the strength to address it yet.

Jackson stands by the door leading back to the hallway, his eyes burning into my face. I can't look at him. I can't let him see the range of emotions coursing through me.

He leads me up the stairs, talking about light fixtures and high ceilings. But all I can think about is how soft the carpet feels underneath my feet, how much I'd love to take a bath in the claw foot tub he shows me in the main bathroom, how I can imagine glancing out the circular window above the stairs with a stained glass center.

I try to take steady breaths to calm my racing thoughts, concentrating as he shows me room after room–how many *are* there?

Eventually he stops at another door, turning to face me. His face is unusually shy. "You good?"

I nod, my mouth dry. I couldn't say anything even if I wanted to.

He rubs his beard once before pushing the door open.

I gasp.

Freshly painted sage green walls greet me and beautiful bay windows let in the afternoon sun, reflecting off the white marble effect crib set against one wall. Above the crib are letters spelling out 'Smudge'.

It's beautiful. Unfinished, but I can already see the vision. The changing table that can sit against the other wall, a rocking chair under the window. In the future, maybe a small toddler bed in the middle, books and toys scattered on the floor.

I see it all before I realize that I can never give Smudge this. All I have to offer her is a small crib wedged between my bed and the wall. A flat that I could get evicted out of after a few missed payslips.

I suck in a breath, blinking rapidly to try to stop the tears from falling.

"What do you think?" Jackson asks, resting his hands on my shoulders, his thumb rubbing in smooth circles.

"It's lovely, Jackson," I say, trying to sound enthusiastic.

This is good. If her mother can't provide this life for her, at least her father can. It's fine. We can make it work. It's only a thirty minute drive, that's nothing. Although, I don't have a car and the journey would take close to an hour on public transport, but that's still doable.

"Come on, there's one more room I want to show you."

I nod, pulling my lips between my teeth to stop them quivering.

He takes my hand guiding me back down the stairs and through the kitchen.

"This is the only room that's actually finished," he tells me, swinging the door open.

A large mahogany desk takes up one wall, a large screen mounted behind it. A comfortable looking armchair rests in the corner. And a chair, identical to the one in the flat, sits underneath the desk.

"Obviously you can change whatever you want, and I left space for you to bring your computer tower."

"What?" I ask quietly, my mind whirring as I try to process what's in front of me.

"Look, I even tracked down the chair for you. I set it up myself. I thought maybe I could see if there was a part missing, maybe some extra padding, but nope it's as it is."

He stands behind it and gives it an experimental swing as he shoots me a cheeky smile.

I take in his expression, the room he's designed, before I glance at the chair under his hands.

And then I burst into tears.

His eyes widen as he crosses the room to me, pulling me into his arms and burying my face in his chest.

"Hey hey, I'm sorry this is too much. It's the wrong time to show you this, maybe I should have waited and got all your stuff in here first. But I just didn't know how to do that without stealing. We can send this chair back and bring your old one in."

I take heaving breaths as I finally choke out. "I hate that chair."

He pulls my face back with a glint in his eyes. "Sorry, can you repeat that?"

I sniff, pushing my glasses up my nose. "I hate it, it's uncomfortable and makes my back hurt and I can never actually cross my legs without my stupid knees bumping into the stupid desk."

"You're saying you hate the chair? Rosie Taylor, after all that."

"I'm sorry," I wail.

His body shakes beneath me with a laugh, and he tugs my face to his chest, letting me bury my face in his soft t-shirt.

Eventually my tears subside. "Wait." I pull back to face him. "Why did you buy it?"

"Well, now I kind of regret it, to be honest. It was a bitch to put together. But you liked it so I wanted you to like it here too." He shrugs.

I furrow my brow. "Jackson, please. What is happening here?"

His eyes widen, realizing that I have spent the past fifteen minutes thinking he was showing off his new house. "I want you to like it here because I want you to live here with me. You and the baby."

I blink rapidly. "You don't—you don't want to split custody?"

"What?" he gasps, eyes widening. "*No!* God no, I want to be with you, both of you. I want you here where it's safe and we can sleep together every night and get a sofa big enough to nap on and a shower separate to the bath."

"You want me to move in with you?"

He nods, wiping away a stray tear from underneath my glasses. "Yeah, pretty girl, I want you to move in with me."

He presses a soft kiss to my lips, still salty from my tears. "I know it's a lot. It's been a crazy few hours, but when you said you couldn't go home last night I just…I couldn't wait for a second longer. I want you to be safe and comfortable. Here. With me."

The thought of going back to the flat already felt hollow. I've spent months worrying about what I'm going to do, how I'm going to raise a baby and afford the rent, and get rid of the stubborn mold that keeps growing in the bathroom.

"I know you love the flat so if you want to—"

"I don't love the flat," I say firmly. "I love it when you're there with me."

I bite my lip, so close to spilling the truth.

I can't agree to move in with the man and tell him I love him on the same day. That would be too much.

"I'll pay you rent." Though would that make Jackson my *landlord*? Gross.

"Absolutely not. Your money is your money and my money is your money." He shoots me his trademark smirk and I tug at his shirt.

"Jackson, be serious. I have to contribute *something*–"

"If you even think about offering to pay rent, I will transfer it straight back into your account."

"You wouldn't."

"Try me." He grins. "I might even add a bit extra to the refund each month."

I roll my eyes as his infectious smile pulls at his lips.

"So, is that a yes?"

I take a deep breath, collecting my thoughts. Can I do

this? Move in with him, let him take the burden of housing me and the baby?

His smirk transforms into a soft smile as he takes my hands and places them over his heart.

"Rosie, I have the means to support you, to support both of you. Please let me. Let me take care of you."

Well. I don't have an argument for that one. My fingers caress his soft t-shirt, and I swear I can feel the strong beat of his pounding heart.

"If you insist."

I squeal as he wraps his arms around me and sweeps me into his arms. "Jackson! I'm too heavy."

He growls playfully into my neck as he spins and carries me out of the office. "Never." He presses a kiss to my lips as his confident strides march down the hall. "I have another room to show you."

Turns out I like the bedroom too.

28

JACKSON

THE RELIEF I FEEL AT ROSIE'S REACTION TO THE HOUSE IS indescribable.

We spent the first night eating takeout and watching Strictly Come Dancing in the bed I'd ordered for the bedroom. I meant it when I said that she can change whatever she wants, but the new mattress is a hundred times more comfortable than her old one, and it doesn't squeak whenever we move.

The sun blares through the windows that we don't have blinds for yet and when I wake up the first thing I see is her. Rosie's hair is sprawled across the pillows as she lies propped up on some pillows and staring at the ceiling.

"Morning," I say, my voice thick with sleep.

She turns her head and sends me a sleepy smile. "Morning."

"What are you thinking about so hard?"

"Smudge woke me up a while ago. Here."

She grabs my hand in hers and places it on her belly. My heart races until I feel a small flutter against my hand.

I bend on my elbow and press a kiss to the spot. "Hi, baby girl, do you like the new house?"

A flutter behind my hand in response.

I glance up at Rosie with a smile, and she grins. "She must like it, she's been celebrating all night."

"Is that right?" I ask again, rubbing my hand across her belly desperate to feel a kick again.

"She likes the sound of your voice," Rosie whispers.

I shoot her a smile and crawl up her body. "And you?" I ask against her lips. "Do you like my voice?"

"I can't get you to shut up most of the time."

"How dare you?" I tease.

She giggles underneath me, trying to push me off her as I bury my head in her neck and gently suck on her smooth skin, my hand still resting over her belly. She squirms underneath me, laughing until I take her lips in mine.

"Are you happy?" I ask between kisses.

"I'm happy." She nods, sending me the sweet smile that makes my knees buckle.

Her hand explores my chest, traveling lower. "So"— she reaches the waistband of my boxers—"Very"—she kisses me —"Happy." Her hand grasps me, and I can't help but groan against her lips.

Later, Rosie's rummaging through boxes in the kitchen when I finally make it out of the shower.

"What is even in these?" she asks without looking up at me.

"No idea," I say. "It's just stuff I got my assistant to pack up from my LA house. I have some in the hotel still, but most of it is at yours."

"All your stuff?" Rosie gapes at me.

I shrug. "Yeah, I can't imagine heading back over there for a while so it would just be gathering dust."

"I'll have to get my stuff over here too," she says around her mug.

I try to quell the excitement rising in my chest. "Shall we go right now?"

"Let me finish my tea first," she laughs.

I tilt her mug and examine how much she has left, but she tugs it back with an eye roll.

"I'm only playing, pretty girl. We can take this as slow or as fast as you want. I know I sprung this on you when you already have so much going on, so we'll go at your pace from here on out. If you want to go back to the flat right now, I'll drive you myself. If you want to move everything over, I've already got movers waiting outside."

She sighs exasperatedly as I send her a cheeky grin and hold my hands up. "Playing still."

"I know this is fast, but that's how we do things apparently." She gestures to her stomach.

"I just know what I want."

"I think I want to go back to the flat today." She bites her lip. "But can I sleep here tonight?"

Don't smile too much Jackson, you'll scare her away. "Sure, we can do that."

The drive only takes forty minutes with London traffic. When we pull up outside the flat I see Rosie glancing up and down the street and it breaks my heart.

She should never have been put in this position in the first place. I've never really considered how famous I am, and unless I'm out with friends who are also in the public eye or I'm on a press tour, I've never really felt the harsh realities of it. When I'm with Rosie or my family, I'm just a normal guy. I think we probably would have released a statement after Smudge's birth, something chill and quiet, but we've lost that now. Lost that privacy. I don't think for one second that our relationship and the pregnancy would have gotten out if it wasn't for Cleo fanning the flames.

I didn't see it coming, but maybe I should have. Maybe I should have considered the ramifications of our situation, but there's nothing for it now but damage control.

I bite down on the anger at the injustice of it all before rounding the car to Rosie's side. Helping her out of the car, she clutches my hand and doesn't let go until we're approaching her front door. Her steps fumble and pull us both to a stop.

There's a letter taped to the door. I rip it down before she can, scanning the words on the front.

The paper crinkles in my hand before I can stop myself.

"What does it say?" Rosie asks me calmly as she steps around me and fits her key in the lock.

I clench my jaw. "What does what say?"

She sends me the stern mum look I've quickly become obsessed with. I follow her into the flat and sigh heavily before handing it over to her outstretched hand. She doesn't look up as her eyes scan the words on the page, lingering far longer than the length the creative sentence requires.

She brushes past me and throws it in the bin immediately.

She steps into the kitchen and starts putting away the dishes she left drying on the rack. I move to her side, lifting a glass and reaching above her to place it in the cupboard. Within a few minutes, the kitchen is back in order and she folds the tea towel neatly over the oven. She takes in the room before saying, "I'm going to go pack a bag, then we can go?"

"You got it, pretty girl."

She nods and I give her a minute, heading back into the living room and gathering the clothes I've left here over the last few months. I don't take everything, not wanting Rosie to think I'm removing myself from her life if she wants to stay here longer.

"Let's go," she says, standing by the door with her suitcase at her feet. I press a kiss to her head and grab the case, waiting for her to lock up behind us.

It's when we're back in the car that she says, "I don't want to sleep there anymore."

I grab her hand and press a kiss to the back of it. "You don't have to."

29

ROSIE

Standing in my flat and reading a note a stranger left for me was probably a low point of my life. I've already tried to forget it existed, but an anonymous stranger calling you a dirty whore is just something that lingers in the mind.

It was an easy decision to move out, pack up the rest of my stuff and close the door on that chapter of my life. If I had a backbone, I would have stayed longer, made more of a point of claiming my own independence before letting a man take care of me. But it isn't just me I need to worry about. I have less than three months until Smudge arrives, and the thought of finding a new place to rent in London that is safe and stable overtakes any pride I have.

Jackson offered to hire a removal team, but I've moved myself in and out of every place I've lived in since I was eighteen years old and I'm not about to let any more strangers into my space than I absolutely have to.

Which is why Jackson, Anya, Danny and myself spend a day boxing up every item of my belongings.

Anya and I are tackling the bedroom while Danny and

Jackson attempt to pack up the heavier furniture in the living room. Jackson has insisted we take everything, even though I know that tiny sofa is going to look out of place as soon as it's in any room in the new house.

Anya's version of packing is taking all the clothes out of my wardrobe and putting them in trash bags. It's very efficient.

The drawers are empty now, so I attempt to lift the corner to pull it out from the wall.

"Jackson," Anya calls out to the boys. "She's trying to lift things again."

I glare at her. Traitor.

"*Rosie Taylor*, blankets and cushions *only*!"

"How many cushions does the man think I have?" I grumble.

"I heard that!" Jackson shouts, from down the hall. "And the answer is not enough."

Anya snorts. "It's cute how protective he is. I love this for you."

I sigh dramatically but can't hide the smile that pulls at my lips as I return to folding clothes on the bed.

"Aha!" Anya exclaims. "I knew you'd keep it!"

She pulls out the long red dress I wore to my nineteenth, folding it over her arm like it's a bridal gown.

I laugh. "I didn't even know that was in there."

I touch the soft material. I fell in love with the dress when I saw it and used almost an entire paycheck from waitressing to buy it. It hugged my curves in all the right places and made me feel like a million bucks...until I got home from my party and found messages from my sister saying I looked like a pig in lipstick.

I shoved it in my wardrobe and never wore it again.

"You should wear it to dinner tonight."

I groan. She has not let this go and it was made even worse when Pip and Cassie flew over this week. The plans have been firmly in place without any of my input.

"I think it's a few years out of style," I soothe. "And it probably won't fit me anymore." I wave a hand at my belly, which I think grows bigger just by looking at it.

I gently lower myself to the mattress before Anya gets any closer to shoving it over my head.

"You might be right," Anya says, biting her lip. "I'll ask Pip what she thinks."

Anya hooks it over the curtain rail and takes a picture. My phone buzzes in my pocket.

ANYA

@Pip what do you think of this for Rosie?

PIP

I see the vision

I appreciate the vision

I already have a dress ordered and arriving
at the house within the next few hours

ME

How did you even get my measurements??

PIP

I have my ways

I chuckle under my breath. "Seems like the dress is a bust."

Anya frowns. "Fine, but I still think you should wear this again." She lays it on the bed next to me, longingly stroking the material.

I don't tell her that I don't think I ever will, that I don't think I'll be able to wear it without thinking of the gut punch I felt when I got home and read that message. I can't get rid of it, but I can't look at it either.

I quickly fold it up, rolling it into a ball in my suitcase.

The wardrobes are basically empty, the drawers bare, and the only thing left are the faded curtains hanging on the rail.

"I think we're done in here," I say, flipping the suitcase closed.

I stand and go to slide the case of the bed, but Anya smacks my hands away. "Don't make me call him in here."

I roll my eyes playfully before following her out of the room. My computer is already packed up and in the van, so the only furniture left is the old desk and chair that I'll be happily leaving behind.

"Rosie, you can't tell me this is comfortable," Danny says, settling into the chair awkwardly.

Jackson gestures as if to say "*See?*" and I groan. "God, let it *go*."

Danny jumps up and helps Anya grab the suitcase. "I've got this, freckles."

"My hero," she drawls.

He lifts it effortlessly, flexing his biceps in his tight t-shirt.

Jackson claps his hands. "I think that's everything, pretty girl."

"I just want to take another look around."

"You got it."

I wander through each room, checking under corners and inside cupboards. Nothing. I've hired a cleaner to come in and do the final deep clean. I know my landlord will dock my deposit for even the slightest mark, but I don't have the patience to get on my knees and inhale bleach fumes just for a tight, scumbag landlord to squeeze the last few pennies our of me to pay off his third mortgage. Screw that.

By the time I meet Jackson at the front door, I'm ready to leave. "I'm ready."

I send him an exhausted smile and reach to swipe my bag from the kitchen counter.

"I'm not," Jackson says, before his lips capture mine and my head empties.

My bag drops to the floor as my hands come around his broad shoulders until they fist in his dark hair. His hands cup my behind and pull me closer. I want to be closer. I want to meld our bodies together until there's nothing that exists in the world but this moment.

He effortlessly slides his hands under my thighs and I gasp as he lifts me onto the counter.

I should protest more, that I'm too heavy, that it's too risky but I've never felt more safe than when I'm in his arms.

I let my thighs open and hook my feet behind his back. His erection rubs against my center, and I moan with pleasure.

"Are you guys—whoa, okay, never mind." We break apart at Anya's voice as she slams the front door behind her.

I drop my head to Jackson's chest with a embarrassed giggle.

"I'm ready now," Jackson says with a smirk, pressing a kiss to my forehead.

I press my fingers to his smile. "Help me down."

He effortlessly lifts me until I'm back on my feet.

"I would like to give you guys a minute or an hour or whatever, but we only really have the van for another few hours before it closes and I refuse to pay extra," Anya says, sticking her head through the door with her hand over her eyes.

"We're coming, we're coming," I laugh.

"In that case, I can give you five minutes at least."

"*Freckles*," Danny's scandalized voice shouts from the hallway.

30

JACKSON

I'M GRATEFUL FOR OUR FRIENDS, GRATEFUL THAT THEY dropped everything to fly across the world in a crisis, grateful that they spent a weekend helping us move into our new home. But I'm mostly grateful when they leave.

"We'll be back at seven to pick you up," Anya says, hovering on the doorstep. "Is that enough time?"

Rosie nods, resting her hand on her belly. "I'm going to nap, but it'll be fine."

"Okay, see you later." Anya presses a quick kiss to her cheek and waves at me over her shoulder before the door closes behind her.

Rosie sighs. "I think I'll make a start on the kitchen before I go lie down."

I cradle her shoulders with my hand, gently pulling her long hair off her shoulder and pressing a kiss to the warm skin at the nape of her neck.

"Or..." I trail my hands down her arm. "We could lie down right now," I whisper against her skin.

I'm rewarded with a breathy laugh as she spins in my arms. "We have to leave in four hours."

"Then that gives me three hours and forty-five minutes to have my way with you."

Rosie lifts her arms to my shoulders, her nails scraping across my scalp.

"I'll probably fall asleep on you," she says with a smile as my hands travel down her back, taking her plump ass in both hand. The leggings she's been wearing to pack have been teasing me all day, and all I want to do is peel them off of her.

"I won't mind if you fall asleep as long as my tongue's buried in your pretty cunt as you do."

Her eyes drop to my mouth as she licks her lips.

"Would you like that, pretty girl?" I run my nose along her jaw, teasing her until she tilts her head, chasing my lips with hers. "Hmm?" The noise rumbles from my chest and I love the way her eyes flutter.

She nods, shooting me a wicked smile. "I'm *really* tired."

I capture her lips with mine swallowing her whimper as I cradle her head in my hands. I feel her tongue flick at my lip, and it takes all my strength to pull away from her enough to climb the stairs behind her, her delicious ass in those leggings causing my dick to swell almost painfully.

We cross the threshold of the bedroom, and I take a second to absorb the changes.

Rosie's green bedding is already on the bed, her clothes hung neatly in the wardrobe and her makeup spread across the dresser.

The past few weeks, the room has felt like a hotel, the drawers empty and the room bare.

Seeing her belongings strewn across the room and mixing with mine, it finally feels like home.

"Where did that come from?" Rosie points to the large

mirror Danny helped me fix to the wall whilst the girls were downstairs.

"I bought it," I say, coming up behind her and resting my head on top of hers.

"God, I look disgusting," Rosie says mournfully, tugging at her t-shirt.

I shake my head, disbelief coursing through my veins. "There's not a single part of you that's disgusting, Rosie. You're beautiful."

She shifts in my arms, attempting to face away from the mirror. "I'm huge and sweaty and my boobs are even bigger than they were before."

I tilt her chin with my knuckle,."You're as beautiful as you were the day I first saw you."

"That's because I was wearing a couture bridesmaid dress and professional makeup."

"Not the wedding, pretty girl. The first time."

She scrunches her brows in confusion.

"At Cassie's concert in Paris."

Rosie's mouth drops open. "I—I didn't know if you remembered that."

I chuckle, gently pulling at her lip with my thumb. "You were wearing jeans that were so tight they looked painted on, and your cheeks were flushed from dancing. I kept trying to talk to you, but you kept running away."

"I was shy," she whispers.

"All I wanted to do was dance with you, tug that clip out of your hair and peel those jeans off you." I thread my fingers through her hair, loving the way her head tilts back inching closer to my lips. "The same way I've wanted to peel these leggings off you all day."

I slowly trace my hand down her side, gently tugging at the waistband of the stretchy fabric.

Rosie scoffs gently. "My maternity leggings?"

"Mhmh," I agree as I gently tug the material down her legs, helping her step out of them.

She gazes up at me with those big blue eyes, the faint rim of her contacts visible as she blinks up at me.

"Arms up," I say, my cock pulsing in my jeans as she silently complies.

I tug her t-shirt up and over her head, letting it fall to the floor. My hands explore her body, curving over her bump before flicking the clasp on her bra. My hands take its place, tracing my thumb across her nipple and loving the whimper it elicits.

"You don't know what you do to me."

31

ROSIE

My blood is buzzing as Jackson explores my body, cupping my breasts in his hands and gently flicking my pebbled nipple. Any residual tiredness I felt earlier has evaporated, replaced with adrenaline and a burning lust that only the man in front of me can satiate.

I tilt my head to his lips, ready for him to push me to the bed and take control. Give me the pleasure I'm craving. He gently runs his nose across mine, teasing me with the brush of his lips. My eyes fall closed in anticipation when suddenly his hands travel across my body again, circling me until I feel him behind me.

"Open your eyes," he breathes in my ear, his t-shirt pressing against the cool skin of my exposed back.

My eyes open and my gaze falls on the mirror on the opposite wall. I'm naked apart from my underwear and Jackson's arm slung across my chest, my body on full display.

Jackson presses a kiss behind my ear as his fingertips ghost across my skin, leaving goosebumps in their wake.

"If only you could see yourself how I see you, Rosie." I

watch him in the mirror as his fingers trace my nipple, lightly tugging before his hand glides over my bump.

I bring my hand to his and watch our reflection as I interlock our fingers. A touch of boldness overtakes me as I guide his hand down further, reaching the crease between my thighs. He chuckles in my ear before he takes over, gently traces my clit through my soaked underwear.

His other hand comes back to my breasts as he gently pulls my underwear to the side, sliding his finger through my wetness.

"You're soaked, Rosie." He nips at my earlobe. "Do you like what you see?" He slides deeper, curling his finger inside me and I arch my back as I nod.

"Yes." I whimper.

I can't peel my eyes away from the mirror, watching his confident hands as one cups my breast and the other disappears between my thighs. The sensations overwhelm me. I feel powerful, like a goddess, revered and adored.

It's not just me he's touching, the Rosie standing in the middle of my new bedroom, but it's *her* too. The woman in the mirror. Confident and worshiped. Beautiful. His thumb flicks at my clit and I nearly see stars. My legs shake and I'd worry I won't be able to hold myself upright if it wasn't for his strong body behind me ready to catch me if I fall.

He flicks his other hand on my nipple in time with his attention on my clit, and I feel my orgasm race to the surface. My eyes fall closed in ecstasy,

"Eyes open, pretty girl. Watch yourself as you come in my arms."

I peel my eyes open as my orgasm rushes through me, his dark stare drinking me in as I grind helplessly against his fingers.

I barely have a second to recover before he removes his

hands from my underwear and brings his fingers to his mouth for a taste.

I whimper as my knees shake, only a few seconds from collapsing into a puddle but I can feel his hard erection against my back and I already know I'm not finished with this man. I don't think I ever will be.

I reach behind me and feel him through his jeans. He groans as he grinds into me. "I thought you were tired?"

I shake my head, finally peeling my gaze away from the mirror to glance up at him.

He presses a searing kiss to my lips, the faint taste of myself on his tongue driving me wild as I turn in his arms and tug him towards the bed.

I pull on his shirt impatiently and our kiss breaks just enough for him to yank it all the way off. "Lie down." I shiver at his commanding tone as I take a seat on the soft mattress, ready to do whatever he tells me to.

"You're being such a good girl for me, Rosie," he says, helping me shuffle up the bed until my head is resting on the pillow. "But you need that nap." He straightens my underwear and rises.

I flick my leg out, stopping his retreat and dragging him back to the cradle of my thighs. "Don't you dare."

He chuckles as he returns to hover over me, shirtless and clad in tight jeans that make it look like he's stepped off a photoshoot. I rake my nails across his abdomen, gently tracing each whirling tattoo before tugging at his belt impatiently.

He stands quickly and shucks his jeans, his cock bobbing at the motion and making my mouth water.

"Like what you see?" he teases.

I groan playfully. How can this man go from seducing

me with his filthy words to cracking jokes that *still* turn me on? "Come and fuck me already."

"Ask me nicely."

I whimper as his hands return to my breasts, and he takes one in his warm mouth, tongue swirling around my nipple.

"Please," I beg. "Please, fuck me."

He presses a kiss to my lips before finally tugging my damp underwear down my thighs and spreading my legs wide. "Hold onto the headboard, pretty girl."

I comply easily, my hands intertwining with the wooden slats.

"Good girl," he praises as he gently slides his hand between my thighs, coating his fingers in my release.

"Fill me up, Jackson," I plead.

He grabs a pillow and gently taps my hip until I tilt up. He slides it beneath me, the new position helping support my weight.

He tugs at his hard cock, and I wish I had free hands so I could do it for him. Feel him warm and heavy in my palm, swipe my fingers through the bead of precum on his tip.

He slaps his cock against my clit, dragging it through my wetness before catching my entrance and slowly pushing inside. I can't help the moan that escapes as I clutch tighter to the headboard.

He tilts his hips, sliding deeper and deeper each time. His hands explore my body as I lay prone beneath him. I want to move, to feel his strong arms and tangle my fingers in his hair but he told me to hold on, so I do.

"Fuck, baby," he moans as he teases his thumb on my clit.

"Jackson," I whimper. "I'm so–"

"You're doing so good, baby." He grinds further into me, his wicked fingers working in tandem with his thrusts until there's nothing I can do to stop the waves of pleasure washing over me.

His hand tightens on my thigh as his own orgasm finds him, spilling deep inside me, just how I like it. His head comes to my chest and he runs his hands up my body, tugging at my wrists until I remove them from the headboard, my fingers stiff from how tightly they were clenched.

I rest my hands on his hair, tugging at the silky strands and pressing a kiss to his head. He slowly pulls out, sliding the pillow from underneath me and gently climbing off the bed.

My eyelids feel heavy, my body spent of energy, and I try to catch my breath.

I feel Jackson return and gently wipe between my thighs, but I can't open my eyes anymore. He slides in bed beside me, pressing a kiss to my cheek.

"Rosie," he murmurs.

"Hmm?"

"You need to take your contacts out," Jackson reminds me, chuckling as I groan. I reluctantly peel my eyes back open just enough to fish them out.

"Sleeping now." I mumble as I climb back into bed and burrow into his arms. "Wake me up in a bit."

He tugs the blanket over both of us and presses a kiss to my forehead, "You sleep, baby. I'll be here when you wake up."

32

ROSIE

THE DRESS PIP PICKED OUT IS TIGHT AND BLACK, SHOWING OFF my growing bump. Paired with knee high boots that I don't think I'll be able to wear for much longer and a jacket that fits like a glove, I almost convince myself that going out will be a good idea.

"Jesus Christ." I spin away from the mirror towards the door Jackson's leaning against.

I awkwardly fix the dress's hem. "You don't like it?"

I turn back to the mirror. Maybe it's too much, too much boob, too much bump.

Jackson prowls towards me, appearing behind me in the mirror, recreating our position from mere hours ago... though this time we're both fully dressed.

"Rosie," he growls in my ear as he curls his arms around me, his hands exploring the dress under my jacket. "Let's cancel dinner and skip straight to dessert."

The laugh under my breath is swallowed by the look in his eyes as he catches mine in the mirror. After he literally fucked my brains out, I had the easiest nap of my life, something that's proven more difficult the further along in my pregnancy I get. My thighs clench together as I remember the words he whispered in my ear. I almost couldn't believe he'd remembered meeting me at Cassie's concert. I remember him winking at me, remember him glancing at me, but I'd convinced myself that he was just being friendly.

His hands appear from underneath the jacket, traveling across my waist and gently tracing against my breasts. I shiver as he gently brushes a sensitive nipple before his fingertips trace the collar of the dress. My chest rises and falls as my head falls onto his chest, allowing his fingers to find the sensitive skin of my neck. He clasps my jaw with his, bringing my face closer to his.

"You're so beautiful, pretty girl," he breathes against my lips, brushing a strand of hair away from my face. The nickname started casually, a tease because I told him to stop, but the more he says it the more it becomes second nature to hear it. Standing in front of my brand new mirror, cheeks still rosy from multiple orgasms and wearing a beautiful dress, I actually *feel* pretty.

I lean up, gently tilting my head until my mouth brushes his. "Let's cancel."

"Rosie, Jackson, the car's here!" Anya calls from downstairs.

We freeze. "This is how it's going to be isn't it?" I say, wryly. "When we're parents."

Jackson clasps my neck, his nose exploring my face as if he's inhaling my scent.

"I'll always make sure there's time to kiss you properly," he says before catching my lips with his.

"Come on," I say, pulling away and tugging at his hand. "Let's get this over with."

The car is a plush SUV, with tinted windows and enough space for all four of us to crowd in the back. Danny and Anya slide into the back seats, leaving the middle for me and Jackson.

Anya leans forward, wrapping her arms around me from behind. "You ready for this?"

I clasp her forearm and shoot her what I hope is a reassuring smile. "I guess so."

"Freckles, please put your seat belt back on."

The first time I attended an official outing with this group, I concentrated so hard on not tripping over my own feet that the thirty second walk from the car to the door felt like walking a tightrope.

Although, that time, the attention was all on the actual celebrities we were with, and no one cared about me.

Still, it was an adrenaline pumping nightmare that took a solid fifteen minutes to get my heart rate to calm down afterwards.

A hand appears on my thigh and I follow the strong forearm until I reach Jackson's black shirt. He's rolled the sleeves up, leaving the collar unbuttoned and his hair loose around his shoulders. I shift in my seat, my thighs clenching. I will *not* get horny in an SUV with my friends before facing a crowd of paparazzi.

His hand curves around my bare thigh, his pinky finger rubbing small circles on my sensitive skin.

I clasp his hand in mine, stopping his movements. I take a steadying breath as he quietly chuckles beside me.

Dick.

"We're here," the security guard says from the front seat.

"You good, pretty girl?" Jackson asks quietly.

I nod my head.

Jackson waits until the car pulls to a halt before sliding the door open. He closes it behind him, muting the flashing lights and shouts from outside. The car is quiet for a few seconds before my door is pulled open and Jackson appears with a hand outstretched and a reassuring grin on his face.

I take a deep breath and step out of the car, careful to keep my legs crossed so I don't accidentally flash any of the dozen cameras waiting outside.

"I got you," Jackson whispers in my ear as his arm comes around me.

"Jackson, when is she due?"

"Rosie, look this way."

"Rosie, any comment on the video?"

I narrow my vision, concentrating on keeping my shoulders back and my eyes on Jackson's hand in mine, caressing me and guiding me through the pushing crowd.

"Give us some space guys," Jackson booms, cutting a path.

The crowd swarms away from us. Anya and Danny must be following. Eventually, the door to the restaurant opens with a smiling host, and we're ushered into the foyer of the restaurant.

"I hate that every time." Anya grimaces as she hands her coat over to the host. "Thank you so much. Sorry about this."

"It's no problem," the host exclaims. "Your friends are waiting inside."

The ceilings are high and golden, with immaculately pressed white cloths covering small tables and the occupants watching like hawks as we follow the hostess through the restaurant. I keep my shoulders back as I finally spot Pip and Cassie in a corner, whispering together.

"Ah, you made it," Pip exclaims, jumping to her feet and nearly knocking the bottle off the table, which Cassie quickly catches.

She rounds the table and I expect her to go straight to

her brother but she comes to me first. "Look at you. You're glowing, darling." She curves her arm around me and places a delicate kiss on each cheek.

Pip is so dainty that I sometimes feel like a giant standing next to her. Even though we're roughly the same height, I feel my shoulders curving in on myself, trying to be smaller, trying to hold my arms in a way that won't show off the bingo wings that my mother points out every time I wear short sleeves.

Pip beams at me, her easy friendship somehow always managing to put me at ease. "The dress! I'm obsessed. I knew it would look gorgeous on you. Come sit, sit." She pulls out a chair for me but I'm intercepted by Cassie. She envelops me in a warm hug of her own, her rose scented shampoo invading my senses.

"Congratulations, honey," Cassie says quietly.

"Thank you," I whisper into her ear before she releases me with a squeeze to turn to the others.

I never thought in a million years that when I finagled Anya to take a job in Paris, that I'd now be hiding from paparazzi, having dinner with supermodels and pop stars and expecting a movie star's baby. But here I am.

I catch Anya's eye as she takes a seat opposite me and we share a small secret laugh. Sometimes it's like she can pluck my thoughts straight out of my mind.

"We've already ordered a couple of bottles, but we didn't know what you'd like to drink, Rosie?" Cassie asks, tracing her glass on the white table cloth.

"We should cancel the wine. It's rude to drink when you can't," Pip insists. "Excuse me?" She tries to get the waiter's attention.

I laugh. "Don't be silly. I'm good with water."

Danny fills my water glass before I've even finished speaking, and I shoot him a grateful smile.

"I'm not drinking anymore, actually," Pip announces. "After the wedding I can't stand the sight of white wine without getting flashbacks to attempting the worm at the reception."

We all laugh as the conversation descends into reminiscing about the wedding.

"Your Aunt was a machine on the dance floor, Annie," Cassie says with a laugh.

She groans into her palms as Danny laughs, placing his arm along her chair. "Claudette really was the life of the party."

"I think she started talking to a studio head about a film idea she had at one point."

Anya groans more, sinking into her seat. "*Why* is she like this?"

"That wasn't the only interesting thing that happened at the wedding," Cassie says, folding her hands underneath her chin and grinning impishly.

I glance at Anya with wide eyes. "I didn't say anything!" she insists.

Cassie cackles, her gold bracelets clanging as she taps her hands on the table. "I knew it!"

"Knew what?" I laugh nervously as my cheeks heat. I glance at Jackson for help, but he just shoots me a wink.

"I saw you two run off halfway through the party. You," she points me, "disappeared and you," she points at Jackson, "came back looking very...disheveled."

I gasp incredulously as Jackson leans his head back with a laugh.

"Wait," Pip interrupts leaning closer to the table. "This all happened *at the wedding*?"

I rest my head in my hands as Anya responds with, "You have to hear this story. You'll never believe it."

I let Anya fill the girls in as I desperately try to sink into the table. Jackson and Danny have a quiet discussion about rugby that I try to listen in to (and contribute nothing to because I know nothing about rugby apart from how much I like Jackson's shorts), but I constantly get pulled back in by Pip as they cackle at my misfortune. Eventually, I stumble into a confession about the months following the wedding until the first course is cleared away.

"I can't believe this," Pip finally exclaims, sitting back in her seat. "I've been dying for the details ever since I found out."

Anya giggles. "Found out what?"

Pip waves her hand between Jackson and I. "This. I've known since like October, was it?" She looks to me as if I have any idea what she's talking about. I glance up at Jackson but he's just as confused as I am. "Uh—"

"You sent me that live photo and it was obviously Jackson's voice in the background."

"Wait, what photo?"

"It records audio?"

"So Pip's known for nearly two months and I only found out two weeks ago?"

"Here look." Pip rustles in her bag and flashes me the photo I sent her in front of her ad.

"*Don't get my bump in it. Looks good, pretty girl,*" our voices echo through the phone.

I gasp and Jackson soothes a hand over his beard. "I can't believe it."

"How have you kept that so quiet?"

"I figured you'd tell us when you were ready."

Danny's head is thrown back as he laughs. "How did you

miss that?" He looks between Jackson and I. "Why didn't I get a picture?"

"You're not on a taxi selling perfume."

"Who did yours?" Danny asks his sister. "I want one now."

"You want to be plastered across a London cab, so my best friend can accidentally out her secret relationship through a live picture she didn't mean to send?" Anya asks wryly.

Danny waves his hand dismissively. "Semantics."

"I did a cologne ad once as a teenager before I went over to LA," Jackson admits as he takes a sip of his wine.

"You did?" I ask with a laugh. "When? And more importantly, is it on the internet?"

Anya's fingers fly on the phone before she giggles. "Jackson, you didn't."

I gasp and scoot closer to my best friend. "Let me see!"

We all huddle around the table as we watch a younger, baby-faced Jackson as he runs through city streets with a gaggle of girls chasing him down, all thanks to the delicious scent of *Pacific Spring.*

He leans back in the booth, his arm slinging across the back. "And I've still got it."

By the time the waiter brings the check at the end of the night, my cheeks hurt from laughing and I almost forget that we have to reverse the circus we had on the way in here.

"Car's out front," Danny says, reading his phone.

We all rise, crowding around the table, and I let Jackson help me into my coat. Pip grabs my arm as we head to the door, "When is the baby shower?"

"Uh, I haven't thought about it."

"Is your family doing it?"

I give her what I hope is an encouraging smile. "My mum might, maybe."

Pip's eyes brighten, "Well make sure I'm on the guest list. I'm going to spoil you and this baby rotten. And if she needs any help with the planning, just say the word."

"I don't think I can survive another Pip Covington party," I grin. When Anya put us both in her bridal party, I knew her vaguely from parties and gatherings, but planning Anya's hen do was an experience that bonded us together like soldiers.

Cassie steps closer as she tugs on her coat. "What are you doing on the first weekend of December?"

I consult my mental calendar, I'll be nearing my third trimester by then. "Nothing?"

"Perfect," Cassie says, clapping her hands. "I've booked us girls a spa day."

My jaw drops slightly, "Oh, you didn't have to do that," I insist, though a foot massage sounds *divine*.

"Too late." Cassie waves her hand. "I've already arranged it all. We'll get our nails done, a facial, it will be great! We'll pick you up Saturday morning."

Pip shakes my arm with a grin as we walk towards the door. "Pre-baby shower."

I laugh at her enthusiasm. "Okay fine, but no presents."

"Try and stop me."

We near the door and I can already see the shadows of paparazzi through the glass. "It'll be over quick," Cassie says, pressing a kiss to my cheek.

"Thank you," I tell her earnestly.

"Of course, honey."

Jackson's hand finds mine and I take a deep breath as he escorts me out the door and into the camera flashes.

33

JACKSON

Tina, our interior designer, is heaven sent. I know Rosie wanted to put as much of a stamp on our home as possible, but we both realized pretty quickly that it would be an overwhelming challenge to decorate a four-thousand square feet house whilst seven months pregnant. All it took was one message to Pip, and Tina was at the door with a color wheel and an armful of brochures. In the weeks since our first consultation, she's spent every day planning with Rosie and has allowed me to design a fully functioning gym in the converted basement so I can do all my training from home.

My trainer trusts that I'll stick to my schedule, so even on my day off I'm pushing sixty reps.

My phone buzzes on the bench next to me, and I let the barbell fall back to the floor with a clatter.

ROSIE

Glitterball

Alarm shoots through me. She went off to the spa this morning with the girls with what I assumed was minimal risk. What could have happened? Is she okay? Is the baby?

Immediately, she sends over a screenshot of a text thread.

DAD

Where are you?

ME

I'm out with some friends

DAD

Do you have a spare key or anything?

ME

Why?

DAD

Because I'm outside your flat

ME

Why are you outside?

DAD

I have a crib for you

I ring Rosie, my brow furrowing.

"What do I do?" Her flustered voice echoes down the line.

"It's all good, I'll handle it. Text me his number."

"Jackson, I cannot deal with this right now. Why has he done this? Nothing from him in six weeks then all of a sudden he turns up with a crib? I don't want them to find the house, Jackson. What if they all show up and expect to stay in the spare room? What if Cleo posts something again and then people com—"

"Rosie," I interrupt. "Take a breath. I've got this. Send me his number."

"Are you sure?"

"I'm sure, baby."

"Okay," she says quietly. "Thank you."

"You good otherwise? You having a nice time?"

She sighs dreamily. "Yeah, we just had our nails done, and we're going for our massages now. Smudge is also enjoying the treatment."

Relief eases my clenched shoulders. "Okay, pretty girl, you relax and I'll take care of it."

We hang up and I wipe my sweaty forehead before dialing the number Rosie sends over.

"Terry," I say as he picks up. "It's Jackson, Rosie's boyfriend." I need to be serious with this man, but I can't help the way my mouth pulls up at the side at the word. *Boyfriend.*

"Hello." Terry greeting is formal.

"Rosie's telling me you've got a crib?" I say, not wanting to beat around the bush.

"I'll wait for Rosie," he says gruffly. "She'll be home soon."

"It's all good, I'll come to you. Can you give me"—I check my watch—"thirty minutes?'

He mumbles something to the affirmative.

Half an hour later, showered and with a hat tugged over my damp hair, I pull up outside Rosie's old flat. I climb out the car but can't see Terry anywhere. I swear if he made me drive all the way over here for no reason, it will be my sixth strike against the whole family. Or is it seventh?

I hear a door close and turn. Terry climbs out of a white van with 'Thompsons Plumbing Co' along the side. He waves me up the road as he crosses to the back of the van.

"I thought you retired." I tilt my chin to the van.

"It's a friend of mine's," Terry replies, opening the side door. "I borrowed it for the day."

I let that bit of information soak in. He borrowed a van from a friend and faced London traffic just to cart a crib all the way here.

He climbs inside, the van shaking at the motion. "If you just take that end," he says.

Silently, I grab a hold of the corner of the box, and we maneuver it out of the van.

I start to walk backwards, minding my footing until we're nearly beside my car. A slight pull halts me in my tracks,

"Are we not going straight up?" he asks, nodding to the door of Rosie's old flat.

I shake my head. "No. We'll get it in the back. I just have to put the seats down."

When we get to the car, I gently lower my side of the box to the ground. "You got it?"

"Yeah, I got it."

The car opens with a beep, and I get to work on setting the seats horizontal.

"Where are you taking it?" he asks suspiciously

"Home," I answer from between the seats.

"Well, this is for Rosie and the baby," he says.

I don't reply.

"Does Rosie know about this?"

No Terry, this has all been an elaborate plot so I could steal your crib from the side of the road on a Saturday afternoon.

"I just don't understand why we're not taking it upstairs," he mutters as I reach his side.

"I don't have to take it, Terry."

He clutches the box tighter. "I'll wait here for Rosie to get home, and then I'll take it up for her."

He is not going to let this go and though a part of me is furious with him on Rosie's behalf, I can't help but pity the man. "Rosie doesn't live here anymore." I admit gently. "She lives with me now."

He blinks at me shocked before looking down at the box in his hands.

"Since when?"

"Since your other daughter leaked this address on the internet and she had strangers outside her door," I say unable to keep the frustration from my tone. My sympathy only extends to the man in front of me, not his other daughter. I slide the box in the car and Terry is still frozen on the pavement when I close the trunk.

"I could have delivered this to her new place."

"From my understanding, she didn't get a lot of notice."

He nods, running his hands over his head. "Yeah, I thought it would be better to just surprise her, but I guess I didn't think it through."

Crib secured, I could just jump in the car and drive off but instead I find myself crossing my arms over my chest.

A part of me wants to shake the man in front of me until he falls to Rosie's feet and apologizes for letting her down. It's hard to imagine my own father in his position, he was always unwavering in his love for his children and loud about it, I never doubted how much he cared for me. But, I get the sense this is a man who doesn't talk about his feelings. This is a man who takes a four hour round trip to deliver a bespoke crib for his youngest daughter without being asked.

"Is she okay?" he asks.

I raise my eyebrows and let out a breath. "She's seven months pregnant, her sister doxxed her, trolls on the internet are sending her horrible messages and she hasn't heard from her parents since. How do you think she is?"

He takes his glasses off and rubs his eyes, the move so familiar I have to look away.

"But you—you're looking after her?"

I nod, turning back to him and looking in his eyes so he can see how serious I am about his daughter. "I'm looking after her."

"Good, that's good." He nods.

I round the car to the driver's side. "Can I give you some advice?" Terry looks up eagerly. "Don't let *them* ruin what relationship you can have with your daughter. And your granddaughter." I add.

"It's a girl?"

"Yeah, it's a girl." I say softly. I readjust my hat on my head before opening the car door.

Terry lets out a breath before burying his hands in his coat pocket. "That's...that's great."

"Terry," I call as he turns away, leaning my arms on the top of the car. "You've got my number now, yeah?"

He nods his head and I climb in the car. Looks like my afternoon plans have changed.

Five hours later, I'm sitting surrounded by a dozen screws, even more cardboard, a half assembled crib and an open beer bottle I had to open just to get through the afternoon. The front door opens downstairs and I hear Rosie call my name.

"Nursery," I call out around the nail clenched between my teeth.

"Whoa," Rosie says as she steps inside and assesses my carnage.

"Good, you're here," I say, shooting her a wink. "How good are you with handheld tools?"

She snorts as she unwinds her scarf and unbuttons her coat, her round stomach appearing beneath a dark green jumper. "You've been busy."

I pull the nail from my mouth and rise to my feet, crossing to her and pressing a kiss to her lips. She sinks into me and I inhale her, her lips still cold from outside.

I pull away gently and nod my head to the crib. "I'm nearly done."

"What happened to the old one?"

I shrug. "I took it downstairs."

She steps towards the walnut crib. From the instructions on the box, I've deduced that it's an advanced style that will see Smudge through all growth stages. It's warm and homely, cozier than the marble white one we had before. I watch as she rests her hands on the wood, and I come up behind her.

"Don't put too much weight on it, I've got too many screws left over," I joke.

"Good thing the baby's not too heavy. I'm sure it will be fine," she deadpans.

I press a kiss to her neck as my hands cradle her belly, taking its weight. She sighs in relief and rests her head on my chest.

"You smell nice." I mumble as her scent invades my nostrils. Eucalyptus and mint.

"It's the massage oil. I can't wait to shower it all off."

"I can help you with that." I tilt my head and press a kiss to her soft skin. "Did you have a nice time?"

"The best," she says quietly as her eyes flutter closed and she leans further into me. "What did he say?"

We sway gently as I tell her about her dad, how he wanted to ask more but didn't.

"I didn't give him the address, but I told him you moved in with me."

She's quiet for a moment. "Was he mad?"

My brow furrows. "Why would he be mad, pretty girl?"

She shrugs gently and it nearly breaks my heart. "Just thought he might be."

I kiss her hairline. "He's not mad. Come on, let's go take that shower."

34

ROSIE

The smell of pine and snow is strong in the air and my boots sink into the muddy footpath. I cling to Jackson's arm just in case I lose my footing and get stuck like a turtle on its back. Getting out of the house is becoming more and more of an ordeal now, especially because I hardly want to leave my new home.

"What about this one?" I ask, pointing to a lopsided fir with a gloved hand.

Jackson tilts his head. "Sure, if you're happy to look at it at a forty five degree angle."

I sigh under my breath and wrap my hand further around his arm. I never would have guessed that Jackson takes Christmas tree shopping as seriously as he takes an exam, but I can't help finding it endearing. Even if we've walked past half a dozen perfectly fine trees already.

"This one," I say, pulling him to a stop in front of a thin, maple spruce.

He hums under his breath. "It's too skinny. It will look like we've dragged a branch in from the street."

"I like the Charlie Brown tree," I protest but he's already moved on.

The tree farm is almost an hour out of London, but when I said offhandedly that I wanted to start decorating the house for Christmas he bundled me into the car and drove me all the way outside of the city to find the perfect tree.

I readjust the fluffy hat on my head and squint at all the options.

"You're going to have to pick one eventually," I tell him. "Before I give birth next to the netting funnel."

"Great, we can catch the baby on the way out."

I bite my lip to stop the laugh bubbling up inside. How can he know exactly what to say to make me laugh?

"Hey, I wanted to talk to you about something," he says casually, slinging an arm over my shoulder.

"Is it about the difference between Fraser and Douglas fir? Because I honestly don't know the difference, they look identical."

"It's unrelated to trees. Related to Christmas."

I look up at him from under my glasses. "Hit me."

"Well, now that we're settled into the house and we're decorating, I just wanted to see what you wanted to do for Christmas."

"Oh." I step out of the cradle of his arm. "Uhm, yeah. Well, I guess I can spend it with Anya and Danny? I already told her that I don't want to be a third wheel on their first married Christmas, but she probably won't let me spend it alone." And I think it's better for everyone if I don't go to my parents house. "So, I mean, I can definitely, like, get out of your hair."

I glance down at my boots, my fluffy jumper and winter coat covering my bump, and I try not to let the blush show on my face. His hands come to my chin as he tilts my head towards his. "Shall I tell you my thoughts and then you can let me know what you think?"

I nod as his thumb teases at the bottom of my lip.

"I would like to spend Christmas with you. I want to wake up in our bed and give you all the presents that I'm going to pretend I haven't bought you already. And then I want to go downstairs and give you some more presents. And, y'know, if you have any for me that would also be okay with me. And then I want to eat some good food and snuggle on the sofa with you and watch Christmas films and then fall asleep full of chocolate."

He doesn't look away as he tells me his plan, his eyes sparkling.

I have to look away to blink the tears that are rimming in my eyes. This man. His communication method should be sold in a relationship guide book. "Uh, yeah, I mean that sounds nice, I guess."

"Nice, you guess?" he mocks as he tugs me closer and starts peppering kisses across my chilly cheeks, nudging the bobble hat he forced me to wear before we left the house so my ears don't get cold. "Just nice?"

"Fine," I laugh. "It sounds really nice."

He finally presses a kiss to my lips.

"Really, really nice," I whisper against him before my tongue finds his again.

"One more thing," he says as I lean my cold cheek on his warm hand.

"Go on."

"My family wants to come over."

I still, biting my lip.

"Before you say anything, they absolutely don't have to come. Say the word, and I'll make sure they stay away, but my mum has not shut up about you and my sisters want—"

"Jackson," I interupt with a smile. "I want them to come. I want to meet your family."

He releases a slow breath. "Are you sure?"

"I'm sure," I say firmly. "You haven't seen them for ages, and we've already spoken on the phone. I'd love to spend Christmas with them."

Jackson's smile is blinding as he cradles my face and kisses me.

"It's a plan."

"But first"— I lift my hands to his wrists— "we have to pick out a tree."

He groans.

"You're going to need to just pick one."

He holds my shoulders and turns me in his arms. "Fine, let me do another lap."

I always thought nesting was an exaggeration supported by companies who want you to buy toys and furniture. But moving into a new house, expecting a baby and in the run up to Christmas? I'm in full nesting mode.

It's helped massively by Tiny the interior designer. I was reluctant until she showed up on the doorstep with a detailed binder and a catalog of designs that felt homely and perfect.

Although I have insisted that I decorate for Christmas myself. Which then resulted in Jackson doing most of it *himself,* after he spotted me on a ladder and forced us both to lie down for an hour until his heart rate went back to normal. I want to create my own memories and traditions that Smudge will experience throughout her whole childhood.

I'm so focused on where the garlands will hang on the banisters and what bedding to add to all the upstairs bedrooms that I've barely had a chance to panic about the Harpers descending on us.

It's best to keep moving. If I stop to think about it too hard, I'll frazzle.

I'm putting the finishing touches on the tree when Jackson appears, handing me a glass of water and taking a seat on the couch.

"What do you think?" I take a step back to admire my work.

"I love it, pretty girl."

I've gone for a country cottage vibe, woodsy and gold, with winter berries and rich green garlands hanging along the mantelpiece. It's really starting to sink in now that this house is my home. It's helped by the fact that Jackson has said yes to every suggestion Tina and I have added. After the downstairs gym, my office and the nursery that he has insisted on putting together himself, he's given me free reign.

"Come here," he says, leaning his arm back on the couch, gesturing to my space.

I toe off my slippers and gently ease back into his arms, resting my feet on the coffee table that he *insisted* we bring from the flat. It's nice to ease my swollen ankles. Working a full time job, editing Kathleen's short, growing a human and the aforementioned nesting, is pretty tiring. Who knew?

"You've been working too hard, Rosie, you need to relax."

"I'm so relaxed," I insist, closing my eyes as I rest my hand on my belly.

"How's the short coming along?"

I nod around a yawn, burrowing into his side. "It's good. I invited Kathleen over before New Years to watch the latest version. Is that okay?"

"Of course, pretty girl. You don't have to ask to have people over in your own home." He tugs at my hair, gently massaging my scalp. I nearly groan in pleasure. "Are you ready for tomorrow?"

I nod very convincingly with my eyes still shut. "Uh-huh."

His body vibrates as he chuckles. "It's not too late to cancel."

"Don't be silly." I tilt my head up to him. "I'm excited to meet them. Besides, they're already in Scotland." As soon as their visit was confirmed, his sister Tara added me to the family group chat, so I've been welcomed with a daily photo dump of their trip across the UK.

Jackson is picking them up at the train station tomorrow after they travel down from Edinburgh. "What time are you going to pick them up again?"

He readjusts and pulls his phone from his pocket. "Train gets in at one."

"Are you sure I shouldn't come?"

"Nah," he sighs. "You won't all fit in the car. Besides, I need them to get all their energy out before they meet you otherwise we'll all get overwhelmed."

"I can handle it." I snicker.

He leans his head back dramatically. "I don't know if I can."

I laugh as I burrow into his side more. I take a look around the room. It's neat and tidy. Quiet and cozy. Soon it will be full of people, full of laughter and conversation.

I know Jackson is worried that it will be too much, but I can't wait.

"I'm excited," I tell him with a smile. "We've always had a quiet Christmas and it's always been...tense."

Jackson gently rubs his hand up my arm. "Why? What do you do?"

"It's just quiet." I readjust my glasses as they slide down my nose. "I spend most of the morning cooking breakfast while they open their presents and then I start on dinner."

"When do you open your gifts if you're doing all this cooking?" He tugs at my hair gently.

I shrug, "I usually get gift cards, so there's not much to open."

He tightens his hold on me.

"Gift cards are fine," I reassure him. "Obviously, I used to get gifts as a kid but the older I got the easier it was to just buy what I wanted myself. Sometimes I head out on Boxing Day and face the sales. I've got some really great stuff there. That bedding upstairs? I battled with a middle aged lady for it in the John Lewis sale one year."

"Who do you go with?" he asks.

I shrug. "I go on my own."

"I'll go with you this year."

"I think I'll give it a miss this year. It'll be nice to just sit around in my pajamas."

"There's a lot of that with my family," Jackson reassures me. "I don't think anyone can fit into their jeans after Christmas dinner."

"What do you guys normally do?"

"We wake up, we watch Cody open all his gifts and embarrass him because he hates the attention, so then we have to open all of ours. The last few years, I've gone quite hard. And everyone gets mad at me for spending so much on them, but I do it anyway."

I smile, thinking about the car that Jackson's ordered for his mum back in Wellington, and the elaborate gifting scheme I've helped him come up with so she has something to open on Christmas morning.

"Then we go outside and swim in the pool until dinner."

"I love that," I rest my head further on his shoulder. "I can't imagine a hot Christmas. We'll have to go out there one year."

"We'll have Smudge to spoil next year too," he says, resting his hand on my belly.

"She won't have a clue what's going on."

He chuckles. "I'll spoil her anyway."

"We should make some new traditions," I say. "For her, as she grows up." I shift in my seat to face him more. "What do you leave out for Father Christmas?"

"First of all, it's Santa. Mum used to leave a bottle of L&P out, but when Cody was a kid we switched to beer so I could drink it." He shoots me a cheeky grin.

"No mince pies?"

"Rosie." Jackson sends me a horrified look. "What the fuck is a mince pie?"

I snicker. "It's just a tiny fruit pie, but that's what we call them. I'll make you some to try."

He grimaces. "I guess if I have to."

"What's L&P?"

"It's like a fizzy lemon drink. I can't stand the stuff, but Ella's addicted to it. I'm sure she's already brought a case over so you can try one."

"Let's compromise. Santa can eat a mince pie and he can wash it down with an L&P."

"Deal," Jackson says firmly, offering me his hand. "And he wears jandals."

35

———

JACKSON

Thank God I told Rosie to stay home I think as my family barrels off the platform and all try to topple into my arms at once.

"Hello, hello," I try to say to them all at the same time as I get hugs and pats from four different women.

"Jackie," Mum wails as she clings to me longer. "You've grown."

"I haven't grown," I laugh as I free myself from her clutches. "It's good to see you too, Mum."

I head over to Cody, who's staring up at me under his lashes. He's definitely grown a few inches. He's already up to my elbow. "Come here, bub." I pull him to me and ruffle his hair as his arms come around me. "How was the train?"

"It was good," he says quietly. "It rained the whole time."

I throw my head back with a laugh. "Welcome to Britain. Come on, I'm parked this way."

I fling an arm around Cody as Nina piles the suitcases onto the trolley I brought, and Mum slots in next to me, clinging on to my elbow.

We head to the exit like a large conjoined hydra head.

"How's Rosie?" Mum asks and I grin.

"She's good. She's been cooking all morning. She says she's not nervous."

Mum waves her hand. "What is she nervous for? We're lovely."

Ella laughs. "We've already been prepped, Jackie," she tells me. "We're all going to be on our best behavior."

"That's what I'm worried about."

Later, when we pull up outside the house, I turn off the engine and turn to the people in the car. "I mean it, go slowly. Do *not* overwhelm her."

All five passengers blink at me before Mum opens the door and darts out, barely leaving enough time for it to swing closed behind her.

Ella, Nina and Tara rush out after her, leaving only Cody sitting in his middle seat. "I don't think all those warnings have done much," he says solemnly.

I sigh and rub my hand over my beard. "You better help me with these bags, because I don't think anyone else is going to."

By the time I've breached the threshold with all the suitcases, Rosie is standing in the center of a Harper sandwich, all of them talking a mile a minute. I glance at Rosie's face expecting to see a look of panic, but she's beaming.

I take a minute to absorb it. Her cheeks are rosy red, and her smile is wide as she nods enthusiastically, allowing my mother to curl her arm around her.

"You're drooling," Cody snickers.

"Wait till you meet someone, bub. Then see if you can keep your mouth shut." I mess up his mop of hair. "Alright, alright. What did I say in the car people? Slowly." I breach the fold and tug on Rosie's arm until she's free from their clutches and firmly in mine. I press a kiss to her head as I wrap my arms around her.

"Honestly," Mum huffs exasperatedly. "You'd think we were wild animals the way he talks about us."

Rosie giggles. "How about a tour?"

An hour later, we're all haphazardly spread around the kitchen, leaning against counters and curled around Mum's iPad as she shows us every picture from their Europe trip.

"This is Edinburgh castle," Tara says, leaning over Mum to swipe through the pictures.

"Whose thumb is that?" I laugh.

My sisters groan playfully as Mum says, "I can't tell where my thumb is! It's not my fault."

"It's an iPad, mother. How is your hand anywhere near the lens?"

"Because I hold it with my right hand, Ella. How else am I supposed to hold it?"

"Like this." Ella holds up the iPad and I pose with my arm curled around Rosie as she snaps a picture.

"That's what I do!" Mum protests.

Rosie giggles into my side as they start to bicker. "You good, pretty girl?" I whisper in her ear.

She nods, her glasses sliding down her nose. "I'm great."

"Where's Cody?" Nina asks, glancing around the room.

"He's uh—in my office. He liked the look of my setup, so I said he's welcome to play a game." Rosie bites her lip. "Is that okay?"

"That's really kind of you, thank you." Ella smiles.

"Of course. Is anyone hungry?"

"Are you going to finally tell us what that amazing smell is?" Mum asks.

Rosie flushes as she steps around the island, reaching into the oven with her mitts and pulling out her giant pot. "It's a Mushroom, Leek and Stilton pie."

She lifts the lid off, and Mum and Nina lean forward.

"Oh, that smells incredible," Nina says.

"I've put it on the slow cooker, so I'll just need to cook some vegetables and it'll be done."

"I'll do that," Nina says, jumping out of her seat.

"I'm going to go check on Cody," I tell the room.

"Oh nice, just when we need the help," Tara chastises.

"I'd just get in the way." I hold my hands up innocently.

I slip out of the kitchen, the sounds of laughter chasing me down the small hallway. I knock politely on Rosie's office door and poke my head in. Cody is hunched over on Rosie's brand new, custom chair, with headphones perched over his ears. He doesn't even look up until I nudge the headphones away from his ear, and I laugh when he jumps a mile.

"Oh, hey," he says, cheeks pinkening.

"You like the setup here?" I ask, taking a seat on the armchair.

"Yeah, it's cool." Cody says, turning back to the screen. "Rosie's got so many games. I saw how many levels she hit on Sixth Temple, it's insane."

"She's got a lot of skills, that one," I smile. "You should play a game together whilst you're here. I know she'd love it."

Cody shrugs awkwardly. "Maybe."

"Come on, I came in to get you. We're having dinner soon."

"Uh, okay. Let me just finish this one game."

I chuckle. "I've spent enough time watching Rosie to know that you've just finished one, so don't try and pull a fast one on me."

He shoots me a guilty look, and I tug the chair away from the desk. "Come on, bub."

He gently places the headphones back on the rest and follows me. "That chair's hella comfortable. Can you get me one?"

I laugh. "We'll see what Santa can do."

36

ROSIE

My cheeks hurt from smiling and my back hurts from the somersaults that Smudge has been doing. I like to think she's as excited as I am, that she can feel the love bursting from every inch of the big house.

My tour was more eloquent than Jackson's first one. He said it wasn't fair because he didn't have enough stuff to show off, but I'm still counting it as a win.

Cody loves my office so I've backed up all my saved games and allowed him free reign over the console. He's only had to be dragged out of there a few times in the days since they arrived, and Jackson and I have been taking turns playing with him.

Cody even said off-hand yesterday that he preferred when I played with him and Jackson's has complained about it nonstop since.

Now, it's Christmas Eve, and I'm peeling potatoes at the kitchen table as Gloria commandeers my kitchen.

"Are you sure I can't help with the—" I ask, attempting to get out of my seat.

Gloria brandishes her knife in my direction, and I

settle back in. "For the last time, honey, you need to rest your feet, not worry about cooking for half a dozen people. Just cook my grandchild, that's your one job today."

I laugh. "But I *like* cooking."

"I'm sure you like sitting down too. Are you sure you don't need a blanket over there?"

I bite back my smile. It is kind of nice to be fussed over, even if I have assured her that a blanket will hinder my potato peeling abilities. "I'm all good, honestly. Let me know when you want me to move onto the carrots."

Gloria puts the turkey into the oven and starts clearing up. I shift in my seat, and she holds up a hand without looking at me. "Rosie, I like you a lot, but I swear if you try and get out of that seat one more time I will tie you to it." She shoots me a wink as she opens the dishwasher. "Besides, this is Jackson's job. Jackson! Get in here and clean your kitchen."

He appears out of the office. "I've already lost five-one to my nephew and now I'm being made to do chores. What happened to the Christmas spirit?"

He steps up to my table and bends down for a kiss. I tug at the Santa hat Tara shoved on his head as soon as we woke up this morning that he's refused to take off.

"How much do you hate being banished from the kitchen?" he whispers.

"How much do you hate losing to a twelve year old?" I whisper back.

He groans dramatically before rounding the kitchen island and attempting to clear away plates.

"What have you been cooking in here anyway? Christmas isn't till tomorrow."

"We're slow cooking," Gloria says, picking up her wine

glass and crossing to my table. "Can I get you a drink, honey?" She starts picking up my supplies.

"I'm okay, thank you." I smile, leaning back in my chair and stretching out my toes. I'll get up in a few minutes and get one, I tell myself as I lean into the stretch.

Gloria bustles back with a glass of water and sets it in front of me. "Just in case."

I stare at the glass, blinking back the heat that burns behind my eyes. It's just a small thing. I could hate the fact that she ignored my answer and got one for me anyway, but I just feel...warm.

"Have you guys had any thoughts on names?" Gloria asks, taking a seat beside me and patting my hand with hers. She shoots me a warm smile that crinkles the corner of her eyes.

"We're not telling anyone yet, Mum," Jackson says from the kitchen.

"Not telling anyone what?" Tara asks, walking into the kitchen with a box of chocolates and offering one to Gloria and me wordlessly. "Are you guys having another secret baby?"

"Just the one," Jackson drawls, bent over the dishwasher.

"We've got a few names on the go," I tell them both. "But until we decide we're keeping it quiet."

"I'm very partial to Tara," Tara says wickedly. "It just rolls off the tongue."

Jackson guffaws. "What have *you* done to be a namesake?"

"Uh, I covered for you when you snuck out at fifteen to go make out with Tia from two streets down."

"Jackson Harper!" Gloria gasps.

"And kept that secret for a good fifteen years until right now." Jackson throws a tea towel at her from the kitchen and

Tara snatches it from the air, rounding the island to snap it at his legs.

Gloria sighs dramatically. "They always get like this when they're home. Fighting like cats and dogs."

Jackson gets Tara in a headlock, and she sneaks out of the hold like a pro-wrestler, cackling in his face as her legs sweep out from under him and she tries to kick out his knee.

"They like each other really, promise."

Cleo and I have never been like this. I never come up with a witty response quick enough and if I do snap back I just end up getting myself into more trouble than it's worth.

"How do you know?"

"What, love?"

"Know that they like each other." I shift awkwardly. "Know that it's not...cruel."

I glance back at the table, tracing the water ring from my glass as it seeps into the wood.

Gloria takes a moment. "Well, I guess it comes from knowing them all. I've watched them as children when they used to have screaming matches. The girls were the worst for it, arguing about stealing clothes and toys and what have you. But eventually, they started ending their arguments with laughter instead, and when I'd try to get involved I'd say, you know 'you're sisters, don't be mean to each other', and they'd just tell me to leave them alone because I was annoying."

I try to smile, but it doesn't fit my mouth right, coming out as a blurted question. "What would you have done if it was? Cruel, I mean."

Gloria looks at me shrewdly before taking my hand in hers. "They bicker and argue, but they're still thick as thieves when all's said and done. They still love each other.

Not all siblings are like that, and I guess it would be really hard if it's not."

I shift in my chair, cradling my bump.

"Jackson told us about what happened," she says softly. "I'm sorry that your sister did that to you."

I shrug, reaching up to adjust my glasses.

"If it helps, the girls were ready to launch an entire smear campaign. It was very elaborate."

My lips twitch at the thought. Before this trip, I'd spoken to the Harpers on an off, the occasional text or a friendly wave through video call, but I already feel more a part of their family than I ever have my own.

"I just never understood why she hates me so much," I admit with a whisper.

Gloria sends me a small smile. "You might never know that, honey. You've just got to learn to love yourself more."

A loud laugh snaps me out of it as I see Tara giggling and showing Jackson something on her phone.

He looks up and shoots me a wink.

"You've raised lovely children," I say quietly to Gloria.

She beams at me. "Well, I wish someone had told me *that* thirty five years ago. I tell you, motherhood is a constant battle to convince yourself you're doing a good job."

I smile and rub my hand against my belly. "I already feel like that."

Jackson appears at my shoulder, gently tugging at the hair that's draped over my shoulder. "I've got to go run an errand."

"An errand?" I ask, narrowing my eyes. "On Christmas Eve?"

He grins impishly. "Important Christmas Eve errand."

"How long will you be?" Gloria asks, checking the gold watch on her wrist.

"Not long," he reassures us both before he presses a kiss to my lips and runs out of the room.

"He's either forgotten something, or he's about to pull off a ridiculous surprise." Gloria tells me, leaning her chin on her hand. I smile, thinking of the car that's waiting for her on her driveway at home. "He's always been that way, going above and beyond. He's been like that since his father died."

Jackson hasn't shared much about his father, only that he'd had an accident when he was younger.

"It was so hard." Gloria's voice wobbles and I rest my hand gently on her forearm as her words tumble out. "I'd lost my Oliver, but I had three kids to care for. Tara shut down, she wouldn't leave her room or talk to me. Ella started acting out at school, getting in trouble and starting fights. "

She crosses her arms across her body.

"Jackson was the glue that kept us together when we were falling apart. He'd annoy Tara until she started laughing again, he would hang out with Ella at school so she wasn't so lonely and then he'd play rugby on the weekends. He just didn't stop, that boy. It was so easy for him to be positive. To look after us."

That sounds like Jackson, I think with a smile, imagining a younger Jackson without the tattoos, with gangly limbs and a fresh face. "I can't imagine how difficult that must have been for all of you."

I've never not had both parents, never had to face the grief of losing one. Despite how difficult our relationship is, I know they're still *there.* Still sitting at the same kitchen table, still waking up in the morning. I could see them again, if I wanted to. I could sit with my dad as he talks about his latest project in the garage, or hear my mum's gossip about the neighbors. There's a part of me that does want that, but I just don't think they do. They haven't reached out since Cleo posted that video. Apart from my dad dropping off the crib and the thank you text I sent that was left on read, they haven't reached out once, not even to invite me over for Christmas. They just don't want me.

Tears burn my eyes but Gloria nudges me with a smile, dragging me from my thoughts. "As soon as he started talking about you, I knew you were the one."

I blush as I shift in my seat, cradling my bump. "Oh, well." I gesture to my bump.

"He was always going to be an amazing father, Rosie," Gloria tells me. "He would be there for this baby regardless. But he's chosen the best partner. You two just…" She shrugs. "Fit."

I feel my eyes sting, and I blink back the tears. I'm unsure what to do with the compliment, with the affection from this woman I've only known for a handful of days.

"I think so too," I admit quietly.

I lean forward, resting my elbow on the table, but Smudge shifts in my belly. I grab Gloria's hand with a smile, pulling it to the side of my belly where Smudge likes to kick. It only takes a few seconds for a flutter to hit the spot, and Gloria gasps.

"She's a twister." She grins at me.

I laugh, before taking a sip of my drink. "I wish she'd be a bit lazier. She's giving my internal organs a hammering."

"I think Jackson permanently dislodged my spleen with a foot once."

I choke on my water. "Huh?"

37

JACKSON

"Hello, Betty," I say, pressing a kiss to Nanny Taylor's cheek, "You ready to go?"

She's waiting for me in the main room of the care home, where an elaborate game of festive charades is being chaired by an over enthusiastic elf.

Betty tugs me closer with a firm arm and whispers, "Get me away from them all, Jackie." She's wearing a homemade jumper that just says 'Sleigh'. A Betty Taylor Original.

I chuckle. "You don't want to play another round of charades?"

The look Betty sends me is flat, and I wink at her as I help her out of her chair. We wander slowly back to her room to find Maryanne, one of the carers, already helping pack a bag.

"There you both are," she says with a kind smile. "Are you excited, Betty?" She raises her voice in the semi-patronizing tone that has Betty replying with a wave of her hand.

"Yes, yes, did you make sure my yarn is in there?"

"I'm just going to sign the paperwork." I leave Betty in Maryanne's care and head back to reception.

"Merry Christmas," I tell Penny as I lean over the desk.

"Merry Christmas." The woman smiles as she hands over the paperwork. "It's so lovely that Betty's getting away. Is her granddaughter excited?"

"She will be."

Am I kidnapping my girlfriend's ninety year old grand-mother on Christmas Eve? Maybe. Will my girlfriend be happy about it? I sure hope so.

I slide the paper back across the desk, chuckling as I finally see Betty's full name. "Thanks again for helping me with this."

"Of course."

It's a plan I concocted a few weeks ago on one of our monthly visits. Rosie assumed her parents would be picking her up but when I quietly asked Penny, she told me no one had informed the staff or requested any paperwork. I knew if I told Rosie, she'd stress and try to get Betty to come to stay with us anyway, so I decided to ease her burden and create a little Christmas magic at the same time.

I wander back to Betty's room. Maryanne has gone, and Betty is dressed in her light pink puffer coat with her bag clasped on her lap and her suitcase by her feet.

"You ready to go, *Elizabeth Taylor*?"

Betty laughs. "Don't you start with that too. I had that from my husband since the day he proposed. He'd tell me I was his Cleopatra. That's where Cleo got her name, you know."

I swipe her suitcase up in one arm and help her stand with the other.

"Oh really?" I ask gently.

"Is she coming for Christmas? Cleo? I haven't seen her in months." I hold my tongue, Rosie and I spent all of Betty's birthday with her last month but none of the rest of the family showed up.

"It's just us and my family." I help her out of the front door, waving goodbye to the staff who are head-to-toe in tinsel. "I can't believe I never put it together," I say, changing the subject back to her famous moniker as we slowly amble to the front where I've left the car.

"It's my secret fun fact," she chuckles.

Getting a small, ninety-year old woman into an SUV is a challenge, but Betty and I persevere. I let her control the radio until we're listening to Bing Crosby dream about a White Christmas. Betty spends the drive staring out the window as the setting sun allows the Christmas lights to flicker on outside the houses lining the street.

Londoners definitely know how to do Christmas. We haven't spent much time in Central London, where the Christmas lights illuminate the busy streets full of shoppers and immaculately decorated trees sit in every window display. But even in the suburbs, lights are strung in front gardens and holiday songs play on the radio twenty four seven. The air smells cold, like snow is just around the corner. I could get used to a Christmas like this.

I shift in my seat. "So, just to warn you there are a lot of people at the house." I reel off introductions to my family. "But my sister-in-law Nina used to be a nurse, so she's already ready to step in if you need to get away."

"It sounds lovely, darling," Betty says, folding her hands neatly in her lap. "Thank you for breaking me out."

"Anytime, Betty."

We pull up outside the house, and Betty tilts her head forward. "Goodness me, you don't do things by half do you?"

"Never," I tell her as I jump out and round the bumper, helping her onto the gravel.

I open the door to Christmas music and laughter, and Betty takes a deep breath beside me. "Rosie!" I call down the corridor.

She rounds the corner with a smile and a tea towel in hand, which she drops to the floor in shock. "Nanny?"

Betty pats my arm with a smile. "I've been kidnapped."

Rosie crosses the hall in a few steps. "Oh my God!"

She wraps her grandmother in a firm hug and gazes up at me with watery eyes. "Merry Christmas," I tell her.

Mum wanders down the hall behind her, and I'm quick to make introductions.

"Come and sit down," Rosie says, ushering her into the living room.

"Oh, it's so lovely in here, darling," Betty says as she gazes around the room. I'm left with Betty's suitcase as all the women in my life convene around the perfectly sized tree.

I'm just about to head upstairs to store the suitcase when I hear Rosie call my name.

I have just enough time to turn before she's in my arms and pressing her lips to mine. I drop the case to the floor and scoop my arms around her, tugging her as close as I can with her belly pressing against mine.

I pull back just enough to cradle her face in my hands and wipe her tears with my thumbs.

"I can't believe you," Rosie says, with a watery laugh. "How did you do it?"

"I have my ways."

She curves her arms around my neck and holds my gaze with hers. "I love you."

Her words settle across me like a blanket, curling around me and squeezing my heart. I've feel like I've waited my whole life to hear those words fall from her lips, and I can barely contain myself.

"I love you too, pretty girl," I tell her. "I have since the day you left me on that balcony."

She grins as I crash my lips into hers. My blood rushes south, and I'm more than happy to whisk her to our bedroom to give her another early Christmas present but my little sister shouts, "Ugh, get a room," as she passes us in the hall, and it's enough for Rosie to pull away with a giggle.

"Let's," I say, pulling her closer.

"We literally have a house full of family," Rosie says with a bright smile as she untangles herself from me.

I tug at her arm as if I can pull her back. "Whose idea was that again?"

"Yours," she tells me, pushing me towards the stairs. "One of your best."

38

ROSIE

"CAN YOU CHANGE THIS TO THE WIDE SHOT?" KATHLEEN ASKS, pointing over my shoulder at the screen hung on the wall behind my desk.

"Sure." I drag the replacement shot onto the timeline. It's a non dialogue scene, so it's an easy fix to slot it into place. The film is coming together nicely. I've been working on it in the evenings when I can, although this is our one and only in-person editing day. Thanks to Christmas and my full-time job, this is my first time even sitting down with Kathleen.

I press play and we lapse into silence again as we rewatch the scenes. I lean back in my comfy, new chair and take a sip of my third L&P of the day. Ella bought a box of the fizzy drink over in her suitcase, and it's quickly become my new addiction.

"Let's cut the last frame of this shot." Kathleen taps her pen on her notebook before sliding it in her curly bun.

We've been at it for a few hours now, holed up in my dark office. When she first walked through the door, Kathleen made the appropriate admiration of the new house, but has largely has remained unfazed by the dramatic changes in my life since I last worked for her.

We let the film run through one final time and I practically hold my breath until it ends. There are always things I normally notice, a continuity error or some noise in the audio, but we pass the twenty minutes and I don't spot anything.

I haven't added the credits in yet, so the screen abruptly cuts to black. I glance at Kathleen, and she stretches her arms over her head. "We did it."

I laugh as she swings back in the over sized chair Jackson sits in when I hole myself up in here.

I scoot closer to the screen, flicking through the edit frame by frame, thrilled that she's happy with my work.

Kathleen tilts her head back on the chair and closes her eyes.

"Do you want a coffee or something?" I ask.

"I need to sleep for a month, I think." She peeks one eye open. "But yes. Especially if it's from the fancy coffee machine I saw on my way in here."

I push my chair back and stand, desperate to stretch my legs.

"Wait, no," Kathleen says, jumping up. "I'll get it myself. You should stay off your feet."

"I have to pee anyway," I tell her with a laugh as I open the door, the brightness of the kitchen causing me to blink behind my glasses.

The house is quiet, a first since the family left yesterday. It's the awkward time between Christmas and New Year's, where the days bleed together and time ceases to exist, and it's more discombobulating without the clamor of voices echoing throughout the house. From the moment they left I missed it all. I missed the laughter and the fact that there was someone to talk to in every room of the house, someone offering chocolates and entertaining Nanny when I couldn't be by her side every second of the day.

That being said, I can't deny it's been nice to have some privacy.

When I told Jackson that Kathleen was coming over to review the fine cut, he made himself scarce in the gym, and I can hear the faint sounds of his music reverberating through the floor.

By the time I finish in the bathroom and return to the kitchen, Jackson has reappeared, his sweaty shirt clinging to his chest and his head tilted back as he gulps water over the sink. I watch the veins in his neck as he swallows and feel heat rush between my thighs.

"Enjoying the show?" Jackson says in a low voice, as he catches me staring.

I cross to his side. "Always."

He tugs me forward and presses a kiss to my lips.

"Oh! Sorry," Kathleen announces as she wanders into the kitchen.

We jump apart.

"Coffee, yes, coming up."

"Hi," Jackson says politely. "I'm Jackson."

"Kathleen." She waves, creeping closer to the counter. "It's nice to finally meet you."

"How's it going in there?" Jackson says, nodding his head towards the office.

"We're finished," Kathleen announces, throwing her hands in the air in celebration.

Jackson laughs as he leans against the counter. "Nice. I've seen bits and pieces, and I think it looks like a great film."

Kathleen's mouth drops open. "You do?"

Jackson nods. "Yeah. I obviously haven't seen your latest cut but I like what I've seen so far."

Kathleen sends me a frazzled look. It's easy for me to forget that Jackson is famous. I faced the media whirlwind when we were outed, the statement that was picked up by multiple tabloids and the overwhelming increase in follow requests on social media, but the news cycle has almost faded by now. When we're just us at home, or with our friends and family, he's just a normal guy, but in reality, he's one of the most sought after actors in Hollywood. Him saying that he likes a film carries a lot of weight.

"Would you like to see the whole thing?"

Jackson rubs his hands together as I finish Kathleen's coffee. "Hell yes. Let me jump in the shower, and I'll be with you."

Forty minutes later, the film has finished, and Jackson leans forward from the seat he's pulled in from the kitchen. "Have you got a screening arranged yet?" he asks Kathleen.

"Not really. We used all of our funding on actually making the thing, so it's definitely not in the budget to host a screening. We've opened up crowdfunding for the festival push though, so maybe we'll have some luck."

"Send me the link," Jackson tells her.

LATER, when Jackson and I are curled up on the sofa, my feet in his lap and a blanket thrown over both of us, my phone buzzes.

KATHLEEN

ROSIE TAYLOR

ME

???

Kathleen sends me a screenshot of the crowdfunding link with a row of exclamation marks.

One hundred percent of the goal reached from a single donation.

I dig my foot into Jackson's side, pulling his attention away from the Christmas film playing on the TV.

"Did you really just fund Kathleen's short?"

He sends me a wink. "It's your short too, no?"

I nudge him again. "I can't believe you."

"I'm a patron of the arts, Rosie. What can I say?"

I quickly respond to Kathleen before I pull up my text thread with Anya.

ME

I think I'm a nepo baby :(

ANYA

HAHAHAH

The first step is acknowledging your privilege.

(That was Danny btw)

ME

Thank you for your support

ANYA

If anything you're a nepo baby-mama

ME

I think that's worse

"Are you upset?" Jackson asks, tugging my foot gently. "I'm sorry, I thought I was helping."

I laugh as he wiggles my socks off. "Am I upset that you just funded an indie short film with the click of a button?"

He looks unsure until I tug him closer by the arm so he's hovering over me.

"Thank you," I tell him. "I love that you did it." I press a kiss to his lips, my hands exploring the warm skin under his shirt.

"You do?" he murmurs against my mouth.

"So much." I nod as I pull at his waistband.

"If there's anything else you need funded, just say the word." He presses a featherlight kiss to my jaw.

"As a patron, of course," I tease.

"Of course," he says as he tilts my head back, and I show him just how grateful I am.

39

JACKSON

Last New Year's Eve, I was in New York with a bunch of people I only see at parties, and we stayed up until dawn drinking champagne and vodka.

This year, I welcomed the New Year curled up with Rosie as we drank a glass of sparkling apple juice and watched the fireworks on the TV, before falling asleep before one am.

It's crazy how quickly life can change, how quickly priorities change.

Before I leave for my first day back on set, I creep back into the bedroom fully dressed and sit on the side of the bed gently.

Rosie stirs, a small tired noise escaping as she turns towards me.

I lean down and press a kiss to her warm cheek, wishing I could climb back in with her.

"What time is it?" she asks groggily, peeling her eyes open.

I rest my hand on her belly, where my t-shirt she's taken

to wearing to bed has risen up in her sleep. I press a gentle kiss to the swell where my daughter is sleeping.

The last thing I want to do is leave my girls for two weeks, to not be able to fall asleep every night cradling the things that are most precious to me. I should be here with her, not stepping out into the cool winter night and driving away for weeks.

But no, I've made a commitment to the job. I have to see it through. One last push before it's wrapped.

"It's early," I whisper. "Go back to sleep." I brush a strand of hair that's fallen over her face back behind her ear.

"Be careful," Rosie says, clasping my hand and pressing a kiss to the palm.

"Always," I promise before leaning towards her and catching her soft lips in mine.

"I love you."

"I love you too, pretty girl. I'll be back in two weeks."

A few months ago, I'd only see her a few times a week and before that, a few times a year if I was lucky. But as I leave our home, I don't know how I'm going to cope not seeing her for fourteen days.

The drive to set is a couple hours, so I spend the time reading the script and getting prepared for the stunts. It's the biggest one of the movie, which is why it's expected to take two weeks to film.

It's a long fight sequence, including one-on-one combat, diving off buildings and driving a motorcycle across two rooftops.

We've been going over the plan meticulously for months, but I've been riding since I could get my license, so I've never had any concerns. I should be ready. I should be excited.

I don't know whether it's the remnants of the festive

break or leaving my woman curled up in bed, but there's a tightening in my stomach that feels suspiciously like nerves.

I don't get stage fright and I haven't hurt myself on this job since I jarred my side all those months ago, and even that was just bad luck. Mistakes haven't been made, everything's gone smoothly, so why do I feel like the other shoe is about to drop?

It's when I get out of the car that it does.

It's still dark, the sky just lightening on the horizon, bathing everything in a cool blue haze as a handful of crew members cross the silent lot. It's almost preternatural, the air chilled and silent, only punctured by my car door slamming behind me.

I can smell the catering truck, but the few crew members standing in front are silent, shuffling from foot to foot. Early mornings aren't anyone's favorites, but by the time I step onto set there's usually enough adrenaline threading through the crew that energy levels are high.

My chest tightens. Something's wrong.

Eric holds the door open to my trailer but I bypass him, my feet taking me to the men crowded around the production truck in a semicircle.

I recognize Marky by his shock of white hair, his shoulders hunched as he rests his face in his hands.

"Marky," I say as I approach. He whirls towards me and pulls his hand away from his face.

"Jackie," he says, swallowing and crossing his hands across his chest.

I rest one hand on my hip before rubbing my beard with the other. "What's going on?" I ask slowly.

Marky takes a deep breath. "It's Tony."

My heart freezes in my chest. "What about him?" I bite out.

I barely register the words coming out of Mark's mouth, —"stunt", "gone wrong", "coma"— but the one that my mind hangs onto freezes the breath in my lungs.

"Paralyzed."

Knees shaking, I barely make it to my trailer before collapsing on the tiny sofa. My palms sweat as I try to take a deep breath, but it gets caught in my throat. I lean forward, dangling my head between my knees and trying to remember the advice my therapist used to give me.

I take a deep breath through shaking lips, trying to count to five before exhaling and repeating the motion. I haven't had an attack like this for nearly twenty years, but I would have one almost weekly in the months after Dad died. If I tripped over my own feet my heart would pound in my chest and panic would grip my throat like a vice. How could a man who was so strong, so healthy, so adventurous, slip in the street and die within seconds? It was only after I started stunt work that I learned how to take risks safely, how to protect myself in a guided fall, how to land from a jump without breaking my knees, that the attacks eased. Over time, my confidence returned, my stunts got riskier, until eventually I was leading projects where I was pushing my body to extremes.

My mouth feels dry, and I press my freezing hands to my face.

Paralyzed.

I ran off before Marky could give me any more information. What hospital is he in? Is Kaia on her way? All Kaia wanted was for him to stop putting himself at risk and now this. Does Masen know? God, *Masen.*

My phone ringing jolts me out of my spiral, and my knees shake as I read Rosie's name on the screen.

"Rosie?" I croak.

"Hey, I wasn't sure if you were on set already so I thought I'd try you. Can you talk for a second?"

"Yes. Please."

"The L&P that your sister sent has arrived! Thank God, because I've already finished the box and I was almost ready to somehow try to make it myself."

Her happy voice soothes me like a balm and I close my eyes as she regales me with the story of how she and my sister bonded over a fizzy drink.

"Jackson?" she asks and I let my eyes open.

"Sorry, I'm here."

"Are you okay?" Rosie asks quietly.

"Uhm…" I rub my hand across my face. "Yeah, nah. It's Tony. He's had an accident." The whole story rushes out, my heart hammering as I spill the limited facts that I know. He was working on a different project, a TV drama that has two stunts in the whole series. The likelihood of him injuring himself was never zero, but they were slim and it still happened.

"That's awful." Rosie's horrified voice echoes my own thoughts. "Jackson, listen to me. He's still fighting, yeah? I'm sure he'll be okay. Is his wife with him?"

"I don't know. I think she's still over in Wellington with Masen." My voice cracks and I squeeze my eyes shut. "I haven't spoken to her."

"Send me her number and I can make sure she's on her way, what hospi–"

"I love you," I interrupt her as she makes plans to look after a family that she's never met.

"I love you too, baby."

I sit in silence for a second, just listening to her breathing over the phone, until a knock on the door interrupts my thoughts.

"Just a minute," I shout hoarsely. I rub my hand over my eyes before turning back to the phone. "I'm doing the motorcycle stunt today."

"*Oh*," Rosie says quietly. "Are you sure you want to do it?"

I don't answer. I don't know how to.

"Listen, Jackson," she tells me. "You've done hundreds of these stunts, and you've got a good team, right? That's what you told me. I trust you, so if you want to do this stunt, then I trust your instincts too."

I nod, even though she can't see me. "Yeah."

"Do whatever you need to do, okay? Just come home to me when you're finished."

Another knock sounds, and Eric pokes his head in the door.

"They're ready for you," he says with a smile. He doesn't know Tony, doesn't know Marky enough to even have heard the story.

There's this enormous news that's kicked my world off its axis, but the rest of the crew is just going through business as usual.

"I've got to go, pretty girl." I tell Rosie as I force my leaden feet to move.

"Okay, text me when you can."

"I will."

The last time I saw Tony, he was determined to keep doing the job he loves. Taking risks is what he's done every day of his life. He was confident, good at his job, probably even better than me, and he still got hurt. I do the safe, practiced maneuvers that the stunt guys like Tony have already workshopped to perfection. The risks I take are assessed and prepared. If something happens to me, the shoot would need to shut down while I recover or get recast. I know this, I've always known this. A waiver is written into all of my contracts so I'm aware of the danger I'm putting myself through by agreeing to do my own stunts.

Paralyzed.

Tony woke up yesterday morning as usual, drank his morning coffee and probably texted his son, and now he's in a coma.

I cross my arms across my body, my feet sinking into the tarmac as if to keep me in one spot, while I attempt to listen to Sam and Shaun.

What would I do if the stunt went wrong? If I jump at the wrong second, or a harness snaps in a freak accident. I've always trusted myself, trusted my gut, known that I wouldn't jeopardize the film by taking on something I can't accomplish, but never backing down. Always jumping straight into the action with a grin at the thought of playing with danger.

I think of Rosie's sleepy smile as she wished me luck hours ago, and the sight of her swollen belly where my daughter is growing.

I imagine her climbing out of bed and answering the call that something's happened, something's gone wrong, and that our lives have been changed in immeasurable ways.

I see Smudge growing up without a father, having panic attacks every time she trips over her own feet, just in case her life changes just like her dad's did. Just like *my* dad's did.

I rub my beard, trying to ignore the shaking in my hand, my ribs twitching in my side in a way they haven't in months.

Can I really do this every day? Step out of the door and put my life and my family's life at risk, just so I can say that I did a cool stunt on a film that probably will be forgotten about in a few years anyway?

Can I risk not coming home to my girls?

"No," I say out loud, my voice firm even to my ears.

Sam and Shaun glance at me with wide eyes as the plans for today's fight scene trail off awkwardly.

"I'm not doing this stunt," I say, catching eyes with Marky. He nods with a frown, his face still pale from the news.

"Jackson, we have to do the stunt today, man," Shaun says, glancing at Sam nervously. "It's in the schedule."

I tug on my beard as my fist tightens on my bicep.

"I appreciate that, but I can't do this stunt today. Or any day." The decision is final and settles in my gut like a stone.

Marky clasps me on the shoulder as I take a step away from the group, my phone already in my hand.

I scroll until I reach Kaia's number, unused for years. I close the door to my trailer as I listen to her sobs from down the line and get her and Masen on the next flight over here.

My mind is on autopilot as I arrange the transfer for Tony to the finest neuro hospital in the city, roping in Eric to help me get Kaia and Masen a rental near the hospital when they get here.

It's a mess, but at least I can do something.

Travis calls with an update about the double that's being brought in to replace my stunts, but it's barely a concern to me now. This is what I want.

40

ROSIE

February arrives and so does my bump. It enters a room before me and I can no longer see my feet. Which works for me as I know my ankles have doubled in size, so at least I don't have to look at them. Jackson still swears I'm beautiful, rubbing my tired feet at night and cradling my bump to take the weight off my back.

Gloria wasn't joking about Harper's being big babies, so her and Ella advised me to start doing perineal exercises over Christmas dinner, which made Jackson go very pale and Cody gag into his turkey.

I told Jackson that he needed to do what he needed to do, but I can't deny that I breathed a sigh of relief when he told me he was stepping away from the stunts. Even though that means the schedule has extended to make up for the lost time arranging his double.

He was home for only a few days before he had to go back to set, this time for even longer. It's fine. I lived on my own for years before he started climbing into bed with me each night and waking up with me each morning. One more week until the film's wrapped and then he's home for good, just a few weeks before my due date.

I can't wait for him to be home more, even though I have to work basically until I'm due anyway.

The guys at work have been strangely supportive, especially Conor and Lee, who have somehow taken it upon themselves to get me anything I want so I don't have to get up from my desk. Even Kevin keeps to himself a bit more, which is a blessing. Gareth has also allowed me to negotiate working from home three out of five days of the week. So generous of him.

It's on one of my office days, when I'm waiting outside the building for my car home, that she finds me.

"Hi Rosie," my mother says, standing beside me, wrapped in a scarf with a trim coat secured around her shoulders. It takes me a few seconds to register that I'm not hallucinating.

"Mum?" I ask, bewildered. "What are you doing here?"

"Well, you've refused to tell us your new address, so I had to take it upon myself to find you." She crosses her arms across her chest.

I blink. "I don't have to tell you where I live."

She huffs, clutching her coat tighter around herself. "Don't be ridiculous Rosalie. Of course your mother needs to know where you're living, especially when you're shacked up with a basic stranger."

I roll my eyes. "Jackson is not a stranger, Mum. He's my boyfriend." She glances away.

"What are you doing here?" I repeat, still absorbing the shock. I turn towards her, placing my hand on my belly as Smudge nudges me.

Her eyes drop to my stomach, and I swear they dampen. "Look at you," she whispers. "When are you due?"

"February twentieth."

Mum looks up. "I've missed so much." Her voice is a whisper drowned out by the London traffic.

I try to ignore the guilt that slithers down my spine. She could have reached out months ago, I remind myself. She didn't.

"Would you like to get dinner with me?" Mum asks, and I almost swallow my tongue.

I can't remember the last time we hung out just the two of us. I don't even think it's ever happened.

"Uhm..." I glance at my phone and the car that's en route.

"Unless you have to get home?"

I bite my lip. My dinner plans are currently whatever I can scrounge from the fridge and I'm *starving*.

"I could eat." I shrug, canceling the car service that Jackson set up for me.

We weave through crowds of tourists as we head away from the office and towards the less populated area. Managing the central London crowds whilst this pregnant is not ideal, but I'm happy to postpone the awkward small talk we're about to have for as long as I can. I try to come up with some neutral conversation topics. Maybe we could talk about the weather?

We end up at a small vegetarian restaurant and we spend a few minutes looking at the menus. I decide what I want immediately, but I keep my head bent over the menu until a waiter comes to take our orders, and my crutch is taken away.

"I almost forgot," Mum says, reaching into her bag. "I brought these for you."

She slides a packet across the table towards me.

"Salted almonds," she says as I warily pick it up. "I used to eat them all the time when I was pregnant with you."

I clutch the packet. "Thanks," I say quietly, pulling the packet off the table.

We descend into silence again as I play with the packet on my lap, my fingers tracing the sharp edge of the plastic, teasing my skin with the threat of a cut.

"So," Mum begins again, "how have your doctor's appointments been? Have you been going to them?"

"Yes, I've been going to my appointments," I mumble, teenage angst rushing to the surface. I swallow it down, and relay her with all I can; measurements, scans, what foods I am or am not eating.

Our food arrives, and we lapse into silence.

"Can you let Dad know we love the crib?" I ask around a bite of mushroom pasta. "It's perfect in the nursery."

"What crib?" Her wrists fall to the table with a clatter of bracelets, as if she's lost the energy to hold them aloft.

She has no idea what I'm talking about.

"Oh." I gulp some water. "Dad brought us a crib just before Christmas, so Jackson brought it to our new place. It's all set up, and we designed the rest of the room around it. It's...it's nice." I trail off awkwardly.

We lapse into silence again, the only sounds the scraping of cutlery on the plates and the hum of our neighbors' conversation.

"And Jackson," Mum asks finally. "How is he?"

I'm grateful for a subject to jump on to, so I tell her all I can about Jackson. His job, his wonderful family, the way he's been there for every step of this pregnancy and how I couldn't have done it without him. She jumps in with questions, even laughs occasionally, and it's pleasant. It's also the longest we've spoken without animosity, or addressing the elephant in the room.

"This was nice," I say to her as we step outside the restaurant a few hours later. I'm still not ready to suggest we do it again, but it wasn't the worst.

"I'd like to throw you a baby shower," she says quickly, as if she's been thinking about it for a while.

"Oh," I say, surprised. I was almost ready to give up on the thought of a shower. Pip wanted to throw me one, but I think a part of me wanted my mother to at least be there, so it was easier to just put it off.

"If you'd like that."

I bite my lip. "Uh... sure, that would be really nice. Nothing too crazy or anything, though."

"Really?" Mum brightens, her eyes crinkling.

I nod. "I have a few friends who've been wanting to throw one so I guess I should."

"How about two weeks on Saturday?"

I do some quick maths, calculating how close that is to my due date, which sits in my mental calendar in a big red circle.

"Yeah, that should work."

"Wonderful," Mum breathes before she steps forward and wraps her arms around me, leaning awkwardly around my bump. The familiar scent of her Dior perfume envelops me, and my eyes burn. I can't remember the last time I got a hug from her.

She pulls back with a bright smile.

"Mum," I swallow thickly. The next words I say will likely ruin everything, start an argument or cause the whole shower to disappear in front of my eyes, but I have to. "I don't want Cleo to be there."

Her smile falls. "What do you mean?"

I straighten my back and rest my hand on my belly. "I don't want her to be there. That's my condition. I won't come otherwise."

Mum sighs heavily, disappointment evident in her voice.

"Fine, Rosalie, if that's what you want." She throws her hands up. "But she's your sister, I don't kno—"

"Mum," I plead. "She's not even apologized for what she did."

"Rosie, I'm not getting in the middle." The familiar saying from my childhood rings in my ears.

Thankfully, my car pulls up alongside me, "Look, I'm not going to fight with you about it," I say, "But I mean it—I won't go if Cleo's there."

Mum huffs as she helps me into the car. "Yes yes, I hear you. Email me your friends details so I can get the invites out to them too."

"I will," I say as I buckle in.

"I'll see you then," Mum says before she shuts the door.

I have the long drive home to ponder if that was a terrible decision or not.

41

JACKSON

THE SHOOT GOT EXTENDED BY ALMOST A MONTH DUE TO THE change in personnel. It's the only regret I have about the whole thing, even though my double Petyr pulled off every impressive stunt without a hit. I watched from the sidelines, but instead of jealousy, I just felt relief that he made it to the ground safely each time.

The film is officially wrapped, and I'm only a few hours away from my girl being in my arms. We've spoken everyday, but any time away is hard, especially these last few weeks. All I want to do now is end every day with her hair tickling my chin and Smudge kicking against my palm.

Wrapping any project is hard. I usually spend the immediate aftermath replaying every scene I've done over the last six months until I'm convinced I am the worst actor in the world. I usually want to stay close to the director, ready to jump back into re-shoots as soon as I can. But this time, I couldn't get my costume off quick enough.

The drive isn't long, and it's barely any time at all before we pull up outside the house.

Eric rounds the car to help me drag my suitcase out

of the trunk, and I offer him my hand. "Hey man, thanks for everything on this one. You've been a life-saver, truly."

"If you ever need—I mean, if you ever want me to work with you again..." Eric stammers.

"You'll be my number one call, Eric," I tell him as I shoulder the door open. "I owe you."

The gravel crunches underneath my feet as I cross the driveway. The lights are on downstairs and I resist the urge to peer in like a creep.

"Where are you, pretty girl?" I call out as I cross the threshold.

I hear a gasp from the direction of the living room and can't stop the warmth blooming in my chest.

"I'm in here!" I hear Rosie call. I toe off my boots and follow her voice.

She's sat on the sofa, a blanket wrapped around her lap, and her big eyes hidden behind her glasses.

I cross to her and rest my hands on the arm of the sofa. "There you are," I say as I press a kiss to her lips. I want to sink into her, feel her soft body pressed against me, but I'm careful not to crush her.

She smiles against my lips as I press kisses along her jaw. "I missed you," I murmur against her skin.

Her hands slide up my forearms until she clutches my biceps. "I missed you too," she whispers against my lips.

I fall to my knees before her and finally catch my breath before tugging the blanket away from her lap.

Her bump looks bigger. I can't believe I've been gone for nearly a month and missed so much.

"Don't say anything," Rosie groans. "I'm huge now."

I frame her bump with my hands, gently pulling her t-shirt higher. I trace my fingers across the gentle line that spans from her belly button and disappears into her underwear.

"Beautiful," I whisper reverently. I press a kiss to her bump, to the only thing separating me from our daughter. "Hi, baby girl."

Rosie entwines our fingers before tugging my hand to the side more. "She's over here."

What once was a little flutter is now a veritable kick that I can feel against my hands.

"Ouch," Rosie hisses.

I press another kiss to where I found her little foot. "It's like whack-a-mole."

Rosie snorts, rubbing her face with her hands. "I changed my mind. I haven't missed you at all."

"Such a liar," I purr, rising to my feet and sliding in beside her on the sofa.

"Are you okay?" Rosie asks, scratching her nails through my hair.

I nod. "Better now."

"Have you heard anything about Tony?"

I close my eyes as she combs my hair back. "A bit. Mostly Kaia's been sending me updates. He's been in and out of it apparently, although he's starting to stay awake longer now."

"That's good," Rosie whispers, pressing a kiss to my head. "I'm glad you didn't do those stunts," she confesses quietly.

"I am too," I murmur as I press a kiss to her lips and cradle Smudge between us. It was worth it for this.

We stay like that for hours, until Rosie's stomach grumbles enough that I start cooking. I've actually perfected my culinary skills under her watchful eye, and it's easy for me to rustle up a risotto.

"I'm going to go visit Tony tomorrow, do you want to join

me?" I call over my shoulder as I load the dishwasher. I don't hear anything so I peer at her from across the island where she's perched on a stool. "Rosie?"

"Uhm, I'm busy tomorrow."

"What are you doing?"

"It's my baby shower."

I'm momentarily confused. Did I forget?

She must see the question on my face, because she says, "It's a last minute thing."

"Where is it?"

"Uhm, I don't know."

Okay, now there's definitely something weird going on.

"What time is it?"

"Uh, afternoon?"

"Rosie."

"Hmm?"

"What's going on?"

"Nothing's going on."

"Why are you being so secretive about a baby shower? What am I missing?"

Rosie sighs and leans back in her chair.

I round the island and lean back against it, crossing my arms.

She tilts her head back. "Mum's planning it."

My arms fall to my sides. "*Oh*." I rub my beard. "I didn't realize you were talking to her."

"I'm not," Rosie says. "Well, I am. Sort of. She was outside my office the other week and we went for dinner and she offered to host it. I felt so guilty that I've not spoken to her in months, and Pip and Anya have been on at me to have a shower, and mum looked so excited when I said yes. I told her about the crib dad got us, so I think she wanted to do something too."

"Hey," I say, crossing to the table and pulling out the chair beside her. "It's okay Rosie, you don't have to explain anything to me. Why was she outside your office?"

She shrugs. "She said she hadn't been able to reach me."

"You blocked her?"

She shakes her head.

Rosie hasn't changed her number and I even gave Terry mine, so why wouldn't she have been able to reach us?

"Are you...excited?" I ask, taking her hands in mine.

"Yeah," she says, *very* convincingly.

I trace my thumbs across her knuckles as I think about how to phrase the next question. "Cleo, is she...?"

"No." Rosie shakes her head. "No, I made it very clear that she wasn't allowed to be there. And Mum even invited the girls to come come."

I nod. "Does your mum know them?"

"No, but she asked for Anya's email and forwarded the invite."

"Hmm," I say, still rubbing my beard.

"What?" Rosie asks, eyes narrowing behind her glasses.

"Nothing," I reassure her.

"You think I shouldn't go."

"No! No, of course I don't think that. I want you to have a baby shower and be spoiled by all your friends. I've wanted that for you for weeks. I just think it's...suspicious."

"Suspicious," she deadpans.

"Not suspicious then, that's the wrong word. I just have a feeling."

"A feeling," Rosie says flatly.

I nod. "I just don't trust it."

"You don't trust *me*?" She slides to her feet.

"No!" God, this conversation has run away from me. "Of

course I trust you Rosie, but it's your mother I don't trust. I just think she might be taking advantage."

"Right," Rosie says, pushing her chair back from the table. "And you think I'm too naive to not notice if someone is trying to take advantage of me."

"No, hell no. Rosie, I'm just trying to protect you."

"Well I don't need protection from my own mother, Jackson," she snaps, placing her hands on her hips.

I could back down, I could apologize and diffuse the tension with a joke, but there's something in my gut that's telling me that something is off.

"Rosie," I say, crossing my arms across my chest. "I just think you should conside—"

"Don't stand there with that Dad stare. It's not going to work."

I mirror her with my hands on my hips. "I don't know why we're arguing about this, Rosie. I'm just trying—"

"Well, stop trying," she snaps. "I'm going to bed."

She turns and storms out of the kitchen, her ponytail swishing behind her.

"Do you need me to help—"

"No," she snaps, over her shoulder.

"Okay then," I say, running my hands through my hair. *That went well.*

42

ROSIE

I FIDDLE WITH THE FABRIC AROUND MY STOMACH, TUGGING IT away from my body as if it could hide my thirty-eight week shape. The material is soft and lightweight, one of the many Pip sent as options when we went out to dinner before Christmas. This is the only one that I even had a hope would fit at this point.

I wipe my sweaty palms on the skirt, liking how it fits along my legs.

I feel pretty, more pretty than I've felt for the past few weeks.

"Beautiful," Jackson says from behind me. I glance in the floor length mirror and see him leaning against the bedroom door.

I fight the blush that rises to my cheeks. "You like it?"

He prowls towards me, wrapping his arms around me and cradling my heavy stomach with his hands as he takes some of the weight. He presses a kiss to my temple, and I can't help but sink into his arms. "You always look beautiful."

I tilt up slightly, pressing a kiss to his lips.

"Are you—" he starts before cutting himself off with a sigh.

I pull away slightly, stepping out of his embrace and into my trainers. Not the perfect vibe with the dress, but my boots no longer fit past my ankles and it's too cold for sandals.

In the mirror, I can see his hands resting on his hips as I balance on the drawers to step into my shoes.

With a huff, he drops to his knees, gently lifts my leg and helps me slide them onto my feet one at a time.

I hold onto his broad shoulders as he takes his time lacing each shoe, and I can't help but let my hands explore his shoulders, reaching the strands of hair that curl around his nape. Now he's wrapped the film, he can cut his hair, but I selfishly don't want him to.

I barely slept last night. Smudge kept kicking my organs to the point where I would wake up every few hours in pain, and then I'd lie there with Jackson next to me, overthinking this whole plan.

Mum knows not to invite Cleo, right? She wouldn't put me through that again. She's just being a mum.

I swallow against my dry throat before looking into Jackson's dark, worry filled eyes. "I'm going."

He looks up at me from his knees, reading the firm expression on my face. He's ready to argue more, ready to push his point, but something on my face must tell him I'm still not budging.

He presses a kiss to my wrist.

"Okay, pretty girl. It's your decision, but glitterball me if you need an escape plan okay?"

I can't help the smile that cracks across my face. It started out as a joke, but I know he's serious. All I need to do is send a code word, and he'll come running. It's something I can imagine our daughter using in the future, the guarantee that he'll be there whenever she calls. "Glitterball." I nod seriously as my phone buzzes on the bed.

"It's Mum," I tell Jackson. "She's outside. I'll meet her outside the gate."

If Jackson has a problem with me sharing our address, he doesn't say anything, just silently follows me down the stairs and helps me into my coat, wrapping my scarf around my neck like a mother hen.

"I don't know how long I'll be," I tell him as I pull my hair from the collar.

He nods. "Danny invited me to watch the rugby, so I'll swing by there after the hospital."

"Don't forget the bag in the kitchen. It's just some cookies for Kaia and Masen. It's not much but..." I made them this morning before starting to get ready, so they were still warm when I put them in the Tupperware.

"Thank you, baby. I'm sure they'll love them." He presses a kiss to my lips and I melt into his arms.

"I have to go," I smile against his mouth as he groans.

"Okay, just send me a text when you're on your way home or if you need me to come pick you up. And if you're in any pain or just get too tired or—"

I reach up on my tiptoes and press another kiss to his lips. "Stop fussing. I'll be fine." At least I hope I will be. "Plus, the girls will be there for backup."

He relaxes slightly as I open the door, stepping out into the damp afternoon. The sky is still suspiciously gray with barely a hint of sun, but at least it's stopped raining.

Our feet crunch on the gravel as we slowly cross the driveway to my mother's familiar silver hatchback.

I wave awkwardly as Jackson tugs the gate open over my

head, and I can see her leaning across the seats to gape at the house.

Jackson tugs the car door open. "Hi Andrea," he says gruffly as he helps me lower myself into my seat.

"Hello," Mum says stiffly, settling back in her seat. "If I'm not allowed out of the car then the least you can do is keep the heat in, Rosie."

Jackson glances at me as he rests his forearm on the door. "Glitterball?" he murmurs.

I bite my lip before shaking my head. "I'll text you in a bit."

"Alright," he says, pressing a final kiss to my lips. "Have fun," he tells me with an encouraging smile.

If I didn't know how stressed out he was, I'd almost laugh at his overprotectiveness.

"I'll see you later."

The door's barely closed before the car is rolling away from the house.

It's tense. Immediately.

I keep my hands clasped on my lap and I keep my head turned to the window.

"You've done well for yourself then, Rosalie. Your big house and your rich boyfriend. Might as well return the gifts." She gestures behind her, and I spot a pink parcel wrapped on the seat.

Her words chafe but I can't help the thrill that lightens my chest. That box is definitely bigger than a gift card.

I turn back to face the front, feeling excitement rather than anxiety bubble in my chest for the first time all morning.

I reach for my handbag to grab my phone to text the group chat. It's barely in my hand before Mum says, "It's rude to ignore me when I've driven all this way to pick you up, Rosie."

Chastised, I place my phone back inside and zip up the bag.

"Sorry," I say, placing it back by my feet. "How was the drive?"

Mum spends the rest of the journey complaining about the two hour drive to get to my house.

I bite my tongue instead of reminding her that I could have arranged a car. Hell, I would have walked there to get out of the awkwardness at this point.

We pull the car to a stop by a large glass hotel. I glance up at the sleek building.

It's not what I would have picked for my baby shower, that's for sure. I would have booked out a small restaurant, or just done it in my living room. But the garden gate was far enough. I'm still not ready to open my home to my mother until she proves that she won't take advantage.

"Come on," she says quickly, darting out the car. It takes me longer than usual to escape the car, having to ungracefully heave myself out, and causing a twinge of pain in my back.

Suddenly, a firm hand is clasped around mine as my mother helps me out of the car. I can feel the rings on the back of her slim fingers, the jewels nudging at my knuckles as her bracelets clang together. I can't remember the last time I held my mother's hand. It must have been as a child, but one day we just stopped, and I never held her hand again.

My eyes mist as I consider the concept of picking up my baby for the last time, even though she's not even here yet.

I blink back my blurry vision as Mum drops my hand and reaches into the back seat for the gift bag.

"This way," she says, tightening her coat around her.

I shake off whatever moment I just had and follow her through the glass revolving door.

The lobby is wide and marble, Mum's heeled boots clicking on the floor as she crosses to the lift. She glances left and right like she's on the run before darting into the lift as soon as the doors open, holding them open for me to follow. I hope I don't have to chase her around the building. I may be in trainers but I am in no position to do anything more than a slow, gentle walk.

Mum pulls out her phone and taps on the screen as I watch the numbers increase until we reach what must be the top floor. I lean against the wall as Smudge twirls in my belly.

I wonder if Anya is already here. She said she'd be arriving a bit later, but maybe it's a ploy and she's waiting to surprise me.

I follow mum out of the lift, and she heads to a temporary rail resting next to the door with more than a dozen coats already on it.

They must be here already. I shrug out of my coat and place it on the rack next to a leopard print, faux fur, winter coat. I know by the feel of the synthetic fibers that Pip has nothing to do with *this* garment.

I hook my bag back on my shoulder but mum's hand is there before it settles, tugging it off my shoulder and hanging it on the rack, "You don't need that, come on. Hurry up, it's started."

How has it started if I haven't even arrived yet?

I rub my hand over my belly one more time, feeling Smudge shuffle as if to tell me she's here with me, before following my mother into the room.

And greet my sister.

43

JACKSON

I'M USED TO SEEING TONY IN HARNESSES, DANGLING FROM wires or covered in protective guards. I'm not used to seeing him flat on his bed, his body tightly braced with medical equipment to help the healing process.

"Looking good, bro," I say, peering over the bed until I catch his eye.

"Get lost," Tony says, coughing out a laugh and rolling his eyes.

I take a seat beside his bedside, resting my bag on the floor.

"Thanks for coming," Tony says. "I've had an itch on my nose that I've not been able to scratch since Kaia left an hour ago."

I dutifully lean over and rub his nose. "What would seventeen-year-old us think if we told them that one day we'd be comfortable enough to scratch each other's appendages?"

Tony snickers. "Why do you have to make everything weird all the time?"

I sit back in the chair with a shrug. "It's just who I am."

"How's the job?"

I rub my hand over my beard. "I uh…" I start. "I've paused the stunts for a while."

Tony peers at me from the corner of his eye, but says nothing.

I lean forward, resting my elbows on my knees. "I just—Rosie and the baby, y'know."

"I get it."

I hear Tony's rattling breath. "I like to think if I could go back in time, I would've walked away the minute Kaia asked me to, but I don't know that I would. I think I'd somehow end up convincing myself that I was invincible and that I could somehow still do the job, keep my family and not end up," he sighs, "here."

"Tony," I say, reaching my hand to his bed but not wanting to touch him in case it hurts.

Tony takes a deep breath, but I can see the tear roll from his eye. "This is my wake up call, Jackie. I'm not giving up on my family, or my life. I'll do what the doctors order and do all my rehab and *live*. And somehow make it up to Kaia."

I laugh. "Good luck with that one."

"He's already working on it," I hear from the doorway. I rise to my feet as Kaia crosses the room, but she leans down to press a kiss to Tony's temple.

"Dad, look what I got from the gift shop!" Masen barrels into the room behind his mother. "It's a book about aerospace dynamics."

"Wow," Tony says earnestly as Masen crowds his bed and holds the book perpendicular to his dad's head so he can see.

Kaia crosses to my side and I pull her into a hug. "Hey Jackie, thanks for coming. And thanks for…everything."

I loop my arm over her shoulder. "Nothing to thank me for," I say gruffly as she gently wipes a tear from her cheek.

I nod my head to the tote bag resting beside my chair. "Rosie sent me with some supplies. I hope you like cookies because there's a lot of them in there."

Kaia laughs softly. "She seems lovely."

"Yeah, when are you going to introduce me?" Tony says as Masen lowers the book an inch. "Are you worried she'll realize she got the worst looking guy out of the bunch?"

"You wish," I retort as Kaia snickers. "She couldn't come today, anyway. It's her baby shower."

"Why do you sound miserable about it?" Kaia asks.

I sigh. "I just have a bad feeling. Her mother's hosting it for her." I wave my hand. "It's a whole thing, but I'm sure it'll be fine."

"Go show Uncle Jackie. He *loves* aerospace dynamics" I hear Tony say before Masen rushes to my side to show me his encyclopedia.

The hospital is close enough to our house that by the time I get to Danny's house for the match, it's only been a few hours since Rosie left. I check my phone as I walk up to his door but there's no messages.

No news is good news, I remind myself as I knock on the door.

Still, I send her a text just to be sure.

ME

How's it going?

I can't even see if it's delivered by the time Danny swings the door open, so I pocket my phone and try to avoid the feeling in my gut that something's off.

44

ROSIE

I FREEZE HALF WAY THROUGH THE DOOR, MY SHOULDERS locking and my stomach sinking to my feet.

"Glad you could make it." Cleo sends me the look I've been greeted with every day since I can remember. A smirk pulls at the corners of her lips, her eyes glittering with the laughter I know will be cruel.

I turn to my mother, questions that don't even need to be asked heavy in the air between us.

She doesn't look at me, her gaze darting around as if she can look at every other person in the room before she can look me in the eyes.

"What's going on?" I ask, hating the way my voice shakes.

"It's your baby shower, silly," Cleo says, turning to me and placing her arm through mine. She tugs me out of the doorway and further into the room. Her phone is in her hand, held up and snapping a picture before I can even blink.

I glance around, finally taking in the surroundings of my

own personal hell. Pastel everywhere, fake pink foliage dotted around the room and dozens of tiered cake stands on doily-covered tables filled with finger food and cold cut meats. There's a guy dressed in black with a camera in hand, zooming in and out of the puff pastries before spinning his camera towards the window.

I skip over the sea of women I've never seen before in my life, desperately searching for a friendly face.

Who *are* these people? And where the hell are my friends?

I glance over my shoulder to see my mother smiling with two women who might have just wandered in off the street for all I know, but she doesn't glance in my direction. Cleo ushers me into an oversized pink armchair that's so soft I basically collapse into it before she turns back to the camera team with a smile.

"Make sure you get a clear shot of the collagen water," Cleo orders them. "The brand wants it to be the thumbnail."

I struggle to get off our sofa at home without Jackson levering me off, so I have no hope of getting out of this contraption.

I take a deep breath to calm my racing heart.

Okay, Rosie, this is fine. Anya will be here soon, I just need to text her—

I groan under my breath as I remember exactly where my phone is and I stare mournfully at the door.

The blonde woman to the right of me shifts in her seat, her leather trousers crinkling against the fabric and I turn to her as if maybe she could help me get up. I'm not above begging a stranger at this point just to help me get out of here.

"Hey—" I start, but before I get any further she stands

with a graceful hair flick and teeters away from me on six inch wedges before walking over to Cleo.

I see my sister glance at me before she turns her attention back to the blonde with a giggle.

My face heats as I glance around desperately. Where is Anya?

My back aches from the awkward position I've found myself in, and I move around until it eases slightly, shifting my weight further into the chair.

I tilt my head back in the armchair and stare at the ceiling, willing the tears to stay in my eyes.

What did I really expect? I should have seen this coming. Why did I think there would be one day where my mother would actually do something nice for *me?*

Now, I'm literally trapped in a room full of people I've never met, as Cleo takes photos holding a bottle of collagen water for what I'm sure is a hefty brand deal, and I'm already blending in with the armchair that's holding me hostage.

I don't know how long passes without anyone crossing my path. I gave up trying to get Mum's attention after her first fly-by without even glancing in my direction.

I keep staring at the door, hoping Anya will walk through any second, but it hasn't opened since I arrived.

"Okay, everyone, it's time for games," Cleo announces, clapping her hands and walking towards me.

I imagine her heel snapping underneath her, or a ceiling tile dropping on her head, or a pigeon flying through the window and shitting directly on top of her sleek curls. As if she can read my thoughts, her lips twist in that familiar smirk.

"First game is guess the size of the belly," she announces,

holding up a tailor's tape and letting it roll out. "Oh," she snickers, as the length cuts off less than thirty centimeters from her finger. "I don't think this one will fit. Wait, let me try a different one." This time, her tape unfurls from her hand and the length disappears under a nearby seat. "Still not enough! I am just *so* bad at this game!"

Giggles erupt around me as the words find their mark. I shift my arms to cover my stomach and sink further in my seat, desperately trying to keep the tears from falling.

The feeling is familiar, the humiliation that bubbles in my chest when Cleo and her friends would laugh when I tagged along shopping with them and couldn't find clothes that fit. It didn't matter that I grew into my weight as I got older, didn't matter that I had what Nanny called 'womanly curves', I was bigger than my sister, and that was enough. Between Cleo's laughter and my mother's criticism, the cruel thoughts settled across my body like concrete, weighing me down until I flattened myself into an acceptable shape.

I want to shrink in on myself, melt into the armchair beneath me, until everyone stops looking at me.

But then, I remember the way Jackson held me in front of our mirror and worshiped my body, the way he grabbed my thick thighs and wound them around his back as he effortlessly picked me up. The man loves my body, he tells me every time he can't let me go, when he kneels at my feet and gazes up at me with admiration.

Smudge kicks at me, reminding me that she's in there. That my body has changed to grow my baby girl.

Rage pierces my insides, boiling through the humiliation and turning to liquid fury to match my scorching cheeks.

I've had more than enough of this. I love my thighs and

my belly that's expanding to grow my baby. I've always loved the way I looked in that birthday dress and I can't wait to wear it again. Why do I care what Cleo thinks? Why have I ever let her words dictate how I feel about myself?

I grab hold of the two armrests and brace my feet on the ground, successfully levering myself up.

I close my eyes and breathe as my stomach cramps from exertion. Shoving my shoulders back, I keep my eyes on the exit as I storm past the crowd.

Just as I'm about to reach the door, it blows open and Anya storms in, her face like thunder. Her eyes widen just slightly before I basically collapse into her arms.

"Where the hell have you been?" I ask, voice shaking. I hold tightly to her elbows as pain shoots down my spine.

Anya's vibrating. "I knew it," she says, gaze locking on Cleo across the room. "We were given the wrong fucking address. We spent an hour waiting in a restaurant in Clapham before we realized something was up. You weren't answering your phone."

"It's in my bag," I whisper.

Anya waves a hand. "We figured that out too, don't worry."

"Rosie, darling, we've been looking–" Pip says, peering around Anya.

"Oh my god," a voice squeals from behind me. "It's Cassandra!"

Suddenly our small group is swarmed by the hoard of women all vying to get a piece of Cassie.

Cassie sends me a wide eyed look. "Friends of yours?"

I shake my head mutely as she gets swallowed up by a swarm. My head is almost fuzzy and I bite back a moan.

"What do you want to do Rosie?" Anya places her hands

on her hips, brown eyes glaring around the room. "I will fight all of these bitches if I have to."

"You should probably help her." I gesture to Cassie's red curls that we can barely see through the crowd of raised iPhones and blow outs.

Anya nods before spinning to face the crowd. "Okay girls, back away from the celebrity. Have some self respect, *please.*"

Anya dives into the crowd, and I finally take a deep breath, my hand resting on my stomach.

"You okay Rosie? You look flushed," Pip says, gently clasping my elbow.

"I'm ready to get out of here."

"You got it, darling. Let me get your coat." Pip leaves me and I brace my hand on the wall to my left as my back cramps.

"This is why you let *me* throw the parties," Pip chastises with a gentle smile as she reappears with my coat. "Afternoon tea? Original."

I laugh. "I wish I'd let you." Pip helps me shrug my coat on, tugging my hair free from the collar.

"Pip Covington?" A simpering voice says from behind me. "Thanks so much for coming."

I straighten my back and turn to face my sister, who has her hand outstretched to Pip. She doesn't even acknowledge me, her gaze fixed totally on the supermodel standing next to me.

"I'm so sorry about the girls," Cleo gestures her hand towards the group still circling Cassie. "You know how they can be. Some people just let the fame overwhelm them. If it's okay with you, there's a great spot in the corner where we can take some photos. The lighting is great, and I know my followers would *love* to see you."

Pip's fan-ready smile fades on her face as she glances at my wide eyes with a question of her own.

"My sister," I say flatly, refusing to even acknowledge her name.

For a second, the familiar fear lodges in my throat. That Pip will be taken in by her just like people always are. But instead, my beautiful friend's eyes narrow as she hooks her arm through mine.

"I've heard all about you," she says in a sharp tone I've never heard before.

"Good things I hope?" Cleo titters, flicking her hair away from her face.

"Is there anything good to say?" Pip asks, tilting her head. I hide a snort behind my hand.

Cleo blinks in shock, glancing to me and our entwined arms before crossing her arms across her chest.

"I don't know what—" Cleo starts, but I cut her off.

"That's enough, Cleo," I snap. "I always thought you were cruel, but now I'm starting to think you're delusional on top of it."

Cleo gapes at me, but I don't stop.

"My entire life I've just been your personal punching bag, a way for you to feel better about yourself by tearing me down. But you know what I've realized? I have a life that's happy and full of people that love me for who I am, and no cruel little pranks or snide comments will take away from that."

"Rosa-pee—" Cleo starts.

"And *enough* with that nickname. You know how much I hate it, but you still say it. You're my sister, and you've always been like this, so I just got used to it. But I'm done. I'm going to walk out of here with my friends and go home to a man who loves me and I'll never speak to you again. I'm going to be a partner and a friend and a mother, but all you'll ever be is a vicious fucking bully."

Cleo gapes like a fish, her cheeks reddening as she glances around for someone to save her.

My mother appears like an apparition, suddenly right in front of me as if she hasn't been blending into the wallpaper all afternoon.

"*Rosalie Taylor*," Mum hisses. "How dare you say that to your sister?"

I raise my eyebrows. "What happened to 'it's none of your business', 'you're sisters, work it out between you'." I scoff. "*Now* you get involved? When I finally stand up for myself?"

I bark a sarcastic laugh and rub my hand across my face.

"Jackson was right. He knew you were planning something like this. I was just so desperate for you to love me that I ignored all the warning signs."

"This is not the time or the place," Mum says with a fake smile, glancing around at the crowd of women peering at us. "You're making a scene."

I roll my eyes. "I don't even know the names of any of these people. I couldn't care less if they hear what a horrible mother you've been and how you raised an evil witch."

Anya snorts behind me as she, Cassie and Pip flank my sides.

"I'm done with this," I say, throwing my hands up. "Thanks for the world's worst party."

I turn and storm out of the room as fast as I can, sensing my friends following behind me.

"I think I'm in love with you," Cassie says as I push the button for the elevator.

"Rosie!" Anya squeals. "That was the most badass thing

I've ever heard. Evil witch," she snickers. "I'm going to comment that on all of her Instagram posts."

"We need to celebrate." Pip says excitedly. "Let's go back to mine. I can throw a *real* party."

"Sounds great," I bite out around a whimper. "But we should probably go to the hospital first."

Three pairs of wide eyes turn to me.

"I think I'm in labor."

45

JACKSON

It's half time. And I still haven't heard from Rosie.

"You sure you don't want a beer?" Danny says as he settles beside me on the sofa.

"Nah, I'm good, thank you. Need to be sober in case I get the Glitterball." I say, glancing at my phone.

"The glitter—what?"

My phone rings, but it's not Rosie's name on the screen.

"Anya?" I answer, shooting a puzzled look at Danny, who shrugs.

"Jackson! Okay, oh my God, so much has happened over here. Yeah—" her voice becomes muffled as she pulls the phone away from her face.

"Anya?" I bark, rising to my feet. "Anya, what's going on?"

"Well, first of all, Rosie's *evil witch* of a sister hijacked the party!"

I squeeze the bridge of my nose with my hands. I knew it.

"But then Rosie stood up for herself like a badass. It was so amazing, Jackson. You'd have fallen in love with her all over again if you'd seen it."

I smile. "I fall in love with her every day."

"Aww, Rosie, he said—" Anya pulls away again, and I can hear muffled voices in the background. "—I was getting there!" I can't help but laugh at the chaotic way Anya is relaying any sort of helpful information, but my laughter freezes in my chest at her next words. "So, Rosie's in labor."

"*What?*" I shout down the phone.

"Yeah, so we're heading to the hospital now," Anya says.

"Put her on the phone," I say to Anya, trying to remain calm as I hurry to the front door and desperately try to locate my shoes.

"Hi," Rosie's pained voice whimpers down the line.

I swallow. "Hey pretty girl, sounds like you've had an eventful day."

I hear her soft laugh on the other end. "Is it too late to glitterball?"

"I'm on my way, baby. I'll meet you there."

Rosie's hair is plastered to her flushed face, and she tries to take a calming breath that comes out shaky.

"You're doing so good, pretty girl," I praise, wiping her hair away from her face and pressing a kiss to the hand that is squeezing mine too tightly.

"How are you feeling, Rosie?" our midwife, Julie, asks with a smile as she opens the door to the hospital room.

An agonized groan is all that she gets in response.

I glance at Julie. "Is there anything you can give her?"

Julie smiles cheerfully from the bottom of the bed. "Let's take a look at you, pet, and we can see what's what."

Rosie nods shakily, taking a deep breath from the gas and air machine.

She briefly lets go of my hand to readjust her hospital gown, and I use the opportunity to flex my aching fingers. My girl is strong as hell.

Raised voices from the hall catch both of our attention.

"No way," says a voice that sounds suspiciously like Anya.

I glance down at Rosie, but she's barely registered the commotion, her eyes closed as she rides out her pain.

"What on earth?" Julie mutters, glancing towards the door.

"She's my daughter. I'm going in there," says the other voice. Andrea.

Rosie's panicked eyes open and latch on mine. "Oh God."

I clasp her flailing hand in mine. "What do you want me to do baby? I'll do it."

Rosie bites her lip as a contraction tears through her body. "Get her out of here," she pants.

I wait until her fingers relax their death grip on my hand before I stand from my seat and press a kiss to her head. "I'll be back in a minute."

Julie sends me a comforting look before she takes a seat between Rosie's spread legs.

I march to the door, swinging it open and taking in the scene in front of me.

Anya is starfished against the door, blocking a red faced Andrea and a pale Terry from entering. I tap Anya's shoulder gently. "Can you sit with Rosie for a second?"

Anya nods her head, shooting a glare at Andrea before ducking under my arm.

"Rosie's sleeping," I say.

Andrea huffs peering into the room as the door swings closed. "Her eyes are open."

"That's how she sleeps."

I raise my arms and start to usher the pair further down the corridor and further away from Rosie.

Irritation flares in my gut. I want to be inside the room with my girlfriend, feeding her ice chips and words of encouragement instead of out here having this conversation. "You both need to leave," I say, guiding them back towards the waiting room.

"I'm her mother. She needs me."

I clench my jaw.

"I don't know why that girl had the nerve to stop me. I had to find out from the staff at the hotel that my own daughter had gone into labor, can you imagine? And the way she spoke to me at her party—"

She tries to brush past my arm and I finally snap. "You being here is not helping Rosie. She doesn't want you here."

Her jaw drops, her slim cheeks gaunt as my words settle in the empty corridor. She flusters for a response, but I raise my hand.

"Enough. I don't want to hear it. I know the stunt you pulled earlier, and I know how you've treated the woman I love for her entire life. Rosie has asked that you stay away whilst she's in labor, and I'm here to make sure you respect her wishes."

"How *dare* you? I'm going in that room whether you like it or not," Andrea seethes, before turning to her husband. "I knew she'd pull a childish stunt like this. I don't know how she's ever going to be a good moth—"

"*Andrea*," Terry snaps, and I'm glad he does because I was more than ready to. "That's enough. I can't do this anymore. I've stood by and let you walk all over that girl her entire life because I thought it was better to not get involved. But I won't stand here and let you speak like that about my daughter when she's next door in agony. I'm ashamed of myself for not doing this before now."

It's the most passionate I've ever heard the man speak, and I'm momentarily convinced I'm hallucinating.

"Terry," Andrea gapes. "What—"

"I want a divorce." Terry announces, standing just that bit taller.

I glance between the two before deciding it's not my circus and these two are definitely not my monkeys. I slowly back away until I'm back in the delivery room.

"*Get over here,*" Rosie wails, and I cross the room in seconds until I'm by her side.

SEVEN HOURS and thirty five minutes later there's tears in my eyes and a bundle in Rosie's arms.

"You did so good, baby," I choke out, pressing a kiss to her head. "I'm so proud of you."

Rosie sobs as she clutches our daughter to her chest, and I think my heart is about to burst straight out of mine.

I wrap my arm around them both. My girls.

Our daughter opens her eyes, and her wails slowly settle until she's staring up at us with big, curious eyes.

"Hi there," Rosie breathes, tracing her finger across her smooth cheek.

"Hi, baby girl," I say, catching her roving hand with mine. Her tiny fingers clench around my thumb, and I know I'm going to be wrapped around this girl's finger for the rest of my life.

I bury my head in Rosie's hair as the tears flood my eyes. My hand covers hers and the tiny body underneath it. "I love you, Rosie," I say as I gently nudge her nose with mine. "I love you so much."

Rosie presses a wet kiss to my lips. "I love you too."

"Now what do we do?" I whisper.

"I don't know." Rosie laughs wetly.

"She's beautiful," Julie asks, peering over the bed. "Have you decided on a name?"

Rosie glances up at me with an encouraging smile.

"Olive." I say, throat thick, "Olive Elizabeth."

Rosie glances up at me with shining eyes. It was her idea to honor my father and I love her for it more than I ever have. It was my suggestion that we make Betty a namesake too.

It's only later, when all our friends have been sent the appropriate pictures and Olive has finally been allowed to leave our arms, that I leave Rosie dozing in bed, her arm protectively curled around the bassinet next to her.

I step outside, ready to call my mother, when I spot a figure in the waiting room.

It's late, nearly four in the morning, and the ward is quiet.

I stop at a vending machine and buy two drinks before taking a seat next to Terry.

"Here, Granddad." I hand him one of the bottles and he looks up in surprise.

"She had the baby?" he asks, his voice breaking.

I nod, unable to keep the pride from my voice as I tell him, "Olive Elizabeth."

He nods his head until he's leaning forward, his head in his hands. I gently tap his back as sobs rack his body.

"I'm sorry," he says, sitting back up straight and taking a steadying breath. "I'm sorry. Olive, that's a beautiful name."

I smile at him. "She's beautiful. And Rosie did so well. Twelve and a half hours in total."

"Jesus," Terry winces, wiping his eyes with the back of his hand. "I'm so..." He raises his hands in front of him helplessly before dropping them with a shrug.

"I didn't realize you'd still be here."

He shrugs. "Andrea left eventually, but I just couldn't." He glances back up the corridor. "Do you think she'll ever forgive me?" he asks quietly.

I sigh, rubbing my hand over my beard. "That's not for me to say." My phone buzzes in my hand. "I have to get this." I gesture to the phone.

Terry nods. "I'll wait here. She doesn't have to see me, but I'll just like to wait. If that's okay?"

I nod. "I'll let her know when she wakes up."

"Jackson," Terry says when I turn my back. "Don't make my mistakes."

"Never," I vow.

Bringing my phone to my ear, I tell my mother about her new grandchild.

46

ROSIE

4 months later

JACKSON HOLDS THE DOOR OPEN FOR ME AS I PUSH THE
stroller into the cafe. Inside, it's light and airy, tall windows
letting in sunlight from the landscaped garden and bathing
the wooden tables in gold. It's quiet for a Tuesday morning
in June, with a few other families dotted around the space,
laughing and chatting quietly, except for the couple sitting
at the far corner of the room.

Dad is buried on his phone, his glasses perched on his
nose. I've seen him more frequently over the last four and a
half months than I have since I lived under his roof. After he
waited at the hospital for hours for Olive to arrive, and then
a further three hours before I was ready to see him, I figured
he'd be allowed some home visiting privileges.

He comes over on Sundays and picks Olive and I up
before taking us over to see Nanny.

He hadn't made the effort in the months before I asked
him to take us, but any awkwardness he felt about seeing his

mother for the first time in nearly a year was overtaken by the desire to spend time with his new granddaughter.

"Hi Dad," I say as we approach.

"Hello, sweetheart." He glances up from his phone and stands, pressing a kiss to my cheek before all his attention is drawn to the giggling baby. "Hello, angel," he coos as he lets Olive clutch onto his finger.

I relinquish my hold on the stroller and chance a glance at my mother. Her back is straight, her blonde hair perfectly styled and her hands clasped on the table in front of her.

She glances at me before her eyes are drawn to the stroller, and the little hand that appears from the lip.

"Hello, Rosalie," she says thickly, glancing up at me.

"Hi, Mum." I haven't spoken to her since the baby shower, since I forbade her to come into the delivery room. Jackson filled me in on what was said afterwards, how my dad asked for a divorce and Jackson asked her to leave.

I tried not to think about it in the blur that was the first few weeks of Olive's life. I had a baby to think about, who needed to be kept alive and fed and cared for. I didn't have the energy to chase after a woman who didn't want me.

Until a few weeks ago, in the car on the way home from the care home, Dad admitted that they'd been talking. He said he knew I couldn't forgive her but that maybe it was worth a conversation. A meeting on neutral ground with lots of backup.

"Hi Andrea," Jackson says, his voice is polite, even if I can see the tight smile he shoots at her.

Jackson pulls a chair out for me, taking the seat between my mother and I. I fidget in my chair before he places his large hand on my knee.

If I could have dreamed up the man who would become the father of my child, I never would have imagined I'd find a man like Jackson. He takes every nappy change, every night feed, forces me to rest when I need it and distracts Olive when all she wants is to cling to my body. Jackson is already wrapped around her finger, and she's just as in love with him as I am.

"She looks bigger," Dad says as he peers at Olive, who beams at him, her little body shimmying in her onesie.

She's a wriggler, always wanting to move. God help us when she starts crawling. We'll never catch her.

"She weighed in at twelve pounds, one ounce at her last appointment," I say proudly.

"Just like you at that age," Mum says softly.

I feel my back straighten before Jackson's hand squeezes my thigh. Olive's a healthy weight, being fed exactly the right amount. She's a perfectly chubby baby and as she grows up she'll still be as perfect as she is now, no matter how much she weighs.

Thankfully, the waiter comes to take our order, giving me a minute to compose myself. I order a coffee and a chocolate cake and notice Mum's lips thin. I brace myself for a comment, but Dad shoots her a sharp look.

Olive lets out a playful little squeak and all our attention is drawn to her.

"May I?" Dad asks, gesturing to her.

I nod my head and gently move her blanket as he swoops Olive into his arms. We spend the next few minutes staring at her in her granddad's arms, her big blue eyes scanning the room around her before landing on the woman next to her.

"Hello, sweetheart," Mum coos softly as Olive's tiny lips curl into a smile.

Jackson's arm comes around me as he tangles his hands in my hair.

I swallow roughly. "This is your Granny, Olive."

Mum's eyes flit to mine, her lip wobbling slightly. She scoots her chair forward, her hands reaching out as if to clutch the baby to her, but she doesn't, instead gently brushing a sock-clad foot.

"You good, pretty girl?" Jackson murmurs in my ear.

I take a sip of my coffee and glance up at him. "I think so."

I tilt my head and press a kiss to his lips.

Olive starts fussing, and Jackson sends me a wink.

"I feel a meltdown coming on," he announces, rising to his feet and rounding the table to Olive. "Come on, baby girl, let's get some fresh air."

He effortlessly plucks Olive out of her grandfather's arms and swoops her into his own. Olive loves being carried by her daddy. I think it's because he's so tall. She gets to see so much more from her vantage point, and I understand too well how it feels to be swept up in Jackson Harper's arms.

"Want to join, Terry?" Jackson asks. Dad pats my shoulder as he follows Jackson out the door, leaving me alone with my mother for the first time in months.

It doesn't take long for Jackson and Dad to appear through the window, wandering around the landscaped garden and pointing out the wildlife to Olive. Mum and I both turn to watch, using it as an excuse not to talk to each other.

"She's so curious," Mum says, and I can see her smile in the reflection of the window.

I nod my head.

"You were like that," she says, still not looking at me. "So curious about the world." She pauses, "And happy. You were such a happy baby. You used to giggle all the time, especially when Cleo would play with you. She used to love playing with you, and even when you had no idea what was going on, you'd let out that adorable little laugh."

I fiddle with my mug, tracing my finger along the rim.

"I barely remember a time we were even in the same room and I had fun," I say, quietly. "I only remember the times I didn't."

Mum turns her head, resting it on a shaking hand for a minute.

"I'm so sorry, Rosalie."

I blink, taken aback.

"I've come to realize that I—" She breaks off. "I haven't done right by you. Cleo always needed so much more attention than you, and she's so much like me that I... It's no excuse. I have no excuse. I'm ashamed of myself. Ashamed that it took your father threatening me with a divorce for me to realize what I'd put you through. I never meant to play favorites—"

"But you did," I can't stop myself from snapping, all my righteous anger that I've tried to let go of since the baby shower bursting to the surface. "I would tell you so many times how miserable I was, how nasty Cleo could be, and you never once believed me. Never stood up for me, never comforted me. I was all alone."

"I know," she whispers.

I can't stop. "She told the whole world about Olive before I did. She stole that chance from me over and over again." My blood pounds in my chest. "And the baby shower? What possessed you to do that? To go along with it?"

She wipes at a tear from the corner of her eye, her bracelets clinking with the motion. "I can't go back in time and fix my mistakes, but I want you to know that I'm sorry for all of it. And if—" She takes a breath, her voice shaking. "If you can't forgive me, I'll accept it."

I watch as a tear drops from her red eyes, smudging her mascara.

In my entire life, I've never seen my mother cry, and I don't really know what to do about it.

I bite my lip as I feel my own eyes water.

"I'm not..." I start before breaking off. I glance out the window, at Jackson, who's already facing me. I watch as his large hands rub Olive's back gently, rocking her in place. I take a deep breath. "I'm not ready to forgive you, for everything. But... we can do this again sometime, if you'd like."

Her eyes widen as she nods her head, sliding her hand across the table towards mine.

"I'd like that so very much," she whispers, her fingers twitching on the table.

I nod my head, glancing back out at Jackson as he tickles Olive's belly until she erupts into laughter.

"Here." I slide the chocolate cake towards her. "Eat some of this before Jackson gets back and inhales it all."

She sends me a beaming smile before grabbing a fork and digging in.

I might not be ready to forgive her, and we might never have the kind of relationship Jackson has with his mother, or Anya with hers, but maybe we can share a slice of cake on a sunny afternoon. And maybe it's a start.

47

—————

JACKSON

"On a scale of one to ten, how bad was that?" I ask Rosie in the passenger seat. She's been quiet since leaving the cafe, giving her dad a hug and her mum an awkward wave before we buckled Olive into her car seat and drove away.

Rosie snorts. "A solid six."

I whistle. "I was expecting a two, maybe a three if we were lucky, so I'll take a six."

"I'm just glad it's over."

I rest my hand on her lap, squeezing her thigh.

Rosie glances behind her at Olive dozing in her car seat. "She's tuckered out now."

"Well she's about to be handed around like a rugby ball in a few minutes." I pull into our driveway though I know we won't be staying long.

I used to take for granted how easy it was to get around before Olive came along. I used to put my shoes on, put my wallet in my pocket and then I would just...leave the house. Now, I have a mental checklist the length of my arm, and a tiny sidekick that needs to be fed every couple of hours.

"Björn or stroller?" Rosie asks as she rounds the car.

"Let's bring both so she can nap," I say, opening Olive's door as quietly as I can. She barely stirs when I pick her up, placing her in the stroller Rosie's assembled without a noise.

When I found this place, I had hoped the proximity to Danny and Anya's house was a sign it was the right neighborhood, but I hadn't anticipated them moving back in full time. We now spend nearly all our time at each other's houses, although they're heading back to LA in a few months for work.

Nearly everyone we've ever met is crammed into Danny and Anya's garden for their anniversary party. The air is thick and warm, and we can smell the start of a barbecue as we get closer.

"Olive!" Anya calls as soon as we cross the threshold. She beelines for the stroller, ignoring Rosie and I until she realizes the baby is asleep and is best not disturbed, a lesson Anya learned her first night babysitting, when she woke her up on purpose and had to suffer through a sleepless night.

"Hello to you too," Rosie says wryly.

Anya pulls her into a hug. "How did it go with the parents?"

Rosie shrugs.

"Wine?" Anya asks.

"I've got enough breast milk pumped to feed a small infant army. Yes please."

"I've got her," I tell Rosie when she turns for Olive.

She presses a kiss to my lips before following Anya back into the house.

I'm glad she's letting loose a bit tonight. It's already difficult with a four month old at home, but losing her mum almost completely has been tough. Thankfully Terry has done his best to be a doting granddad to ease the sting, and my mother came over for the first two months to help, but I know the distance has been hard on her.

Olive wiggles in the stroller, her tiny arms stretching as she stirs. I can't resist pulling her into my arms. She fusses for a few seconds, staring up at me with her big blue eyes so like her mother's before she conks back out on my arm, face smushed into my tattoos. She just wanted a cuddle.

I spot Danny near the grill and wander over. "Hey, bro."

Danny turns ready to hug me but spots the sleeping baby in my arm and awkwardly waves instead. "She looks comfortable."

I chuckle, swaying side to side as Danny reverently touches Olive's toes.

"Nice day for it," I tell him.

"Yeah." He turns back to the grill. "Though I'm sweating over here. I'm never doing this myself again."

"As if Anya will let you hire a cook."

Danny laughs. "It was a struggle to let her get a cleaner to come twice a year to deep clean. And even then we pay her double."

Anya and Rosie are the same, as stubborn about clinging to as much normalcy as possible. It doesn't matter that her husband can afford a fleet of staff, Anya would never allow it.

"God, that smells good," Cassie says as she appears at my side, her red curls bouncing as she jumps on the balls of her feet.

"Here. You can have this non-burnt one." Danny offers her a burger from the side.

"Non-burnt, you say?" Cassie asks as she assesses the charcoaled burger.

"You should have seen the ones I made before this."

Cassie laughs as she takes a bite, her eyes rolling to the back of her head with a groan.

"Do you want to take one to your *friend*?" Danny asks her with a wiggle of his brows.

"A friend?" I ask, rounding on Cassie with a grin. "Who?"

Cassie takes an exaggerated bite of her burger, gesturing to her full mouth helplessly before spinning on her heel and escaping back into the crowd.

"Who's the friend?" I ask Danny scanning the faces gathered. I don't see anyone I don't recognize.

He snorts, "Showed up just before you guys did, I haven't had the–fuck's sake," he mutters as his attempt at flipping a burger ends with half of it splattered on the ground.

"I'll go put the baby down and take over," I pat Danny on the arm.

"That might be for the best."

I turn back to the house and glance down at Olive who's starting to blink back awake. "Let's go find Mummy."

48

ROSIE

"Well, at least Cleo didn't show up," Anya says, clinking her nearly empty glass to mine. I've spent the majority of my glass recounting my afternoon.

I laugh dryly around my glass. "I think she's learned that lesson now."

"I'm proud of you for going, Rosie." Anya squeezes my hand.

"I'm proud of myself too." I wave my hand, ready to stop talking about the whole thing. "Anyway in other news. Did I tell you about the short?"

"No?" Anya says, sitting up straighter.

"It's just been approved for feature film funding."

Anya squeals. "That's amazing."

I nod, giddy at the news. Jackson's quiet contribution meant that the film was shopped around at over twenty festivals, where it eventually found enough momentum to be commissioned into a feature. "I start editing next week."

"That's so exciting! Have you told the girls?"

"No, I'll tell them now. Where's Pip?"

"I don't know, she had a phone call and she's been holed up upstairs ever since."

The patio door slides open and Jackson appears with a wide awake Olive in his arms. "Someone's up."

"Yay!" Anya squeals, abandoning me for my child.

"She's probably hungry," I tell her, standing up from my bar stool and heading to the bag where I packed my milk.

"I'll do it," Anya coos, pulling a smiling Olive into her arms. "You guys go eat before it's all gone."

"I think the worry is *if* it's all cooked," Jackson agrees as he comes to my side, wrapping his arm around my waist as I pull the milk out of the bag.

"You have to—"

"Rosie, I've got this," Anya assures me, "go and enjoy, please. It's my party, my rules."

"Come on, pretty girl." Jackson pulls me back outside, but before we can rejoin the others, he tugs me around the side of the house to a shadowy alcove next to the fuse box.

"Is the grill back here?" I tease but my giggle is cut off when Jackson backs me into the brick wall and kisses me breathless. It's easy to sink into him, letting my tongue dance across his lips and my hands slide up his bare arms.

He nudges his leg in between mine, widening my stance until he can hook my thigh across his hip.

"Jackson." I laugh, breathlessly. "We shouldn't."

"Isn't this familiar?" Jackson asks, raining kisses along my neck. "This time last year, we snuck away from the same party."

"I just went out for some air." His hand clutches my backside and I groan as he grinds me against him. "You were the sneaky one."

"Semantics," he breathes.

"It's not even dark out, everyone can see."

"I don't care." He tugs me closer, his hands exploring my body.

"We're parents now, we have to behave."

"Never."

"I...okay, I'm out of excuses," I admit, tugging his mouth back to mine and kissing the smirk from his lips.

I need him closer. I scrape my nails against the hair at the back of his neck, curling my fingers in the strands of hair he kept long because I asked him to. Both his arms curl around me, squeezing me closer to him.

Jackson runs his hands across my hips, my stomach, my breasts, down to the crease in my thighs. The man worships me.

"Stunning." He slides his hand under my shirt, lightly teasing the cup of my bra. "Ravishing." He plants a kiss across my jaw. "Breathtaking,"

I pull him back to my mouth as he whispers the final word on my lips. "Beautiful."

I grind myself into him further, teasing him with every movement.

"You're not bad looking yourself," I tell him wickedly.

Jackson throws his head back with a laugh, and I let my head fall forward, resting on his shirt.

"Come on, let's get back to the party." Jackson tells me, stepping back and readjusting himself in his jeans. "I'll ravish you when we get home."

"Promise?" I tease, tugging at his waistband.

"That's a promise, pretty girl." Jackson claims my mouth in a final searing kiss, and I have half a mind to abandon the party and take him right here. But I don't need to. I can wait. I know we've got a whole lifetime ahead of us.

EPILOGUE

JACKSON

8 months later

"ARE YOU EXCITED FOR THE PLANE, OLIVE?" ANYA ASKS THE giggling girl in my arms.

Olive babbles incoherently, wiggling impatiently until I let her fall into her favorite aunt's arms.

"She slept most of the way here, except when she kept trying to press the call help button," Rosie says, collapsing on the patio chair beside me. The sun is setting and it's nearly Olive's bedtime, but we can't keep her away when she knows there's people around. She's loved being in Wellington with the family, and she loved it even more when Anya and Danny arrived laden with birthday gifts and toys.

Rosie kicks her feet up onto my lap and I cup her ankle with my palm. Her pale skin has tanned in the Southern sun and she's taken to wearing the purple jandals I bought her everywhere she goes.

It's warm and balmy, the coolest breeze of autumn in the air, but we've both loved it here. We flew over back in

December so my girls could experience their first warm Christmas, and we used the opportunity to explore my home country. It's been years since I spent more than a few weeks here, so spending the last two months driving, sailing and hiking both islands has been as much for my benefit as Rosie's. I told her she'd get to go traveling.

"You can sit with us on the way home, Olive Oil," Anya tells my daughter. "I need to stock up on all my Olive cuddles."

I chuckle. "It's only been two months. And you've had a photo every day."

"It's not the same," Anya insists, swaying Olive in her arms.

"She's loved the sun," Rosie says.

"It is miserable in London," Danny says, "Dark and wet and cold."

"I'm sorry your birthday's in the winter," Anya says to Olive seriously. "Auntie and Uncle should have gotten married in September, so you would be a summer baby."

Rosie groans as Danny and I laugh, causing Olive to peel into giggles too.

"She *is* a summer baby," Rosie insists. "In the Southern Hemisphere."

"What's so funny out here?" Mum says as she pulls open the sliding door behind Rosie. Mum spent the first few months of Olive's life living in a flat down the road from our house. She suggested it casually, not wanting to intrude on our settling in as parents, but it only took a few weeks before we were both relieved every time she came to help. She never stayed longer than necessary, only coming to take Olive for a walk so we could rest, or dropping off some home-cooked meals. When I had to go on a press tour for six weeks, she came back and stayed in the guest room so Rosie wouldn't be alone.

For a girl who's been alone in her own family, she's loved having her new one around.

"I've already had my new neighbor, complaining about all my new plants." Mum says perching on the arm of the chair by Rosie's head.

"Oh, is that all he's talking to you about?" Rosie asks, wiggling her eyebrows.

Mum waves her off with a laugh, "Don't you start."

"Start what?" Anya says excitedly.

"Nik, the silver fox from across the street." Rosie giggles. "He miraculously keeps finding an excuse to come and knock on the door."

Anya gasps as my mother *blushes*. "Get it, Gloria."

"On that note," I say as I stand up dislodging Rosie's feet as everyone laughs. "It's bedtime."

"I'll take her," Mum says, laughter still rolling off her tongue as she pulls Olive out of Anya's arms. Olive loves her grandmother, resting her head on her chest and grabbing the neck of her t-shirt in her fist. Mum leans her head on Olive's. "I'm going to miss you so much, bub."

Danny and Anya say their good night's as the sun officially sets on the horizon, crickets chirping in the distance. I settle in next to Rosie as her eyes drift closed. I'm going to miss it here for sure, but I know that as long as I'm with my girls, I'm home.

"I can't believe she's a year old." Rosie says, digging her foot into my side.

I catch her foot and pull her down the seat until she's lying underneath me. "Remember when she could fit in the palm of my hand?"

"You used to carry her like a rugby ball," Rosie giggles.

"She loved it."

I fall in between her thighs and press a kiss to her lips.

"She's a happy baby, isn't she?"

"The happiest," I tell her, shifting so the box in my pocket doesn't press into her thigh.

"Are you happy?" I ask her, pressing a kiss to her lips.

She sighs beneath me. "So happy."

I carried the ring around with me the whole trip. I thought I'd maybe do it on Christmas morning, but the day was so hectic that I lost track of time. Then I carried it in my pocket ready for the final day of our hike up Taranaki Maunga, the same route my dad and I used to take, but Olive had a meltdown so we had to cut the hike short. Then I'd planned on doing it when we visited Tony and Kaia in their new house near Paraparamu beach, but I couldn't get her on our own the whole two days we were there.

But now, on the evening of our daughter's first birthday, in the garden where I used to play with my dad and eat lunch with my sisters, it feels right.

I shift underneath her, pulling her until she's sitting back up. "I *was* happy," she grumbles.

I cup her chin with a laugh. "Rosie Taylor," I tell her, gently tugging at her lip, "I need to ask you something."

"I'm *really* happy Jackson, honest," she giggles.

I roll my eyes, gently wetting my lip. I'm not an anxious guy, but I'm shaking with nerves as I slide off the seat and onto one knee.

"Rosie," I say quietly as she gasps. "I have loved you since the day I first met you. I loved you when you ran away from me on that balcony, and I loved you when you burst into tears when I showed up at your door. I loved you when you made me watch your dancing show and dragged me to look at old buildings—"

"That was *you*," she chokes out.

"I love our beautiful daughter so much that I can't believe I ever lived a life without her. Without both of you. I'm so glad that your birth control failed."

Rosie laughs wetly, eyes shining behind her glasses. Her hair falls in tendrils across her shoulders, as she sits up straighter, her long legs falling to one side.

"Being with you has made me the happiest man in the world." I break off as a sob blocks my throat and I sniff, attempting to compose myself. "Marry me, Rosie." I pull the ring box out of my pocket, clicking it open.

Before she even looks at it she falls into my arms, nearly knocking me back with the force. "Yes," she cries as she presses her lips to mine, our tears mingling.

"Really?"

"Yes!" she laughs. "Of course it's a yes. I've been waiting for you to ask me for months."

"How did you know?" I chuckle as she peppers kisses across my cheeks.

"Unless your dick turned into a cube, it was pretty obviously in your pocket." She giggles as I gasp scandalously. "Plus, your mum looks at my hand first thing every morning in case you've asked me overnight."

"Right, never mind I take the whole thing back." I attempt to rise to my feet. "Forget it ever happened."

She kicks out her leg as I crowd her back against the chair, tilting her hips until we're tangled together. I grab her left hand and slide the ring on her finger.

"Never."

THANKS FOR READING!

I hope you enjoyed Jackson and Rosie's story!

If you liked this book, please consider leaving a review, I'd love to hear from you!

Want to read Anya and Danny's story?

Read the first two chapters of Keep It now...

ANYA

I GAVE MYSELF ONE YEAR. ONE YEAR TO 'MAKE IT' BEFORE I packed it in for good and got a job flogging insurance or office supplies or something in a depressing, solid nine to five. One year. That's it. Then obviously, one year turned into two and two into two and a half and so on and so forth until I ended up here, four years later a jack-of-all-trades at the bottom of the film industry ladder willing to be paid in meals and *experience*.

The film isn't a bad one. It's a surreal short about a woman who's being stalked by her past self and — yeah, okay it's not great. At least it's a job. A job in the middle of nowhere with fourteen hour days and a two-hour commute there and back. So what if I have to stuff extra bread rolls from the soup at lunch into my backpack so I can eat some form of dinner? It's experience. So what if I have to take a four hour round trip to pick up a smoke machine last minute and pay five hundred pounds out of pocket just to be told it's *no longer necessary*?

It's experience. Experience I need if I want to get anywhere close to fulfilling my dreams.

I just really didn't think the final tether holding my dream in my hand would be a power cord connected to a smoke machine.

"Yeah, we don't need that anymore. The director says it would make the scene look too cheap." The producer, Beth, tells me.

I really didn't think I'd give up on my dream on a foggy afternoon in Kent but standing in the middle of the forest with an apparently redundant smoke machine, is evidently enough to tip me over the edge.

A burst of laughter comes out of me. "You're joking."

In my university days, I would have held it together until I found my best friend Rosie on set and ranted to her about the audacity of sending me on a fool's errand in the middle of shooting. Rosie, of course, is nowhere near the outskirts of Kent since she had walked into a job in a post- production house the day after graduation. I wasn't jealous when Rosie was offered her job, we were going to be in different departments after all, but I couldn't help feeling bitter thinking about her glamorous city life working on the next wide-release feature while I've been stuck working for pennies on under-funded shorts.

"No," she says, turning her attention back to her iPad.

I close my eyes. After more late nights than I could count, over a hundred hours of driving and likely the same amount of pilfered bread rolls, I've had enough.

"That's it." I slam the smoke machine on the floor. "Fuck this. I'm out."

That makes Beth look up. "You what?"

"I quit. This is so not worth it. Find someone else to be your errand bitch. I'm basically a glorified delivery person."

Beth says nothing, her mouth slightly parted. "You can't quit, we haven't hired you."

I laugh, slightly manically. "*I know.*"

I grab the smoke machine from the ground and walk away, finally feeling a weight fall off my shoulders. I'm going to go home, order a takeaway, drink a whole bottle of wine and watch a property development show.

"Wait!" I hear Beth shout from behind me. I don't stop.

"Do you know anyone in the market for a smoke machine?" I ask Rosie, holding my phone between my cheek and shoulder as I unceremoniously throw the forsaken thing on my passenger seat and start the engine.

"Why are you selling a smoke machine?" Rosie laughs.

"I've rented it for three days and I am not driving back to fucking Slough anytime soon." I sigh as I put my foot down, my little car already spluttering from the miles I've already put it through today.

"Okay, I feel like I am missing some very important pieces of information here."

I fill her in on my day from hell, gripping the wheel with both hands and trying to concentrate on the drive.

"You need to stop settling for crummy experience jobs, Annie," Rosie says after I finish my story, using the nickname she gave me in our first week as housemates in first year. "You need to aim higher."

"I am aiming higher," I protest. "It's just no one higher wants me."

"No, we are not having any of that self-pitying bullshit today, missy." Rosie scolds.

I groan and rest my palm on my forehead. "I can't *not* drown in self pity at the moment. I feel like everyone is already where they need to be and I am still basically at the same point in my career as I was when I was nineteen. I think I need to get used to the fact that I peaked in uni and pack it in."

Rosie sighs."Have you started drinking already?"

"I wish."

Rosie laughs."Okay, first of all, don't give up yet. One shitty

job—"

"Many shitty jobs. In a row!"

"Okay, fine, many shitty jobs do not mean you are a shitty filmmaker. Besides, you want to direct your own. Why don't you make your own film?"

I pout. That is a solution I had been playing with for months but I'd been making people's low-budget, non commissioned shorts for years now and they're always terrible. I want to direct my own film, sure, but I'd want to at least be commissioned for a mid-budget feature and not a kickstarted short. I can't get commissioned without at least having my name on a successful production and I can't get on a successful production without already being on a successful production. Besides, there was the stubborn voice in the back of my head that liked to question whether I even really wanted to direct anymore, but I wrote that off as insecurity and stamped down on it whenever it cropped up.

"I just—ugh, just let me moan for a bit before I start thinking about all of that. I've mainly got to figure out how my landlord will accept the bread rolls I've been paid in as rent. I'm going to be out by next week."

Rosie laughs. "Okay, why don't you come stay with me for a bit, just to get you on your feet. You can sleep on the couch and earn some money in the pub over the road and then reassess whether you want to pack it in and go home."

"Would you actually?" I ask quietly.

"Babe, I've been dying for you to come crash here since I moved in," Rosie says.

"You're so good to me you know that?"

"I know, I get funding from the government for supporting the sad and unemployed."

After we hang up and my breakdown starts to progress into a slightly throbbing headache, I feel a little bit lighter. I might not have solved all of my issues tonight but at least I have a semi-plan. And that nagging voice in the back of my head can shut up.

THREE WEEKS later I'm all moved into Rosie's London flat. And by moved in, I mean my two suitcases are open at the end of the bed and I spend my time rummaging for clean underwear. Rosie has even managed to get me a few shifts at The Old Crown working behind the bar for a cheery old man named Steve. It's not the nine-five routine I imagined as my backup but at least the money lining my bank account is relatively steady. Plus, it's better than standing outside in the freezing cold with a smoke machine (which I returned...eventually).

I still feel that nag of something — definitely *not* jealousy — when I see Rosie leave in the morning in her stylish work wear on her way to her cushty production house in Soho, but I'm making money and getting back on my feet.

On one of my only Friday nights off, I'm waiting for Rosie to come home so I can open the bottle of vodka in my suitcase without feeling extremely alcoholic. Checking my phone for an update on my temporary roommate's ETA, I glance at the exchange we shared earlier.

ROSIE

Send me your CV

ME

Why

ROSIE

Send it and I'll tell you why

ME

CV.dox

Why do you need my cv

Why

Rosie

Why

Using my closed laptop as a table, I paint my nails whilst watching a rerun of the *Robin Carlson Show*. Jackson Harper is on making everyone laugh on the press tour for the new action blockbuster *Starboard Bound*, a film about the hijacking of a big boat, or cruise ship or whatever. He's joined by his co star Danny Covington who sits sulkily lapping up Harper's jokes and barely answering questions with more than two words. *Spoilsport*, I think bitterly.

"Honey, I'm home." Rosie shouts from the door as she kicks it shut behind her. "I brought food. Don't tell Steve because I got it from the Chinese place down the road and I don't want him to hate me."

I stand with a mock gasp and move into the kitchen, "Not the Golden Dragon, Rose. They've been competing for months. The amount of fliers I've already had to hand out over there is going to give me carpal-tunnel."

"Well, we'll hide the packaging so he will never need to know," Rosie says, pulling out boxes of noodles.

"What's the occasion, anyway? You never order in." Unlike me, Rosie is a healthy person and believes having more than one meal a day of entirely processed and salted foods is bad for you.

"We're celebrating," Rosie says promptly.

I crunch my brow as I shovel egg fried rice into my mouth

directly from the container. "Wha arr ee selebrashing?" Rosie dishes up her food and grabs a wine bottle from the rack before we head back to the couch.

I wait for Rosie to tell me what we are celebrating, but instead she pours two glasses of wine. She hands one to me with one hand and snatches my plate away with the other, gently placing it on the coffee table as I'm still trying to stab a piece of broccoli with my fork.

"Oh my god, why bring food if you won't let me eat it?" I ask.

"*Because*," says Rose, "I am trying to tell you why we're celebrating."

"Okay, hit me."

"Our house just finalized a deal with Gwendoline Marcs." Gwendoline Marcs is an up-and-coming director. They say up-and-coming but she has already had a few nods for her last and first feature *And Then They Met* and there are rumors she has another project lined up. She started directing when she was younger than me and now in only her mid-thirties, she's basically established herself as the next Scorsese in the making. I am, reasonably, obsessed with her.

"Oh my god Rose." I hug her. "That is so cool"

She grins. "I know we are all so buzzed. Grant brought

us a round of drinks at lunchtime to celebrate. But that's not why we are excited tonight."

"What could possibly be more exciting than you working with Gwendoline Marcs?"

Her grin grows. "*You* working with Gwendoline Marcs."

I laugh. "As if."

"I am deadly serious."

The look in her eyes makes the laughter on my lips fade. "Wait— huh?"

Rosie tries to smother the grin on face, but her sparkling eyes give her away. "I don't know too much about the film yet, today was just an excuse for a piss-up. But basically from what I can tell it's being filmed exclusively in France and the main actor is a complete nightmare. It's all under NDA so no juicy details —although I bet they're a real diva."

I wait for Rosie to take a swig of her wine, vibrating with apprehension.

"*Anyway*," she continues, "apparently they're looking for a PA/assistant/runner person."

I gasp, "I'm a PA/assistant/runner person."

"I know," Rosie cackles. "So I was like, 'that's crazy my best friend is currently looking right now.'"

I am on top of the world.

"But they said no."

I fall, pitifully, back to earth.

"But *then* they said that they needed a French speaker." And I'm up again. "I speak French!"

"I know!" Rosie laughs. "I told them you are fluent and half

French and have a French passport and everything and guess what?"

"What?" I ask breathlessly, already knowing my best friend is going to pull through for me.

"They wanted to see your CV."

"*Shut the fuck up.*" I jump to my feet "Where's my CV?"

Rosie laughs. "You literally sent it to me earlier."

"You didn't tell me it was for Gwendoline Marcs, I didn't even double check it!"

"I looked at it before I sent it. Relax."

I place my hands over my pounding heart. "You did not do this for me."

"Of course I did this for you, have you met me? I'm amazing."

I laugh. "You are. If you get this for me I will marry you so you can have your EU passport."

"You were already going to do that, I was just waiting for the ring."

I laugh but say quietly. "This is—this is a lot right now."

I can feel Rosie smirking but don't look at her, instead I put

my wine glass down and cover my face with my hands.

"I don't know if I can do it."

Thwack.

"What was that for?" I raise my hands against another pillow onslaught.

"Of course you can do it, you muppet! You're on the ball, you're great with cast *and* crew and *you speak French.* If you waste this opportunity because you're scared I will never speak to you again."

I groan. "But what about my job with Ste—"

Thwack.

"If you dare consider turning this down for that goddamn

takeaway shop downstairs I will murder you in your sleep," Rosie hisses between hits.

"Fine! Would you—*ow*—would you stop that? It's just —whew, you know?" I breathe.

Rose exhales and loops her arm around my shoulders. "Okay, take a deep breath. I think this is your shot. You've got

this Annie, I can feel it. This is gonna be it for you."

I close my eyes and breathe in deeply. I can imagine myself on set with a headset and clipboard, shouting at people to get to where Gwendoline Marcs needs them to be. I'll bring her coffee and she'll say, '*thanks Anya, good job*' and then she'll take me under her wing, mentor me until she eventually says in her Oscar's acceptance speech "I wouldn't be here today without the support of Anya Bonnet."

"Yes. Okay, yes, you're right. This is my shot."

DANNY

I KNEW IT WAS GOING TO BE AN INTERESTING DAY WHEN I WAS pulled into a glass conference room for a meeting with my father. I could hardly remember the last time I have spent time with my family without the polished glare of a conference table between us. Even meetings with my sister happen across a table, albeit at a restaurant over a bottle of wine.

Swinging in my office chair to look out the tall glass window, I watch the workers outside with my chin in my hand. The professionals heading out on their lunch breaks with their blue suits and lanyards swinging from their necks. I've never had a lanyard and wonder idly if I could use one, even if just for my house keys.

The door opens and my father walks in. Charles Covington is an imposing man, his deep set frown lines marring the face so similar to mine. Charles raises his eyebrows and drops a script on the table with a thud, the paper sliding across the glossy surface.

I cough a laugh, my hand covering my burgeoning grin. I learned a long time ago to find humor in everything my father did. Not only does it infuriate Charles Covington but it makes the tension that fills my body fizzle away a little. I reach forward and grab the script.

Resting my ankle on my knee and flicking through the pages, I wait for my father to break the silence. I will read this script cover to cover just to avoid speaking to the man.

"You leave for Paris next week." The deep American voice drawls from the other side of the table. Charles has never lost his American twinge, even after all the years spent in London with my English-rose mother. I tried hard to cling to the home counties accent I developed at school, refusing to be associated any more with the man who raised me than I have to.

"No audition?" I ask mildly.

"Don't be smart, Daniel," Charles clutches the chair in front of him. I haven't auditioned since *Better You Know.* "It's with Gwendoline Marcs and it's a summer shoot. On location in Paris. You can't fuck it up."

I run my fingers through my hair, "Do I even get a say?"

Redness starts spreading up my father's throat, his tell that he's about to explode. "No, you don't get a say. Do you know how many strings I pulled to get you this gig?"

I'm sure the *strings* he pulled were sending a single email. Pip has already told me that Charles was producing a new feature. Pip always gets the news before I do.

"What if I don't want to do it?"

"I don't give a fuck if you don't want to do it, your contract is signed."

"Hmm, I don't remember signing anything." It's truly second nature to be as ornery as possible with my father.

"You will do this job, Daniel. You will behave perfectly, you will do a good job, you will promote the shit out of this film and you will be goddamn happy about it."

"I'm not listening to this." I stand up, throwing the script back on the table. I move to push past my father but he blocks my way.

"You will listen and you will do this," my father's beady eyes glare.

I clench my jaw and take a seat, my blood boiling.

"You'll have top billing."

As if that's an enticement.

"What's it about?" I ask, leafing through.

"Do I look like Wikipedia? Read it yourself for Christ's sake. I'm sure you remember how to."

I flick through the script. Conveniently, what are evidently my lines have already been highlighted, most likely thanks to my father's PA Georgia. Of course, I won't even be allowed the dignity of going through my own script.

I worked with an actor years ago who combed meticulously through every page, considering every word and inflection. I watched her study her book like she was preparing for an exam, and I couldn't help but credit it with her enviable performance. I had wanted to learn from her, and really pay attention to the words coming out of my mouth, not just memorize like a robot. The next time my father handed me a project, I had asked for a clean script. He didn't even reply.

The script in my hands feels heavy, thick, long. Picking out lines at random, I have a small tickle in the back of my brain that this job might be different from the other superficial projects I've had before. Closing the book and placing it back on the table, I turn my attention back to my father.

Before I can open my mouth my father opens his. "We're hiring you a personal for this one."

"Eric?" I say, referring to the PA I have used before. I like Eric because he was more like a chill cousin than an employee, he never pressured me to do anything I didn't want to do and mostly just left me alone.

Charles guffaws. "Not a chance, you'll get a PA through production."

I glare at my father.

"And before you complain, I don't have anything to do with it," he says, throwing his hands up in mock surrender. "That's all. You'll get the train on Sunday, Georgia will send you an email."

"The train?" I ask.

"Production is focusing on its carbon footprint." Charles stands, pushing his chair back under the desk. "I'll fly out in the first few weeks to see how you're getting on." *To make sure you stay out of trouble.*

Charles turns and pulls the door open. "Don't fuck this up and don't embarrass me, Daniel." He doesn't even look at me as he strides from the room.

I lean back in my chair, content to wait for my father to be well out of the vicinity. Heaven forbid I get stuck in the elevator with the man.

Stuffing the script in my bag, I run my hands through my hair and take a breath. *It's one more job,* I tell myself, *one more.*

Slinging my bag over my shoulder, I stomp to the elevator. My hand itches in my pocket on the long descent to street level.

Stepping out into the fresh spring air, I pull my vape out of my pocket and take a drag of the cherry flavor. I switched from cigarettes after some nagging from Pip. I had rolled my eyes when I first started to find the little pink sticks in my empty cigarette cartons but I appreciated what my sister was trying to do. It's taken years to have anything resembling a close relationship with my sister, so now I'll do anything to make her happy. Even if it means using the poor substitute for the real thing.

Pulling my headphones in and blasting a rock song, I shoulder my way down the street. I take a deep breath and watch my feet, glancing up under my lashes at everyone who passes me by. The tension in my shoulders aches, and I know I will have to lock the door twice behind me when I get home just to feel secure.

Checking the time I decide it's early enough to get the tube home without any issue. My father pays for a car service, but my reluctance to use his money sometimes overtakes my need for privacy — today being one of those days.

The tube carriage isn't crowded but I stand near the door, facing away from the rest of the carriage. I learned a few years ago that this was the best way to remain inconspicuous.

I finally take my first easy breath when my front door slams behind me. I dump my bag on the floor and flop onto the couch. The ticking of my watch echoing through the empty room like a metronome. Opening my eyes I glance at my bag, the corner of the manuscript poking out.

I pull it out and settle into the couch.

One more job, I tell myself, *one more.*

Keep It available now!

ACKNOWLEDGMENTS

Firstly, thank you for picking up *Forget It*! If you're new here or have been here since the beginning thank you for taking a chance on me!

I have so many more people to thank this time so here goes:

Aimee, I am sorry that I named a side character after you and then decided that character was going to have a whole book and then decided she was going to get railed by a 6'5 movie star with a praise kink...or am I? I wouldn't have been able to do this without you, let's keep doing it forever.

Gee, I don't think this book would have existed if you hadn't asked when Rosie and Jackson were going to get a book. As always, thank you for your constant grammar support, sourcing some expert midwife advice and being my resident star sign queen. Also, I am sorry for making you read all the spicy scenes...kinda.

To my friends and family who have been nothing but supportive since I shyly confessed that I'd published a book. Aimée thank you for recommending *Keep It* wherever you can and Cara thank you for getting pregnant right when I needed some first hand knowledge. Sophie thank you for travelling to New Zealand before I ever met you and having great instagram pictures that I could stalk. Esther, Clive, Amy and Lydia, thank you for your love and support (but please don't read this one).

To my fellow authors who have been so welcoming,

supportive and loving–thank you for lending your ear when I've needed it most. Meg Jones, thank you for being so kind (and for helping with my marketing, you queen).

Thank you to my amazing beta readers, Hannah, Emily, Lisa and Jordyn.

Mum, thank you for supporting me even when you have no idea what I'm talking about. I love you to the moon and back.

And finally, thank you Joey for everything. I love you. You're always the best part of my day.

ABOUT THE AUTHOR

Francesca Shaw is a twenty-something author living in London with her partner. When she's not writing romance novels, she's juggling a full time career in the film industry and reading every romance book she can get her hands on. She also lived in Paris for six months and will not shut up about it.

Follow her on Instagram and TikTok @authorfrancescashaw

ALSO BY FRANCESCA SHAW

The It Girls

Keep It

Forget It

Book 3 (Coming Soon)